Scared to Death

MATT SERAFINI

BASED ON THE SCREENPLAY BY
WILLIAM MALONE

AND THE STORY BY
WILLIAM MALONE & ROBERT SHORT

ENCYCLOPOCALYPSE
PUBLICATIONS

CONTENTS

CHAPTER
ONE

J anie Richter saw a face staring at her from outside the
bedroom window.

A man peering in from the tiny patch of lawn. A simple
shard of moonlight casting immobile features, a permanent
sneer beneath cruel and searching eyes.

People didn't look like that.

Not even in Los Angeles.

The phone on the floor beside Janie's bed rang and startled
her. Her foot caught the cradle and she went tumbling, kicking
the receiver off with a ding as she fell face-first against the glass,
getting a good view of the lonely sidewalk and the empty cul-
de-sac beyond it.

Whoever had been there was gone now.

A homeless drunk, she figured, as had been the case many
times. It happened when yours was the last house on the street,
and the only thing outside it was a curved guardrail holding
back the trees.

People used that turnaround all the time. People looking to
get off the beaten path, wanting privacy without having to go
trekking into the hills on Mulholland in order to do it.

In the time that Janie had lived here, a little over a year

now, she'd seen a lot: A silver Porsche probably belonging to some studio executive, pulling beneath the shadows so the young and hungry starlet riding shotgun could disappear into his lap.

Or the steady stream of high schoolers who came here with their headlights already off, thinking they were being sly, settling in to either smoke up or make out, and usually both.

And then there were the homeless who shambled to and from the woods, as if there was some hidden enclave out there, almost always carrying fresh paper bags in their fists. One had knocked on her door once, jiggling the knob, asking if Eleanor was in there, over and over, while Janie hid in the closet with a meat tenderizer and waited forty minutes for the police to arrive.

That's all it had been, right? Another drunk looking in? Spotting the bedroom light from the street and getting curious?

Getting a show! Janie realized, thoughts interrupted by a full-body shiver that made her remember she was standing against the window in a towel that barely covered her thighs.

The air suddenly colder than ice.

She drew the curtain and felt much better. An illusion, just some plastic flap dangling over a thin pane of glass. But out of sight, out of mind worked just fine most nights. And if only she'd remembered earlier to pull it down, she wouldn't have seen that awful face at all. Wouldn't be on edge right now.

Janie took the towel away from her body and draped it over the clanking cast iron radiator as she turned up the heat.

On the floor, her big toe nudged the overturned phone receiver where a caller was asking, "Hello? Hello?" into the air.

"Oh," Janie said, bending down to answer as small scratches fell against the back door. Slow brushes on heavy wood.

She imagined that monstrous face again, hunched on the back steps now, peering into her kitchen, glimpsing pieces of her life while weighing a decision to take it.

Janie's blood turned to ice against that thought, the light

brown hairs on her forearms rising to attention beneath pocks of gooseflesh.

Down by her ankles, the voice was still coming through the phone receiver: "Hello? Uh, is… anyone there? Is everything cool?"

Janie didn't hear those questions, just stood immobilized, knowing she had to hang up and dial the police, realizing that she was unable to do so. She was unable to do anything — some irrational prevention in her brain suggesting that any motion might suddenly provoke the knocker to action.

In that moment, every awful thing in Los Angeles stood conjured outside her door, every awful front-page headline and news broadcast wrapped inside the shadows of her imagination, eager to get in.

You should've listened to Dad, she thought. Community college back in Minnesota.

Except that all dads existed to make daughters paranoid, perpetually aware of dangers, real and imagined.

A frustrated yowl rose to replace the clawing and Janie's tension melted, her thumping heart dialing way down with the arrival of one very obvious explanation: Kasey.

Her stupid tiger-striped kitty appeared in the window, leaping up onto the hanging flowerpot hooked there. Pink paws tapped against glass, begging to come in for nightly Friskies.

From the floor, the caller said, "I can hear you breathing, you know. Pretty hot."

Janie scooped the phone and placed the cradle on top of her bureau, tucking the receiver between her neck and shoulder. After the mini-heart attack she'd given herself, she was grateful for some company.

"Sorry," she said. "Tripped over my phone."

"Yeah?" the voice gave a naughty little giggle, delighted to be talking about any part of her body. "How is your poor foot?"

Janie reached for the pink nightie that swayed on the hangar in her closet as the question dawned on her: *Who am I talking to?*

It could've been Kurt, the blond surfer from trig, more sculpted than any college senior should be. Only he spoke in that chilled-out Huntington Beach long drawl that was absent here.

Darn. She wanted it to be Kurt. He'd cornered her after class the other day with that casual "Hey," then asked her out to burgers with a confidence that suggested he knew what her answer would be. A confidence this caller lacked.

Janie was shivering, eyes glazing, daydreaming about her upcoming night out with Kurt – burgers at The Apple Pan over on Pico.

"I could… like, you know," the caller said. "Come over and totally rub it."

"Walter," Janie said, unable to get the sigh out of her voice. The lanky film student with whom she shared a lit class last semester, whose timing had been so bad that he'd asked for her number during finals, four months ago, and only now worked up the courage to call.

"As charged," Walter said.

"Great." Janie barely remembered Walter. Cute enough, she supposed, skinny, always nervous. In constant struggle to find conversation without knowing enough about the opposite sex to understand that curiosity was all you needed.

Just ask good questions, dummy.

"So," Walter said, dragging out his vowels as if waiting for Janie to come to his rescue. "What, um, happened with your foot, anyway?"

"Nothing. It's fine. Was just reading." Last thing she wanted was to tell him that she was standing naked in the middle of her bedroom. Didn't need him getting the wrong idea because he already had the wrong idea.

"And now?" Walter asked, teasing his question out, fishing for extra details.

"And now… I'm talking to you."

"Well, hey, that's good news."

"Why is that?"

"It means you're around tonight!"

"For...?" Janie slipped her nightie overhead while somewhere outside, Kasey wailed as if in heat. And inside, the heat refused to click on. She shivered again. A full-bodied tremor.

"A movie or two?" Walter answered. "There's a Maria Ouspenskaya film festival at the Vista."

"Could you say that again? In English?" Janie reached for the cherry red nail polish atop her bureau, wiggling her toes, visualizing that color, wondering if she should go instead with peach. No matter the choice, there wasn't a boy in Los Angeles whose name wasn't Kurt that could pry her away from tonight's task.

"Maria Ouspenskaya," Walter said, failing to keep the nerdy disbelief out of his voice. "A film festival. Look, come see some movies you haven't seen before."

"I don't know, Walter," Janie shivered terribly. "It's already late." Next to her, the radiator clanged, pushing heated water from the boiler. Somehow, it was even colder in here.

"It's eight o'clock!" Walter countered. "And you're twenty years old."

"Yeah, well, *Dallas* is on later, okay? I don't want to miss it."

"*Dallas?* Who needs *Dallas* when you can watch *The Wolf Man*? Two Wolf Man movies, in fact, and Tarzan for good measure."

"Is Patrick Duffy in any of those?"

"Um..."

"How about I call you later, Walter? If I'm still hanging around?"

"I'll be at the movies..."

Outside, the sound of trashcans toppling, tin skidding across pavement. Janie yelped and Walter giggled, which only hastened her impatience. "Look, Walter, I have to go. My cat just knocked over my trashcans."

"Yeah, sure," he said. Four months of practicing this conversation in his head, working up the nerve to make this call, and being defeated by garbage cans.

"It's true," Janie said, suddenly annoyed that she was having to prove to this dork that she was telling the truth. "She does this when she thinks she's being ignored."

More scratching followed, every bit as deliberate and precise, from somewhere that wasn't the back door. Its source, difficult to locate. An animal's nails scraping into a surface – louder and more pronounced than tiny cat claws on the bottom of a door.

Janie's heart was pounding now.

"How about I call you tomo—" She slammed the phone down and stepped into the hall. It hurt to walk, her body chemistry so riled that her veins felt like they oozed Vaseline.

Everything had gone silent, even her own footsteps on laminate were strikingly muted.

"Kasey?" Her voice wobbled while taking slow and protracted steps toward the kitchen, trying to blot that grey face from her imagination. She felt it leering through each of the hallway's windows as she moved past them, too scared to look because her paranoia was off the charts.

Janie tried to call for her kitty again, but her voice refused to comply. Once in the kitchen, she pulled a cutting knife from the drawer. It wobbled in her fist like it was made of rubber and she went to the rear door and peered outside.

Her teeth chattered. It was so impossibly cold now that her breath gusted past her lips. Logic that defied all explanation. This wasn't just a night in anymore, but a nightmare.

On the other side of the glass, the world seemed balmy and warm, and Janie couldn't get there. Would never go outside with that face waiting in the darkness.

There was a smell now, too. It turned the air sour. On the idea of spoiled trash or fresh roadkill, but nothing her nostrils could place. Janie's throat heaved as she pushed her mouth into her forearm, staving off a retch.

A shadow passed in front of the kitchen door, shifting the light around, dampening it.

Janie crouched to the floor, whimpering, as outside came a cat's anguished wail.

"Kasey," she mouthed.

The next yowl was keen but distant, and Janie realized that Kasey had retreated into the night, offering throaty protests. Some kind of signal or warning. Giving her owner a head's up.

Janie lifted her face to the half-paned window on the door. The fenced-in back yard seemed quiet. And empty.

She looked down at the knife in her fist, knowing the drill. Time to call the police. Again. She wondered if they'd keep her waiting even longer this time.

She started back down the hallway, shoulders heaving. The biting cold was everywhere. Her breath gusted like some haunted house spirit. She had visions of her pipes freezing, stress she shouldn't burden herself with, but couldn't help thinking about. The absurdity of everything.

She passed the bathroom and her peripheral vision clocked motion inside the darkened space. Stirring shadows. She gasped and took off running, breaking hard right at her bedroom door, following the corridor around to the living area and the entryway beside it.

The front door was off its jamb, the wood around it, splintered. Janie's eyes bulged. That face had lured her to other side of the house and then looped back around to breach.

It had gotten as far as the bathroom before Janie decided to come back through the house.

Behind her, the intruder's growl was the harbinger for a sudden explosion of plaster. Janie shrieked and fumbled through the blinding haze, a prowler's vague outline materializing, stepping toward her.

Janie had no time to scream. A huge palm squeezed her

throat, taking away her voice. But not her nose. The smell was toxic, setting her lungs on fire.

The plaster haze thinned and the intruder's free hand wiggled fingers against Janie's face.

She clawed at the forearm, which was hard and scaly and slathered in some type of goo that stuck to her fingers like wet cement.

The wiggling fingers were tipped with claws that slashed down and tore Janie open, blood bubbling up through her throat, exploding past her lips. Her head lolled so that her chin scraped against her breastbone. From this angle, she saw her organs spilling from the gashes in her body.

The killer carried her in its fist, all the way through the hall, squeezing her windpipe tighter, pressure building in Janie's face. It moved into her bedroom and tossed her on the bed. Janie bounced off the mattress and crashed onto the floor, landing in in a pile of magazines, alongside yesterday's newspaper, already coated in her gushing blood.

Her nails clawed through the newsprint as the killer reached down and slashed her back.

The last thing Janie saw was the headline atop the torn and bloodied periodical beside her. The one she'd been looking forward to reading later tonight.

The one that read: IT'S SUMMER IN LOS ANGELES, 1980.

CHAPTER
TWO

Ted Lonergan eyed his reflection as though it were a stranger's.

The man staring back from inside the glass seemed weak in his tan blazer, and the yellow Polo shirt beneath it told an even clearer story, unwashed and disheveled, its collar resting in two different directions.

Ted never was comfortable on the days he had to dress up. A hog in tuxedo for as natural as he felt. Even beyond the clothes, his features had softened in a way that distressed him. He seemed too comfortable, too naive for a man who'd seen what he had.

"This is your life now, huh?" Ted asked the mirror, his voice infused with grim disbelief.

It hadn't been that long in the grand scheme of things, but this is what two years' worth of martini lunches and intolerable politicking did to a man. Turned your face soft while your brain went to mush. It was easier to dismiss reality in this life: runaway children, domestic violence, brutal murder. This blazer turned those things into newspaper anecdotes to be absorbed from afar, and then forgotten. Something to briefly tsk about in conversation before getting down to the business of novels.

The sum of those grim anecdotes had once been the entirety of Ted's life. And though it hadn't been that long, two years of relative cold turkey, his past felt like a dream. Experiences that belonged instead to some of his characters.

Ted Lonergan eyed his reflection and had to admit, he did not like how soft the author had made him. He worried what another five years might do.

"Can't fight change," he grumbled and then laughed at the idea of giving himself a pep talk inside the bathroom of the Cock 'n Bull English Pub, like some nervous waiter on a job interview.

"What'd you say, buddy?" the question came loudly from behind a stall door, pants pushed down around ankles, black socks up to the knees. The speakers in here gave good acoustics. The song was 'Million Dollar Face' by Rick Springfield, and it sounded better in the shitter than on Ted's car stereo.

"Nothing," Ted said while flashing on a memory. Seventeen years old and cruising the valley in his dad's old Ford Sunliner. Radio tuned to KHJ as he drove to Amy Nelson's house in the Hills where he would smoke a joint and spend the evening floating stoned in her swimming pool, looking up at the stars, imagining the alien life that must exist out there among them.

This nostalgia teased a smile out of Ted before the immediacy of the afternoon came roaring back. The task he needed to accomplish. He took a deep breath and thought, *Just an hour... Lunch. You can do this.*

He grabbed a paper towel off the sink and scrunched it around his hands. Then he hurried out into the dining room where every swivel stool at the bar, an entire restaurant of power lunches – agents and clients and executives – turned to size him up. Make sure he wasn't anybody to note.

He wasn't.

Victor was where Ted had left him, looking pensive while staring out the window with his hands folded, watching lunchtime foot traffic bustle down Sunset Boulevard. He didn't look at the table until Ted was fully seated, at which point he turned slowly and glared. "So, when can I see a first draft?"

Ted took a sip of coffee to stall this question further. *Probably by July 4th*, he thought, but Victor didn't have to know that. If Ted's response was, "Two months," then Victor would demand another book this year.

He didn't have that in him.

Ted was halfway through his most recent manuscript, *Red Tide,* about killer cuttlefish wreaking havoc on a Colorado lake. He could barely stand to think about it, though the process of writing it was hardly brain surgery. Some vaguely scientific McGuffin to set things in motion. A couple core characters to push the story along. Lots of fish fodder, gratuitous sex, the more salacious the better, according to Victor. Oh, and keep it around sixty thousand words so not to offset printing costs.

It was all about protecting those profit margins, after all.

Ted might've traded in his old life to become an artist, but he wasn't making art.

"Ted..." Victor said. One simple word that somehow managed to sound like, *"I have more important things to do today."*

"I hear you," Ted said. Killer cuttlefish was in good shape. All he needed was to think of a climactic carnage set piece, doll it up with some excessive gore, and then figure out how the hero cop could convincingly eradicate the threat.

Or unconvincingly. Sometimes that worked better, and Ted liked to amuse himself by seeing what his publisher would allow him to get away with. Like the climax to *Blood Brains*, a novel that had been written at Victor's behest. An attempt to replicate the success of Farris' *The Fury*. It involved a husband-and-wife team of psychic spies from the U.S.S.R. whose mission was to poison America's water supply with experimental psychotropics that would render the entire country docile and controllable. And they would've succeeded, if not for the telekinetic American teenager on their trail. An explosive confrontation atop Mount Rushmore that resulted in Teddy Roosevelt's head exploding into rubble, sending the spies tumbling to their deaths, while debris rained down upon the Fourth of July celebration below.

Ted's best-selling book to date.

Point was, *Red Tide* wasn't going to take much more time. Rest of the summer, probably.

Across the table, Victor leaned in, afraid he might miss Ted's answer. Ted picked up his BLT and took the last few bites. Victor's face, his business casual smile beneath his bushy moustache, began to twitch.

"You really are a pain in the ass," he growled.

"Good to hear. I don't feel like I've got the whole 'artist thing' down, yet."

"Getting better every day."

Ted raised a finger, gesturing 'one minute' as he swallowed his food. Victor leaned even closer, a third of the way over the table now, hanging on every gesture. Ted nodded as if about to speak, then reached for his coffee and took another sip.

Victor sighed and pushed away, gesturing for the check. "Should've ordered you a Moscow Mule. You woulda fessed by now."

"A what?"

"Vodka and ginger beer. Served in a brass cup. They invented 'em here, ya know?"

Ted looked at his coffee mug and clucked disappointment. "Now you tell me."

He'd already delivered one novel this year, *Dark Neighborhood*. About a housewife who gets bitten by a vampire and spends the book infecting her family one-by-one, and then, eventually, the entire neighborhood where she lives, the whole thing climaxing at a bloody fondue party. Vampires, because Victor wasn't finished chasing the success of *Salem's Lot*.

Ted never believed his take on bloodsuckers would set

Booklist on fire, but that wasn't going to stop Victor from trying. *Dark Neighborhood* was out in two weeks and this lunch had been intended as Victor's gesture of good will. A way to keep his talent happy. They had talked a little publicity already. Radio shows. Book signings. A couple conferences across the country, even one in London this fall where Ted would sit on panels with guys like Farris and Masterton and alongside other newcomers like Jerry Williamson and Bari Wood.

A great opportunity to rub elbows with readers while pretending this lifestyle was meant for him.

But at last they had reached the point where Victor was out of patience. Where the only thing that mattered was the only thing left to discuss.

"I don't want to be an ingrate" Ted started, "but maybe you should complain about the bacon. Wasn't quite crisp enough. Might be worth mentioning—"

Across the table, Victor's eye was doing that twitch thing whenever he didn't get what he wanted. "One day a trained monkey is going to be able to do what you do."

Ted laughed, wishing he had one of those world-famous Moscow Mules right now so he could toast that sentiment. "You're probably right."

The waitress dropped the check off and Victor picked it up with a sigh. "Not my best investment."

"I'm working on it," Ted said. "That's all I've got to report for now."

"This summer?" Victor asked, one eyebrow cocked.

"I'm working on it."

"Jesus. You know, maybe it is for the best I don't rush you."

"See that? It's settled."

Victor's cheeks pulsed, projecting a kind of disdain he was no longer interested in masking. "Nothing's settled," he said sharply. "I wasn't going to mention it, but maybe it's time you learn some new tricks."

"What does that mean?"

"It means the reviews for *Dark Neighborhood* ain't pretty."

"Oh, come on, your *critics* don't read these things. They're too afraid of getting cut off. No more free books."

"If you say so."

"They look to see who's putting it out, who wrote it, and they adjust their reviews accordingly."

"They read this one."

"It has some of my best stuff."

"You wrote a scene where the family eats their youngest child for Thanksgiving dinner."

"*'Depraved, more depraved, Ted!'* Sound familiar? You're sending me mixed signals."

Victor rose and dropped a five-dollar tip on the table, storming off like a jilted lover. The curious patrons looked between Victor and Ted, trying to understand their dynamic. Ted met their eyes with a shrug as Victor reached the vestibule, rifling a Marlboro from a crushed soft pack.

Ted got up and followed him to the sidewalk, catching a plume of smoke in the face as Victor exhaled at him. Ted squinted, glancing up at the City National Bank building towering above them as Victor rushed off.

Ted hurried to keep up.

"Five books per year," Victor growled.

"I did that," Ted said. "Last year. I delivered five books."

"Five different books. Not the same crapola over and over again."

"That's why you're getting killer cuttlefish this time. Nobody's done killer cuttlefish."

"Sounds like that piece of shit movie I saw at the Avco last year..."

"The one with Paul Bartel? You know, it wasn't bad."

Victor clenched his jaw, unsatisfied with that answer.

"What do you want, blood, Victor?" Ted rolled up his sleeve as they walked, tapping the soft flesh on his forearm, tenderizing the area. "Why don't you bite right here? We'll start the marketing for *Dark Neighborhood* today."

"Oh, that's very funny. Very funny." Victor stopped and swiveled on his heels. "But it won't be when I stop the checks."

Ted reached into his pocket and took out a package of pop rocks, tearing open the paper sleeve and pouring some on his tongue, the sugar beginning to sizzle. "Victor," he said. "You're an idiot. And I can prove it. You know why you're not going to stop the checks? Because those tired old plots are the same ones that gave you a home in Bel Air, and that Rolls Corniche right over there."

Victor laughed.

"So, lighten up."

"You know, you guys kill me. Every writer thinks his is the great American novel. You know what it is, Ted? You know what it really is?"

Ted poured more pop rocks onto his tongue in anticipation of the answer.

"It's garbage."

"It *is* garbage. But you buy it."

"Contract or no contract, shape up or I'll yank that rug right out from under you." Victor stormed across the street, disappearing into the mouth of the parking garage.

Ted watched him go, somewhat satisfied with the way things had gone. He'd gotten an extension by not delivering a deadline. This line of work was supposed to be easier, but Victor busted balls harder than Ted's old superior, Captain Warren. If not harder.

His yellow Mazda sat in the restaurant's side lot. He unlocked the door and dropped behind the wheel, picking up the spiral notebook on the seat beside him. He rolled his eyes while he rifled through the notes. "Killer cuttlefish," he sighed.

Doesn't matter, though, because you did it. The rest of the day was clear skies and calm waters. With the flick of a key, the

Mazda rumbled to life. Ted poured a few more pop rocks into his mouth and shifted into reverse, rolling back toward the street, slamming into something. The heavy sound of grinding metal bounced the Mazda's frame around without allowing the vehicle to move, bringing him to an unexpected stop.

"Ah, Christ!"

In the rearview mirror, his bumper had dented the side of a much fancier car, the driver's head down against the steering wheel. Ted popped the door and marched toward the silver Jaguar, his mouth full of dissolving sugar rocks.

"Why don't you look where you're going?" he said lightly, hoping a joke could evaporate any tension.

A sandy blond sat behind the wheel, hand covering her face. She lifted her head slowly, eyes narrowing. "You hit me." Her voice wobbled.

"What?"

"I said, '*You hit me.*'"

Ted stepped back and surveyed the situation performatively. His Mazda, halfway out onto the street, backed right into the rear right side of her Jaguar. "Oh, yeah," he said. "I guess maybe I did."

The woman's glare was cutting glass now.

"Well, hey," he said. "Did you ever think about getting a smaller car?"

"You've *got* to be kidding me."

"Just saying…" Ted slapped the Jaguar's side wall. "This thing is like a Bolt Cruiser, ya know? Kind of hard to miss. Like a tank."

She cracked the door and got out, her teal blazer opening to show a pink shirt beneath. "I don't want another car," she growled. "I like this car." She slammed her purse down on the roof. "And I especially like it without any dents."

"Yeah, it probably would look better without the dents."

She went around the rear bumper to the point of impact.

"Look what you've done!" she hissed. His bumper had put a few dings in the area around the wheel.

"Rear quarter panel," Ted said. "Going to be really hard to get parts for this car. Especially that little chrome strip there. Tough to find."

"You know what? You're a real jerk. This car has been in my family for years without any accidents. It's never going to be the same. And you didn't even look. You just thew your car into gear and smashed right into me. How in the hell did you ever get a license?"

Ted held out his candy as if it were a flask. "Would you like some Atomic Rocks?"

"What is wrong with you?"

"Atomic Rocks. They fizz on your tongue. Would you like some?"

She gasped. Spun in a circle as her face cycled through every emotion, bewilderment morphing into anger. "I think you're crazy."

"Juicy Fruit. I think I've got a stick of Juicy Fruit."

"Stay right here," she growled. "I'm going to call the police."

From the corner of Ted's eye, Victor pulled out of the garage, the Rolls Corniche convertible top down. He spotted Ted, the collision, and gave a conciliatory honk, breaking into laughter before speeding off in the other direction.

That was somehow the worst part of today.

Ted took the purse off the roof and jogged to catch the angry woman. "Miss," he said. "Oh, miss…"

She was already halfway to the restaurant and started walking faster.

Ted caught up and handed over her purse. "You forgot this."

She snatched it back.

"Hey look," Ted said. "I'm sorry I hit your car. I understand why you're upset."

"Wow, that's really great of you."

"Let me give you my card." Ted reached into his pocket and fished out his last business card, bent, crumpled, pathetic. Her eyes clocked his name and occupation.

"An author?"

Ted pointed to it. "My address is on there. Come by my office any time and I'll pay for the damages. I really am sorry this happened. And it really was nice to meet you."

"I don't believe any of this."

Ted started back toward his Mazda and the woman was giving chase, heels clopping after him.

"Hey, wait!" She grabbed his blazer tail to keep him in place. "You're not leaving?"

"Well, yeah, I've got to get back to work. See, I've got a deadline and—"

"I've got to call the police and report this."

"Okay, call up the desk sergeant and ask for Barry Watters. Nice guy. He'll send a squad car over and—"

"I don't think so. You're staying here."

"Oh, I can't. Here, have some Atomic Rocks." He placed the package of candy in her palm.

She exhaled.

"Oh," Ted added. "What's your name?"

"Jennifer Stanton."

"Great, I'll see you later, Jenny."

Ted walked back to his Mazda and got in, pulling away from the twisted metal with a loud screech. From the sidewalk, Jennifer grimaced at the sound of further damage being applied to her car. He dropped the window, called out, "Sorry!" and then cut the wheel to get around her, slipping into traffic, flipping through a few radio stations before settling on KROCK, where the song was 'Him' by Rupert Holmes.

He took a slightly longer route back to his office down Laurel Canyon Boulevard on the way to Burbank, trying to drive off the guilt he felt over leaving Jennifer high and dry. He knew she'd call in a day or two, and if she didn't, he had ways of finding her. Had no intention of stiffing her on the bill, just couldn't bring himself to talk to the police. Everybody on the force knew Ted Lonergan.

Many of them blamed him for what happened.

That was another life now, a proverbial stranger's dream, and while Ted did mourn the direction that his life had taken, it didn't mean he wanted his old one back, either.

Ted glided the Mazda into one of the sidewalk spots, his building a few feet away. He climbed the stairwell to the top floor, which he shared with one other business, a bail bondsman named Costas Salvi, who seemed to only work nights.

Ted unlocked his office door and froze in the doorway.

"You're a tough guy to get a hold of." The man said from behind Ted's desk, grinning with his arms folded across his chest. Lou Capell. Ted's only friend.

Ted's stomach turned sour as the memories returned in an unwanted flood. He flashed on Gracie Stanfill, the one image that haunted him still, her standing alone with a widow's bouquet in her fists, looking down at the fresh-covered grave, mascara droplets wobbling off her chin.

He hadn't spoken to her at all that day. The day of Lyle's funeral. And he recalled the pressure that had driven him to try and rectify that. But Gracie hadn't wanted to see Ted at all, smacking his face preemptively.

Sometimes, you just had to be the bad guy in someone else's story.

"This is breaking and entering," Ted said, dryly. "I should call the police."

Lou stood and placed his hands on his hips, where his detective badge was visibly clipped to his belt beneath the Roebuck & Co. blazer. "They've been a bit busy lately."

"Then maybe they shouldn't be wasting any time talking to has-beens."

"Come off it, man. Figured you might want to catch up a bit."

Ted studied him carefully, searching for ulterior motives, finding one, but being far too tired to push back. He walked inside and reclaimed his seat from Lou.

Lou nodded, then sat down in the seat opposite the desk.

"Then how 'bout a game?" Ted asked. "For old time's sake?"

CHAPTER
THREE

The chess board was largely decimated.

Lou reached out and rubbed the head of his queen between his dark fingers, weighing every possible move. Then he sat back to study the board anew.

"Oh, for Christ's sake, Lou, would you move?"

"Don't rush me, man. That's how you make mistakes."

Ted was relieved that Lou had been willing to play. He was the sort of the guy who never just "dropped by" and Ted couldn't stall the conversation forever. He knew why Lou was here. Even without the particulars, Ted knew.

"You've been working on that for two days now," Ted laughed, tearing the top off another sleeve of Atomic Rocks. He shook the bag and poured half of it onto his tongue. "You'd have to try hard to *not* move into check."

Lou's fingers fell again around his queen, eyes clocking Ted as he zipped his majesty past the maelstrom, placing her on the far side of the board. Away from Ted's king.

"That's your move?" Ted asked.

"Damn right."

"What the hell are you doing?"

"What do you mean?"

"You just threw away your queen."

"I got a plan." Lou reached into his coat, taking the opportunity to glance around Ted's office. The place had an old-time look, a frosted glass door with Ted's name stenciled across the window. TED LONERGAN. Beneath it, smaller letters scratched off, though the ghost words still lingered: PRIVATE INVESTIGATOR.

"Maid's day off," Ted told him, sensing Lou's disapproval and shrinking beneath the detective's quiet judgment.

Dust moats floated around stacks of books, newspapers, and magazines. An asthmatic's nightmare. Ted couldn't remember the last time another person had set foot in here, so there was barely enough room for movement, just a winding path toward the bathroom off to the left.

"You got a plan, huh?" Ted asked, attempting to steer Lou's attention back to the game. "Regicide?"

Lou slipped a few Polaroids from his coat pocket and dropped them on the board. Ted glanced down and then wished he hadn't. He looked away but it was too late. His mind was already absorbing them like a sponge, all the gruesome details slathering through his brain, infesting his thoughts. Putting the Writer to work.

None of this should've been a problem for a man like Ted, who made a living at schlock fiction. In fact, the page that currently wobbled around in his typewriter contained a half-written scene where a cuttlefish chomped through a lifeguard's scrotum.

Ted could write gore all day long, and often did. It wasn't uncommon for him to chuckle over the sound of his own keystrokes once the creative fires got roaring. There had to be a certain demented poetry to the bloodshed in order for it to stand out, after all. But when it was a real human being beneath all the shredded skin and missing limbs, such as the person in the Polaroids currently sitting in the middle of the desolate chess board, then the grief he felt was indescribable.

"Wish you would've just called, Lou," he said flatly.

"I'm sorry about this." Lou looked remorseful. "I wouldn't be here if—"

"No."

"Look at the photos, man. Please."

"I looked at them."

"I mean, really look. Get the scent back."

The Scent. Would if it were that easy. Ted had been running from "The Scent" since turning in his badge. For a while, he thought the private sector had been the answer to his problems. Take what he'd learned at the academy, on the job, and simply use those tools to take the gigs he wanted. Easy stuff, like cheating husbands, missing persons, erroneous disability claims, nothing too taxing.

Nothing that would haunt him.

But "The Scent," to use Lou's term, was more like a stain in that it lingered and couldn't be removed. Ted's last job as a private investigator was two years ago. He still had nightmares about it.

Lou cleared his throat, the sound pulling Ted out of his mental rabbit hole. Reluctantly, he turned back to the Polaroids where the macabre details drew him in. In a moment, he was locked on. A young girl, blond and nearly nude, awkwardly sprawled across what must've been her bedroom floor. One leg folded up beneath her torso. The other, torn right off.

Ted closed his eyes. In the darkness there, the Writer got to work, keys clack-clacking, stringing together words that Ted struggled to read. In a moment, his mind's eye had half a page.

Half a page he didn't want to read.

The page described a girl. Alone in her house. Killed sometime after nine, the Writer guessed, based on her skimpy nightie, and the way her intact thigh was splattered in peach-colored nail polish. She had been settled in and ready for bed when she got interrupted. And the psycho who had done this to her, not just amputated a limb, but slashed her flesh to ribbons and took several bites from her neck, had tremendous power.

"Janie Richter," Lou said, causing the page in Ted's mind to tear, the Writer pulling the unfinished sheet from the typewriter's carriage and slotting another. "Twenty years old. Nursing student. Waited tables to make ends meet."

He plunked down another photo, this one showing what Ted guessed was a middle-aged man if the steely grey chest hair on his torso was any indication. That was all he had to go on because the victim's head was missing.

Plop. Another photo. Another girl. This one's chest torn wide open, the wound messy and undisciplined. Whoever had done these murders wasn't just powerful, but angry, too.

"Lou…"

Lou gathered the photos and slipped them back inside his coat. "I wouldn't be here if I wasn't desperate."

"You're going to have to get by without me."

"Can you just go to the Richter girl's house, get me a read on what's happening. Do that for me and I'll—"

"Lou."

"Don't do it for me," Lou said. He lifted his chin and gestured to the photograph on the file cabinet behind Ted.

"Low blow." Ted swiveled in his chair and pushed the photograph down, more harshly than intended. The picture was of he and his partner, Lyle Stanfill, while on a fishing trip up at Big Bear.

Ted recalled the way Gracie had warned Lyle then about drinking too much that weekend, citing Ted as the bad influence when really their friendship had been symbiotic. Friends that supported each other's strengths and weaknesses.

He remembered again the pain of Gracie's slap and felt that sting in his cheek even now.

Lou was barely looking at him. "I'm up against it, Ted. Please."

Ted poured the rest of the Atomic Rocks into his mouth and

gave a humorless laugh. A borderline scoff. He remembered what it was like to be up against it. "How is the asshole, anyway?"

"The chief? Still an asshole."

"And you want me to come back."

"No," Lou said. "Just... advise. Drive out to this girl's house and—"

"I don't want anything to do with Warren. Guy's got a real knack for getting in the way. Stop you from winning."

"Forget Warren. Focus on the people dying."

"Warren never has," Ted said. "To him they're just statistics. Maybe that's the key to a good night's sleep."

"Come on man, you're too sharp to be a thirty-four-year-old has-been."

"Maybe, but I still don't need your hard sell."

Lou dropped a manilla envelop beside the board, scattering a few of their discarded game pieces. "I didn't mean that. Shit. I just... I need you to go out to her house and take a look, alright?"

Ted closed his eyes and the typewriter there had a fresh sheet of paper in it, keys already striking out, the Writer branding the page with a description of Janie Richter's death. Her body dropping onto the stack of periodicals on her bedroom floor, ruby-red blood coating them like spilled paint.

"The Scent," as Lou called it, building out a mental picture. While that description wasn't entirely accurate, Ted had nothing better with which to replace it. He thought of it as "pure empathy." Hyper emotions that formed pictures like building blocks. It had been a while since he felt it last, but now it was clawing up out of his subconscious and Ted hated it.

Lou tapped the envelope again, then stood up. "I should be going."

Ted watched Lou go to the door and pull it open. His mouth popped, about to say something else, when he leapt back in surprise at the sight of somebody else in the hall, just beyond the jamb.

The woman from this afternoon, looking a bit startled now that she'd been caught eavesdropping. "Is this…" she started to speak, eyes roving over Lou's shoulder, finding Ted behind his desk.

"Jenny," Ted said, grateful for the interruption. The tenor of the room lifting on her presence.

"Jennifer," she corrected.

Lou raised his hands. Here was tension he didn't need. "I think I hear Captain Video calling me on the Opticon Scillometer."

"Umm," Jennifer offered, as if Lou had suddenly stopped speaking English.

He flashed a quick smile. "Just a little childhood humor."

"Oh," Jennifer said. "Don't leave on my account. I'm just here about my car."

"A Jag," Ted added, flashing his eyebrows as if Lou should be impressed.

"The Jag," Jennifer said. "Have you hit any other cars lately? Or do you have a really short memory?" Her tone warmed a little, an indecisive smile beginning to stretch.

Lou snuck past her with a polite nod, turning around in the hallway. "Ted, the address is in that folder, will you—?"

Ted waved him out and stood up to greet the woman he hadn't expected to see again today. "Come in, Jenny, um, Jennifer. Please."

She did, scrutinizing every detail of his place, her nose wrinkling at the inches of dust that coated everything.

"Maid's day off," Ted repeated.

Jennifer sat down where Lou had been and fished a crinkled piece of paper out of her purse.

"Care for a game of chess?"

"Mister Lonergan, I hate to be blunt but—"

"You want me to pay for the damages to your car."

"Yes, well, I went right over to the garage after you stranded me and—"

"I didn't exactly *strand* you. I mean, I slammed into you in a moment of complete distraction, but—"

Jennifer dropped an invoice down over the chessboard. "It's going to cost twelve hundred to repair the damage... It sounds like you're still willing to admit it's your fault?"

"It sure was, but I can't give you a check."

Jennifer sighed. "First, you don't have insurance—"

"It's un-American."

"Now you don't have a bank account."

"I don't trust banks."

"Mister Lonergan..."

"Ted."

"Mister Lonergan."

Ted rose and wound around the various magazine stacks to the far side of the room. A bookshelf stuffed with author copies of his own novels. Jennifer followed him with her eyes as he pushed aside an entire stack of *Blood Brains* to retrieve a thick envelope behind it. He removed a few bills, put the envelope back, and then returned to the desk, handing over the money. "That's yours."

Jennifer held the crisp, fresh-from-the-bank, currency with uncertainty. "Um. There's a little over two thousand dollars here."

"That's in case you have trouble finding parts," Ted said. He scribbled down a name and number on a notepad, then tore it from the binding and handed it off. "Here's the name of a guy who can help you. Hewitt. Scottish, if you can believe it. Nice guy, though."

Jennifer just stared, confused.

"You're driving a Mark IX Jag, right?"

"Yes," she said, relief washing over her face. "Thank you."

"I am very sorry that I hit your car. I was in a ridiculous headspace this afternoon and that doesn't excuse my behavior one bit. Just…" He stopped because Jennifer didn't need to know his life story. The more people knew of Ted Lonergan, the less they wanted to know. "Well, I know sometimes people can become attached to things like cars and I'm truly sorry for the hassle I've caused you."

"You are so odd," Jennifer said.

"Fair."

"And you're right," she added. "My car does have sentimental value. Um, excuse me for saying this but… this is not the reaction I expected to get. After this morning I thought I'd be dealing with a real head case. I even talked to a lawyer."

"And now?"

"And now… thank you."

"I am in contact with Earth. Occasionally."

Jennifer folded the money, along with Ted's reference, and placed both in her handbag. She rose and started for the door. "It was nice meeting you."

Ted got up and rushed around the desk, toppling a stack of files. "Gee, maybe we'll run into each other again."

"I hope not." Jennifer laughed after she said it. After realizing how harsh it sounded.

"Let me take you out to dinner," Ted suggested. "Make it up to you."

"Oh, I don't think so. Besides, you've already made it up to me." She flashed a lovely cherry smile – the best and nicest thing Ted had seen today. A display of beauty to make the world less harsh for a moment. And then she walked out of his office.

He followed Jennifer into the hall and watched her go, trying to hang on to the pleasantness she represented, trying to forget about the terrible pages the Writer was producing even now, all the chaos and destruction packed into his words.

"Good afternoon, Jennifer," he said, rather desperately, voice echoing down the empty hall.

Jennifer pushed through the stairwell door and glanced back

with a fresh smile, hesitation in her eyes. "Bye, Mister Lonergan."

Then she was gone, and Ted still didn't want to go back inside his office. He thought of Lou's folder and couldn't stand the idea of being alone with it. All the ghosts swirling around inside the cover.

Now, Lou's words were echoing around inside his head.

"Just advise."

That's what they always said. *"Just advise."* Because so few of them knew any better.

Lyle had known. Lyle had understood. But Lyle was dead.

Some even claimed it was Ted who had gotten him killed.

He shook that debilitating thought from his brain and then headed inside to read Lou's file.

CHAPTER
FOUR

Ted spent the afternoon working on *Red Tide*, hoping to exorcise some of the encroaching darkness. He wrote a chapter called "Ghost Fishing" in which an unscrupulous father and son duo of petty thieves planned to swim underwater to the rich side of the lake and loot a few of the vacation houses there. Only they get entangled in a web of discarded casting net and become bait for the crazed school of flesh-hungry fish.

The world of crazed cuttlefish held little comfort for Ted, given the way Lou's file weighed on his mind, implying a certain responsibility whether he wanted it or not.

So, around eight, he drove out to Janie Richter's apartment in North Glendale, a quick ride down West Glenoaks Boulevard. It was dark by the time he got there and parked at the end of the cul-de-sac beneath a yellow sign ominously marked END.

The two-family house was little more than an unbroken shadow far outside the streetlight glow that covered the rest of the road. Poor Janie Richter might as well have been living in outer space.

Ted cracked the Mazda's door. The warm May air pushed against him. He shivered as "The Scent" tightened around his head. Keyboard keys clacking there, the Writer's fingers striking, a scene spilling out across the page.

He tucked Janie's file beneath his arm and climbed out of his car, turning to face the Brand Park Forest that surrounded him on three sides.

The typewriter showed a completed page already. It described someone spying on Janie from the refuge provided by this foliage. Night after night. A study of her rituals and rotations. Visitors, if she had any. A lover. Friends? What nights she worked. The ones she didn't. What time she got home.

No, the Writer suggested, tearing that page from the cradle, crumpling it.

"Waste of time." Ted agreed. Everything about the murder had been impulsive. Decided in the moment. Theirs wasn't a patient boy.

Ted stepped on a broken sewer grate as he crossed the dead-end road, eyeing the bay window that jutted out over a small stretch of grass.

According to the police report, the second-floor apartment was empty because the grad student that rented it had accepted a job offer in Colorado but was keeping this place on the books until August in the event he didn't like the gig and decided to move back. Lou had two witnesses placing him out of state yesterday evening.

"You saw her from the window," Ted said, matter-of-factly, as he approached the glass. The scenario could only start one way. The Writer was typing again, describing what the perpetrator had seen from this vantage: Janie in her nightie, pink and see-through. She stood at her bureau, mulling her nail polish choices while the killer watched, face against the glass, like Ted right now, aroused by the sight of her young, barely clothed body. Something he wasn't supposed to be seeing, emboldened by the darkness.

"Go on," Ted urged, as these terrible thoughts sifted over his brain. "Who's going to know, right?" The Writer was already onto the next scene, typing a moment similar to the movie *Halloween*, the killer's lumbering point-of-view perspective as he glided through the shadows, slow stepping down the driveway. His mind made up. The girl inside about to die.

Click. Ted's flashlight beam carved a path through the night. He followed the killer straight along the pavement toward the back of the house.

Except, Ted turned back around and pointed his beam at the trees that swayed gently above his Mazda.

According to the report, witnesses saw no strange vehicles yesterday. No delivery vans or utility trucks. That didn't mean that someone hadn't happened down this road, caught wind of the house at the end of the street, noticed the half-naked girl standing behind the glass, and decided to—

No. The Writer discouraged Ted from even building out that profile. It wasn't correct.

"Then where'd you come from, pal?" Ted wondered. According to the report, Lou and his guys had even canvassed the surrounding streets for suspicious vehicles and persons in the event the killer had gone into the woods there and used the trees as cover to creep around to Janie's street. Nobody had seen anything.

Ted went all the way down the driveway, using his light to peer through every window. He imagined the murderer creeping along, knowing the darkness would conceal him every step of the way. The Writer described Janie in her skimpy nightie, walking parallel to the killer, all that separated their bodies was a few inches of drywall, a couple of glass panes.

"You watched her," Ted said. "But it was dark out here, she couldn't see you."

Up ahead, trash cans were scattered. Ted hot-stepped around them. The killer had accidentally stumbled into them while spying, entranced and aroused by Janie.

Except, that conclusion prompted the Writer to rip the page from the cradle and crumple it, leaving Ted lost for a moment.

The Writer slotted a new page and the paper wobbled in place, crisp and blank. Janie hadn't been sexually assaulted. She wasn't robbed. For their man, this was strictly about taking lives. And Janie hadn't been his first.

"You were trying to draw her to the back of the house," Ted said, realizing then that the spilling trash cans hadn't been an accident, but bait.

The landlord had left a key beneath the mat for investigators. Ted retrieved it and clicked his way inside through the back door, locking up behind him, feeling a shiver as he considered a scenario where the murderer returned to the scene of his crime. But no. He didn't think that was right. Janie was already old news to their boy.

There was a mess around the kitchen sink: a dinner plate, a few dirty glasses, a bag of Wonder Bread with two slices missing.

"You knew she was alone," Ted said, moving into the hallway. "Knew you could get away with doing whatever you wanted." That appeared to be the only consistency in the attack pattern. The killer chose people in isolation. Always at night. Hardly surprising, but each profile had to start somewhere.

Rage, Ted thought. Perhaps the *who* of it didn't matter at all, so long as their perp got to kill. But for what reason? Repressed sexuality? Gender resentment? Religious intolerance? Societal ostracization? None of those felt exactly right, and the Writer agreed, fingers hovering over the keyboard, on standby. "What's eating you, pal?"

Ted passed the bathroom on the right, a complete mess of broken tile and scattered plaster. A warzone, part of the wall entirely decimated, showing through to the front hall beyond it. His shoes crunched debris as he walked.

This destruction introduced more questions, and Ted was disquieted by the reality it suggested. The murderer was powerful enough to break through the bathroom wall. Meaning he'd done it fast, probably without the aid of weapons. It wasn't enough for this guy to be some kind of carnival strongman, that kind of power was almost—

"Wayyy too many horror novels," Ted said, catching his reflection in the bathroom mirror. He looked different than he had at lunch. In the darkness of a dead girl's bathroom, Ted Lonergan suddenly recognized himself. The grimness in his eyes like hardened cement. A renewed sense of purpose. A bloodhound back on the trail.

The Scent.

Ted shook his head to try and exorcise that train of thought. This was a murder investigation. Not a paperback. Lou deserved his best possible assessment and the people of this city needed it even worse.

The hall led into Janie's bedroom. It also snaked off to the right, which is where the bathroom wall had been broken through. The hall then banked to the left, leading to the front door and living room.

"You lured her to the kitchen so she wouldn't hear you slip in the front," Ted said. "Because you'd already bought yourself access to the front." He glanced at the bathroom again, pieces clicking into place. "You didn't hear that part, did you, Janie? Because you were in the shower."

Ted entered the bedroom next and sat down on the victim's bed, smiling sadly at the indiscriminate blood spatters that stained the old carpet. He looked around the room, at the calendar with one day circled later this month. The name *Kurt* scribbled in red sharpie, followed by two exclamation points.

Plans and dreams, snuffed out by someone's indiscriminate rage, turning Janie into a ghost. A bundle of memories that lived on only in the minds of others now.

Ted opened the file and shuffled through the pages, reading parts of it aloud. "A sticky and unidentified substance coated the body," he said. "Remnants of that same substance was discovered in the bathroom, and on the door jamb as well."

The Writer typed a single letter on the empty page, then pitched the paper into the garbage.

"It *isn't* semen," Ted said. The report was careful to note this. Whatever the unidentified substance was, was at the lab for analysis.

This triggered something of a reset in Ted's brain. His already wafer-thin profile crumbled away, a contradiction to everything he'd been building. Every crime scene was coated in this slime.

Time for another theory. The Writer had already begun working on a fresh page, but Ted didn't want to read it. He resisted, because what would Lou think if Ted came back with a conclusion similar to the plot of one of his books? If Ted had learned anything during his years on the job, it was that real life was never as fantastical as we wanted it to be.

He thought back to those hot August nights as a teenager, floating in Amy Nelson's pool, stoned and watching the skies, dreaming of the future, of infinite possibilities that felt so eventual at that age. Life on other planets had always been his favorite fantasy, inspired by the words of Isaac Asimoff and Robert Heinlan, Cordwainer Smith and all the other yellow-paged dime store paperbacks that had fueled his imagination then.

Why was his mind so jumbled now?

And on the topic of this strange, translucent slime, what in the hell was it?

"You ripped her leg from her body, tore her hair off in clumps." Ted rose from the bed and crossed the room, frowning once more at Janie's bubbly, excited handwriting, the enthusiasm with which she'd written the word, KURT!!

It wasn't Kurt who'd done this to her. But what about another man?

A girl so beautiful surely had other suitors. Was guaranteed to have left a few broken hearts in her wake. Someone who felt rejected might wish to destroy a girl like Janie. Might feel nothing but hatred and anger in his heart. And maybe the pattern was there. The murderer linked to all victims, avenging a series of unknown wrongs, imagined or otherwise.

That didn't explain the slime.

In each of these cases there were no fingerprints. No witnesses. The police had checked gyms, athletic clubs, and any other place where someone in possession of this kind of strength might hang out. Lou had also checked every mental hospital on the west coast. No escapees, or releases of anyone who might fit this bill. Nothing. A big zero.

Which is what Ted was coming up with too.

"Except there is something here," Ted said. There should be more consistency in these attacks. A pattern in how the murderer engaged with each victim. Similar cuts or bruises. A little exploration was to be expected as the killer earned the confidence to take things further, but these attacks were so chaotic you could make the case they weren't even done by the same person.

There was at least one working theory in the file that suggested a disparate cult of nomads up from Nevada, wayward hippies who trawled around town in a rusted red van, and who had grown emboldened in their recruitment efforts, lashing out at those who rejected their end times treatise. At least one killing in Redondo Beach had been attributed directly to them. Perhaps each of Lou's victims had encountered them, but that was going to be difficult to prove without a lucky break.

And that still didn't explain the slime. Nothing explained the slime.

Something settled into Ted's mind in that moment that he'd never say out loud.

And never to Lou.

"Too many novels," he repeated, still fighting the conclusion. But the dread was already in his bones. No use lying to himself. He could pretend they were looking for some rabid lunatic, a nomadic cult, or a skewered vigilante who felt he'd been wronged, but none of that was the truth.

Suddenly, Ted regretted his decision to stop carrying. He'd only recently grown accustomed to the naked hip, and now that there was no sidearm to cement his security, he felt like he needed one.

Because whatever had been in here last night, whatever had mutilated Janie Richter, was something to be scared of.

Ted collected his things and rushed from the apartment as though it were haunted. He hurried to his vehicle. And while he wasn't a superstitious man, only playing one for the rubes who plunked down seventy-five cents to own a copy of his gibberish, he was badly shaken up tonight.

Cuttlefish, vampires, aliens, crazed fetuses, demons... That's why his brain was pushing hard for this conclusion, right? The Writer, trafficking in well-worn territory because Ted had left reality behind long ago. The Scent, like any muscle, was dull from lack of practice. It pushed fiction because Ted no longer dealt in fact.

He closed his eyes as the Mazda idled. The Scent swirled. The Writer wrote, pushing him toward the truth even as he resisted it.

Ted's profile, the one he wished he could turn over to Lou, an angry man on a killing spree, refused to materialize past silhouette. The Writer couldn't articulate what he didn't know, choosing to put forward something far more unsettling. Pages that described a hulking figure with a powerful gait that would tear anyone who crossed its path to pieces.

That was the perpetrator they sought.

"At least you'll shred what's left of your credibility and that will be that," Ted told himself. He pushed the Writer's work from his mind, cursed his loyalty to Lou, and shifted into drive. The Mazda sped off, leaving Janie Richter's place immersed in the same darkness that had likely cemented her demise.

His hands trembled as they squeezed the steering wheel.

This resistance caused them to shake harder. The Writer pounded keys with furious determination, hammering out a creature double feature. Gnarled claws dripping with slime, something crawling up from the bottom of a murky forest bog with murder on its brain.

"I'm not going to let you do this," Ted said, voice trembling. He sounded desperate. He felt weak and helpless, knowing it was all going to get worse from here: the murders, his mind, everything.

He shuffled his thoughts, settling first on Victor and the unfinished manuscript waiting back at the office. The easiest problem to solve. Stop off for a fresh bottle of Jack, then zip back to Burbank. Post up over the keyboard, pecking away until those killer cuttlefish were burning in hell.

Next, he thought about Jennifer Stanton. The lovely woman for whom he'd caused a tremendous amount of grief. That she seemed content upon leaving his office this afternoon, happy with both the money and the reference, should've been enough. But there was also a kindness in her spirt that Ted was attracted to.

The way she looked at him, it was as if he mattered. It was the kind of thing you realized you couldn't go without once you got a taste of it again. And after spending the evening with the ghost of Janie Richter, along with all the spirts that Ted Lonergan had failed to put to rest, he recognized a desperation for that sort of connection.

He cruised the 101 with the windows down, Kenny Loggins' 'This Is It' on blast while the late spring breeze soothed his anxiety. The weather wasn't enough to exorcise the Writer's troubling thesis, but at least it got his panic under control.

On Sunset Boulevard, Ted pulled up to a meter and eyed the all-night drug store beyond it. Two hookers stepped from the shadows as if on cue. One white, the other black, both of them in neon negligee.

"Take you around the world?" the black girl asked, a curious eyebrow cocked high.

Ted liked her smile. Liked her curves even more. And he especially liked the enthusiasm in her voice. She was probably skilled enough at her job to be able to sell the façade of companionship.

"I'm afraid to fly," he told her, smiling sadly and then wedging himself into the phone booth on the corner. He dropped a coin into the slot and dialed Lou, who answered so quickly he must've been waiting by the phone.

"Ted?"

"Just came from Janie's. I don't know."

"Will you think on it?"

"Don't have much choice."

"I know," Lou said, sounding ashamed. Fully aware of the burden he'd placed on his old pal.

"Let me ask you," Ted said. "The report mentions a slimy substance found at the scene."

"Yeah. A real mess."

"Got an ID on it?"

"Not yet."

"Talk soon." Ted ended the call and walked into the store. He grabbed a bouquet of red roses out of the water pail by the register, then counted two of his novels on the paperback spinner, temporarily relieved by the sight of them. A reminder that Ted Lonergan was more than a tortured detective. That there was another version of him in this world now.

You don't have to go back, he thought.

Except The Scent had already returned. He felt it now, swirling through him, sharpening dulled instincts. As he approached the counter with the flowers, he realized he was already transformed. The Ted Lonergan he'd been earlier today, the fraud in the blazer, looking out from behind the bathroom glass at the Cock 'n Bull English Pub, was wilting, ceding ground to the career detective who'd always intended to return.

Ted paid for the flowers and jogged back to his car.

"This boy's got real game," the hooker joked, watching him climb into the Mazda.

Ted waved before driving off, recalling Jennifer Stanton's address off the repair estimate he'd seen this afternoon. She was in Santa Monica, ten minutes west of here, right off San Vicente Boulevard. Her street was dark, save for the slight sodium glow of sporadic streetlamps.

He parked and scribbled a note on a sheet of paper, getting out, carrying the flowers toward her door, imagining the killer as he walked. Lou's madman crawling through the shadows, searching out prey.

Ted's own hand became a gnarled talon. He imagined it closing around Jennifer's throat, squeezing, watching her bulging eyes blister in disbelief.

"Stop it," he whispered, and had to close his eyes to make everything disappear. Then he skipped up the steps and placed the flowers on the welcome mat, sliding a note beneath them:

Jennifer, I hope this is the right color.

He turned to go and felt the change. An urge to go to the window. Peer inside. Maybe he would find Jennifer there, perhaps in a state of undress. If he were to see something like that, what urges might follow?

The Scent was already driving him. Flashes of wicked things. Jennifer screaming, her leg torn away. Her hair being pulled from her scalp in wispy strands anchored by patches of torn flesh. What she would look like while writhing on her back, blood squirting from her?

He grabbed his head as if that was a way to make it all stop.

"Don't say it," Ted growled as he dropped back behind the

wheel of his Mazda. He was shivering now. "Don't go there." But it was much too late. His brain had gone there hours ago. The Writer had figured it out and the pages in his head were cleaner than they'd ever been. Ted was going to have to admit it.

Because it was the truth.

Whatever was doing this wasn't a man at all.

CHAPTER
FIVE

I t moved through patches of trees, toward the call of detached voices that hovered in the far-off night. Its footfalls were heavy, lumbering and graceless, pounding dirt as it advanced.

In its head spoke a different voice. One both familiar and constant, echoing through its mind. A static cadence. Always the same words. In the same order. Never stopping.

The words that lived inside its thoughts had been part of its life since the beginning. The first notes of consciousness that it could recall. Words that it had committed to memory without understanding the meaning behind any. In fact, it understood almost none.

It was learning, however, and had zeroed in on one specific word, intuiting somehow that its meaning was in reference to its very existence.

Syngenor.

That's what the voice called it. The Syngenor.

The Syngenor walked, transforming the air around its body into a snap of bitter cold. Its skin swallowed humidity as it moved, carbon dioxide flushing out through its hard and scaly pores, transforming the immediate atmosphere around its shoulders into something akin to winter frost.

For the Syngenor, this was breathing. The process also calmed its fury, which was constantly mounting inside of it. Fury because everything here was new and intimidating.

The creature scanned the nightscape, searching out a specific noise it believed was calling to it. Provoking it. Everything provoked it because everything in this miserable place was an assault on its senses.

Whirring machinery shouted at it from everywhere, zipping along roads and rails, assailing the sky. Technology that encased melodic beats inside of metal bones. Layered beneath all that chaos were the endless voices, whimpering animals, chirping insects. A symphony of unending chaos thriving inside its head.

As bad as it was, the daylight hours were so much worse.

The Syngenor preferred the dark for this very reason, and because people were simply easier to catch after night fall. Oblivious to the danger until it was too late. They were lesser beings that way, soft and lacking in any sort of survivor's instinct. The Syngenor thought of them as cattle, herded for its own specific need.

It turned its head, honing once more on the noise that caught its attention. One interesting voice, soft and honey-tinged, more pleasant than the others. Certainly better than the one running through its mind on repeat.

The creature's large, muscular limbs swatted down a bundle of dried branches, cracking them right off the bark. Then it stomped toward a clearing up ahead where the trees receded and became pavement. Beyond it was a scrawl of homes that ascended all the way up the hillside.

A thrill moved through the Syngenor as the creature considered for a moment what it was looking at here: a slaughterhouse. Just one sprawling mountain of unsuspecting bodies.

It cocked its massive, elongated head and listened to all those hearts, pounding in concert, voices mumbling from behind a hundred walls, all the laughter and the crying. Moaning. That permanent assault on its senses again. The Syngenor's inability to filter any of it out, cementing its natural state as agitation.

For as long as the Syngenor lived, peace was unattainable.

It stood lost inside a nightmare, a dark fantasy that established itself inside the creature's consciousness. Right here were all the bodies it could ever need.

But not just yet.

Right now, it searched for something closer. For the source of that sweet, diffusive voice calling out.

Two flickering headlights danced across a stalk of close-knit trees on the creature's left, a car gliding up around the bend. Carefree voices floating in the air.

"That's me!" the voice cried out. "Up ahead."

Headlights carved through the darkness, becoming more pronounced as the vehicle appeared. Its growling engine shredded the Syngenor's sense of safety, and the creature felt its body brace instinctively against it.

It took a reflexive step back into wooded cover, slashing at the nearest tree, its six-inch claws cleaving off a hunk of bark. The soft rumble in its throat became a growl that sent woodland creatures scurrying for their lives.

Twenty feet away, the car pulled to a stop. Indistinct laughter from every voice inside of it. The one the Syngenor was interested in was especially wobbly. "I... I can walk from here, I think."

"It ain't the walking part I'm worried about!" another voice added.

"You better not wrap your car around a tree."

The creature studied these sloshy inflections, concluding there was no threat here. The sensation of balmy air passing into its body relaxed its stance. It watched the girl pop the door and get out, her sneakers clopping down on pavement.

The Syngenor inched forward, all its attention and interest locked onto her as she giggled and leaned back through the open window. "Listen, guys," she said. "I'll call you tomorrow."

"Not from the hospital you won't!"

"I'm not that drunk!" she snorted, then tapped the trunk of the car with a suddenness that made the creature wince. A gesture it interpreted as antagonistic.

Could it have been wrong about her?

The car pulled away from the curb. "Good night," she giggled, wiggling her fingers. Then she pumped an excited fist into the air. "Woooooo!" she cried as she staggered across the creature's field of vision. "What a night! What. A. Night!"

She headed for another vehicle parked in the shadows.

"What a *cold* night!" she said, shivering in the sudden absence of humidity.

A couple of feet away, the Syngenor was on the move, dropping onto its limbs so that its stomach raked along the ground to better prowl her.

The young girl walked faster, as if sensing a presence. Her car was tucked on the bend of the road, right against the curve of this paved half-circle, the street looping up into the hills above.

"Keys?" she wondered, an etch of panic in her voice.

The creature crawled onto the pavement, killing claws clacking against the tarmac. Its elongated body was exposed out here, and anyone passing by would see it crouched on the far side of the vehicle, listening to the girl currently fumbling through the bag that dangled off her shoulder. It paused, considering for a moment the full auditory spectrum of the area, then decided there was time to make its move.

The girl stopped.

The Syngenor froze too.

She craned her neck toward the trees but saw nothing. Stood there a moment and then something rattled in her fist.

The creature crawled to the vehicle's rear.

Click. The door swung open. The girl dropped down behind the steering wheel. Her breathing was labored now. A series of harsh and unpleasant scrapes that the creature did not enjoy hearing.

It always ended this way. Humans becoming hostile in its presence. The Syngenor had believed this one, with her soft voice and innocuous tone, would be different. Would want to help.

Another click and the car screamed to life. The creature, close enough that the vehicle's deep grumble startled it into standing upright.

Inside, the girl sighted a monster moving vertically across her rearview. She shrieked, began fumbling with the shifter.

Only the creature was faster, tearing the driver's door straight off its hinges, tossing the metal hunk to the pavement. She shrieked again, scrambling across the front seat and fumbling for the far door.

The Syngenor closed its hand around her ankle and squeezed, turning her bones to dust. It tugged on what was now a limp and fleshy sock in its palm, yanking her toward the driver's side and slashing her shoulders, turning her clothes and skin into one indistinguishable tangle of ribbons.

She howled as it sliced her again. The Syngenor felt an unexpected surge of resentment now. It slashed her a third time for this betrayal, nails driving so deep inside her body they scraped against bone.

It yanked her ragdoll body from the car, throwing the carcass against the idling metal frame. The Syngenor's slick black tongue glided from its mouth, flicking against the bloody mess it had created on her back, slithering along the pulp like a curious snake.

Until its tongue found its way against the bone that joined her spine to her skull. The pronged tip of its scaly muscle pierced that area, beginning to suck, siphoning fluid from it.

The Syngenor glimpsed its reflection in the car's window. Its silver eyes rolled back, draining her of spinal fluid, taking every last drop so that its pores began to ooze with that clear, crystalline substance.

Only then did it begin to feel lighter. And with its night business completed, it worried all over again about the work ahead.

How little time was left to accomplish it.

CHAPTER
SIX

It was early morning in Venice, and Sherry Carpenter was being led out of the aerobics studio by two men in suits. She still wore her pink dayglo tights, and her frizzed hair was pulled back across her scalp, ponytail swaying against the small of her back.

"In here," one of the men told her as they stepped onto the sidewalk where a dark sedan idled. The back door open.

"No, it's fine," Sherry said. "Really, I'm fine."

"Then you have nothing to worry about." That came from the man in the tan suit. His eyes hidden away behind dark Ray-Bans. Brown hair buzzed all the way to his scalp, where a small patch of hair was missing on the round of his skull. A scar that formed a white T all the way down the back of his head.

The other man went around to the driver's side and climbed behind the wheel, flashing a smile that was intended to reassure her. Though when two men barged in on your morning workout and demanded you come with them, it was difficult to feel reassured of anything.

"Listen," Sherry said, her voice ticking up so to arouse the attention of morning joggers and other passersby. "I don't know who you guys are and I'm not getting in this car."

"We're the good guys," the Tan Man told her, flatly and without conviction. He only needed to spin the lie, didn't have to sell it.

"We just want to talk," the driver shouted from within the car. "About your employer."

"Ed?"

The Tan Man gestured to the back seat.

From the front, the driver continued: "Time is a factor, and once you've spoken to *our* employer, we *will* bring you back here."

"Yeah," the Tan Man added with a leering smile. "We'll even help you get cleaned up if you want."

"Quite alright." Sherry took a reflexive step back and the Tan Man pressed a hand against her shoulder, using his arm to guide her forward through the opening.

"Compliance," he said as he followed her into the vehicle, pulling the door closed behind them. "Never let them fool you into believing it's a bad thing. It's what makes the world go round."

With them inside, the driver shifted and eased away from the curb. "Don't pay him any mind, Miss Carpenter. My partner gets hung up on the clout, likes to remind people he's in charge. Shoulda seen him in Saigon."

Sherry turned and looked out the window at calm pacific waves breaking on the beach.

Who were these men? What could she tell them about Ed that they didn't already know? She stuffed her hands beneath her thighs to hide the fact she was trembling. She'd just been abducted by men who hadn't — and wouldn't — identify themselves. Sherry hadn't wanted to make a scene in front of her class, the exclusive club she'd just paid through the nose to join. And how stupid was that? Putting her life at risk over manners.

Now she was in the back of what she assumed to be a government sedan, watching small pockets of commuter traffic roll by as the driver swung a right and started away from Venice.

"Do I get to know where we're going?" Sherry asked.

The Tan Man stared straight ahead, his task completed, his screed on compliance, delivered. He had no more purpose until they reached their destination. And Sherry realized she knew more about him than perhaps he intended. He expected compliance because he practiced it. Whatever he'd been like in Saigon, he probably followed orders to the letter.

In the front seat, the driver took a left onto Wilshire, the car rolling to frequent stops at every red light. "You don't live anywhere near here," he said.

"No," Sherry agreed, self-conscious about her workout perspiration. It was souring up the car. This enraged her, the idea that she could be anything other than defiant in this moment. Here she was, kidnapped, and still feeling apologetic about something beyond her control.

Timidity is a curse, she thought.

"Well," the driver pushed, "why come all the way out here?"

"I find the ocean inspiring."

"Do you need inspiration?" The driver grinned in the rearview mirror, then angled the glass to get a better look at her. "Your line of work?"

"Everyone needs inspiration."

"What is your line of work?"

"Thought you knew?"

"I wanna hear it out of your mouth." There was slight anger stitched around these words, the driver's impatience beginning to surface.

"I am cooperating, you know."

On this, the Tan Man beside her turned and frowned. His lips were thin, almost amphibian, and his mouth nearly disappeared off his face when he closed it. Something about his flat, clenched expression made Sherry more nervous than she already was. *"I am cooperating,"* she'd said, but his reaction, this gesture, was its own silent response. *"Yeah, but I really wish you wouldn't."*

"Hey," the driver said. "It's a long drive. I'm making conversation."

"I don't have much to say. I'm a research assistant."

"For Amberdine Research?"

"That's right."

"You work closely with Doctor Amberdine?"

"Sure," Sherry said, thinking about her answer, deciding that nobody really worked that closely with Ed. "I mean, I guess."

"Who else works with you?"

"Nobody."

"Nobody?"

"There used to be an office manager, Marci Howe, but she left a month ago and Ed didn't seem all that interested in replacing her."

"Business bad?"

"Don't think so. Ed has no shortage of grants—"

"What exactly do you do for him?"

"Research assistant," Sherry said, slower. "My nose is to the books most days. Lots of fact checking and verification. When Ed's putting together an experiment, I price the parts, anticipate labor, break everything out into line items."

"Very interesting," the driver said, patronizingly. "And where do you work?"

"I already told you."

"Physically," the driver said. "Where do you go to work?"

"Um, our office is in Hollywood—"

"This town," the driver laughed. "Even the lab geeks gotta get their abs tight, in case they're discovered."

Sherry shrunk down in the seat. "I am cooperating. You don't have to treat me this way."

"How are we treating you?" the driver asked, angling the mirror further down for a better look at Sherry's spandex thighs. His menacing grin was the only thing in the glass, and Sherry was certain he wanted her to challenge him.

She just shook her head.

"I would like to know," the driver pressed. "How are we treating you, Miss Carpenter?" The Good Cop, Bad Cop routine had been abandoned somewhere along Wilshire, way more severity in his tone.

"Well, you... you showed up back there like you knew how to find me."

"And?"

"And that's a little weird. You knowing how to find me."

The driver clapped in amusement. "You are an innocent one, aren't you?"

"If you wanted to talk to me about Ed, all you had to do was ask."

"We did ask."

"Oh," Sherry said and decided to leave it at that.

"My job is to bring you from Point A to Point B," the driver said. "If you're not interested in making conversation, then what can I do to make this drive more pleasant?" He gestured to a corner restaurant. "You want to stop and grab a bagel? My treat?"

"I'm fine," she said lowly and ashamed of how vulnerable she sounded.

The Tan Man angled himself ever so slightly, sensing this weakness. He stayed positioned that way, as if Sherry required constant eyes. She felt them from behind the impenetrable tint of his Ray-Bans and turned away, counting the southbound cars while the sedan cruised the length of Wilshire, heading, she assumed, downtown.

"Well," Sherry said, challenging the car. "Do I ever get to know where you're taking me?" She tended to speak more when nervous and, in this situation, thought it could make these men see her for the human being she was, rather than some job.

They might be less inclined to—

Stop, she chided herself. *Don't go there.* As the driver had told her, somebody had questions. And given the ones he'd asked so far, Sherry kind of believed that. If they wanted to kill her, they wouldn't have been so brazen about abducting her in front of a dozen people.

"When was the last time you saw Ed?" the driver asked.

Sherry thought back. It had been raining that night. Inches of water sluicing against the office's front windowpanes, putting the traffic outside at a complete and utter standstill, the way rain always did to Angeleno commuters.

That endless parade of headlights glinting in the deluge as Ed shuffled notes into his satchel bag, grousing about having to meet some business partners for dinner.

"Ten days ago?" Sherry said. "Eleven?"

"Is that common?"

"In the four months I've been working for him, yes."

She didn't know Edward Amberdine all that well. He'd hired her, had shown great interest in bringing her into the fold and often talked about mentoring her. But Sherry had the sense that Ed didn't trust her yet. Didn't seem to trust anyone. Marci Howe, the former office manager, had given Sherry that spiel on her way out the door, and while she often saw Ed several times a week, he just as often worked off site.

She didn't know where.

He was the kind of idealist who couldn't ever stop talking about how he was going to change the world. His special brand of progressive idealism had won Sherry over in grad school, and while other jobs offered more pay, along with superior stability and upward mobility, none of them had what Ed offered.

The future.

"Where are going?" she asked, more pointedly.

"Business district." The driver zipped through an

intersection on a yellow light and caught a horn from one of the side streets.

"That's a half hour drive."

"Next time we'll fly," the driver laughed.

The Tan Man angled his head a little further. In her periphery, Sherry saw the handgun holster looped through his belt. Her eyes clocked up to his face and caught him grinning.

She took the hint and slumped back, staring at the sun-blasted apartment buildings that jutted up above the sporadic palm trees that lined the road and waited for those few downtown skyscrapers to finally come edging into the horizon.

One of the highest buildings there was emblazoned with the logo NCS. Norton Cyber Systems, which Sherry understood to be Ed's most direct competition. They had made several offers to poach Sherry. Ed had both known and anticipated this, promising that he was on the verge of changing the world. And amidst this discovery, she would become the *de facto* daughter to it. "Your face on the cover of every science journal on Earth, a role model to a legion of young women."

"That you?" she gestured to the NCS letters on the top of the building and the driver laughed, shaking his head.

It took forever to reach the Business District, but the sedan finally swung a right at some lights and then a quick left, slipping beneath the street, into a subterranean parking garage where the vehicle's interior went blacker than night, rolling right up against two oversized cargo doors.

Then it was just the three of them sitting in complete silence, as if the men had forgotten their cue and nobody could progress beyond it.

The sedan idled there for what felt like forever.

Until the elevator finally slid open and a man stepped out, lit only by the weak sodium glow of the elevator cab behind him. He grinned ear-to-ear, looking like a nervous jack-o-lantern in the low light. "Miss Carpenter!" he said, beaming as he approached the back seat and pulled open the door. "What a pleasure to meet you. A pleasure!"

Sherry got out and stretched, starting to relax as she studied him. Unlike the men in the sedan, the Driver and the Tan Man, there was nothing menacing about his pasty, sun-deprived skin, perpetually greasy hair, and comically wrinkled clothing. She'd known two dozen boys just like this one in college. Recognized a lab geek when she saw one.

"Please..." he stepped aside and gestured to the elevator.

"Thank you, Mister, umm..."

"Did you have a nice trip?" Mister Umm placed a hand on the small of her back and ushered her along. Behind them, the sedan reversed and rolled off before the elevator doors were all the way closed. Then they were ascending out of the ground, toward the sky.

Sherry looked at her fellow lab geek, thinking for a moment that question must've been a joke. But Mister Umm was a cliché all the way around. Nervous about being with the opposite sex. Just like all those boys back in school. This was an example of the only conversation they knew how to make. Awkward.

"Not really," Sherry said.

"Oh." Mister Umm was seemingly distressed by her answer. "That's a shame. A shame. Because what we're doing here today is really just debriefing."

"Debriefing?"

"A debrief," he repeated. "Edward Amberdine. A debrief."

"Look," Sherry said. "I really don't understand what this has to do with me."

"That is, umm, too bad." The elevator slowed, then rose a couple more feet before stopping. The doors slid open and revealed a gloomy, abandoned office space.

Sherry leaned out and surveyed the floor of vacant and unused desks, rows of endless doors, each one closed and unmarked.

"Please," Umm said, stepping out into the unoccupied space. "Right this way."

Sherry followed him shoulder-to-shoulder, down a dark hallway that spanned the entire length of the building. "Are you guys just starting out or—?"

"No, we, umm, well, we travel light." Umm rounded a corner where the hallway was suddenly brighter, one whole wall of floor-to-ceiling windows that looked down on the business district, people scurrying around down there like ants. "All the way down," Umm said.

Sherry, still studying the sidewalk below, stepped back, hand to collarbone. "What did you just say?"

"Oh," Umm said, shaking his head. "No. No. Not like that." He gestured to the far end of the hallway, to a corner office door that was half open, a waft of cigar smoke bellowing out like early morning fog. Sherry smelled the deep grass aroma from here. "I mean, all the way down the hallway." He leaned against the glass, smiling as if this was all some simple misunderstanding.

The whole of this journey had been intentional, Sherry realized. Designed to keep her off-kilter and disoriented. She hadn't much life experience beyond the classroom, though she'd always been perceptive enough to see things as they were. As such, she had intuited that whoever was in the room up ahead would seize on her discomfort. Exploit it. Suddenly, she felt ill-prepared and didn't want to go in.

"Right down there," Umm said, flicking his wrist as if shooing her away.

"This as far as you go?"

He tightened his smile and said nothing more. The script, exhausted.

Sherry placed one reluctant foot forward, then another as she started down the hall, nose wrinkling against the overwhelming presence of smoky pepper and eucalyptus.

An overweight man in brown slacks paced in front of a desk,

phone to ear. He wore a thin blue button-up too tight for his body, with an unfastened tie swaying down from both sides of his collar, as if he hadn't gotten around to knotting it yet. The phone cord was wrapped around his torso, which dragged the receiver all the way across a largely empty desk, and the only other item on it was a blank ceramic ashtray. He stared at Sherry as she entered, forced a smile that attempted to hide his intentions.

He lifted a finger and signaled "one minute."

"It's a goddamn mess," he said into the phone. "We trained those sons of bitches, didn't expect them to turn around and shoot an archbishop." His eyes ticked back to Sherry, wider and more nervous than they'd been a moment ago. One house secret he hadn't intended to spill in mixed company.

Or had he?

Sherry looked away, glancing back through the door, finding an empty hallway. Umm, long gone.

"As of today, El Salvador's on its own," he said. "At least as far as the company's concerned." He looked at Sherry again, smiling wider. "I'm onto... something else." He slammed down the phone and cleared his throat. "Miss..."

Sherry said nothing.

He searched the air for an answer, eyes becoming slits. "Carpenter," he said this in a protracted, agonized way. Then he twirled around, untangling himself from the phone cord. A strange and almost comedic routine that betrayed his steely, deadened expression.

He stepped out from behind the desk, rocking on his heels, and Sherry realized how close they were in height. And he wasn't rocking on his heels, but was instead rising on his toes, trying to steal the vertical advantage away from Sherry. Trying and failing. This Big Boss.

"Amberdine Research," he said, studying her reaction for what felt like an eternity.

"That's... where I work."

"Worked."

"Excuse me?"

"Christ, you really don't know." He plucked his cigar out of the ashtray and puckered his lips around it.

"What don't I know?"

"Ed Amberdine is dead."

"What?"

Big Boss studied her again, softening his face into one of those "come on, it's just the two of us…" expressions.

"What happened?"

"Ten days ago, his body was found floating in Silver Lake."

"He drowned?"

Big Boss took a deep breath and closed his eyes. Sherry's ignorance was not the reaction he wanted. "Amberdine did not drown," he told her. "Police picked up a homeless man that same night, some schizophrenic streeter, who had the good doctor's identification, among other valuables, on his person. While in custody, that man confessed to dumping Amberdine's body, then went to his grave swearing he didn't murder him."

This was shocking. Until now, Sherry hadn't known anyone who died, save for distant relatives she'd only met a handful of times. It was strange to reconcile the idea that there would be no more Ed in her life. Her mentor, suddenly passing into memory.

"Before the suspect swallowed his tongue, he gave an eyewitness account that…" he stopped for a second, discomfort riding his features. "Described the devil himself, stalking the good doctor down some city sidewalk, cleaving hunks of flesh from his back. Whole time this guy's watching from a dumpster, claims the devil's got glowing eyes that beamed a message straight into his brain, commanding him to hide this body. And so that's what he did. Dropped the doc's corpse in Silver Lake. Quite an undignified end to Amberdine's story."

Sherry wiped a tear from her eye over the uncharitable way this news was delivered, and also because of the outlandish nature of his demise. A deranged eyewitness account, a robbery gone bad, and none of it of any real consequence to the man puffing his cigar, letting her ruminate in misery.

"I'm going to ask that you think carefully before answering my next question," he said. "I will only ask it once, and if I'm happy, you can get back to your workout."

Sherry nodded, sniffling.

"During your admittedly brief tenure at Amberdine Research, did you ever visit Ed offsite?"

"You mean, at his house?"

"I'm talking about the existence of a secondary work site. Some place beyond the Hollywood office."

"No."

He nodded. "Did he ever mention another location? You ever see an invoice, or any type of paperwork that might've suggested one?"

"No. Nothing."

"My people have combed through your office. They haven't found anything useful."

"Maybe that's because…"

He lifted his chin, and Sherry proceeded with caution. Big Boss wasn't simply a driver or hired muscle. He controlled those resources. And if there was a conclusion here that Sherry was not cooperating, well, this was the one person authorized to destroy her. And in the sanctity of this abandoned office space, who would know?

"Because?" he challenged.

"I don't know everything that you know," she said, delicately. "But maybe there isn't another location?"

"What you're saying, Miss Carpenter, is that maybe our genetic researcher was actually killed on some anonymous street by a ten-foot-tall devil? Who then proceeded to instruct a homeless man with a history of debilitating mental problems to chuck his body into the river?"

"I'm not saying that."

Big Boss smiled big. Like everyone else today, he got off on the prospect of intimidating the helpless. Sherry, in her neon pink spandex was about as harmless as a hamster. But that didn't seem to matter to any of them.

Or maybe it was exactly the point.

"Did Doctor Amberdine ever mention to you who he was working for?"

"The people behind the grant funding?"

"Us," Big Boss said. "He worked for me. Which means you do too. And though it is a tragedy that he is no longer with us, he was on the hook to deliver certain... results."

Sherry nodded, making every effort to prevent the twinge of disappointment she felt – Ed's idealism bankrolled by government stooges — from registering on her face.

"We recovered experiment notes," Big Boss told her. "They are... vaguer than we would like. Given everything, including your admission that Ed wasn't always in your office space, I've no choice but to conclude that he was working in secret."

"Ed had two labs?"

"Smart girl."

"I wish your men had just asked me after my workout. I could've saved you all some time."

"I wanted to look into your eyes."

"And you believe me now?"

"Maybe."

"I graduated last December. Started working for Ed in February. And I only ever worked at the Hollywood office. If there was another site, sir, I'm sorry, but it's news to me."

Big Boss studied her for a long time, his nods becoming more pronounced as he decided, yes, he probably did believe her. "Miss Carpenter," he said. "You are our final link to a very important project. Please do not leave the city."

"I won't."

"My people will be in touch." On that he spun toward the

window and waved a dismissing hand through the air, so that she knew she was free to go.

Sherry took a taxi back to Venice, the traffic much slower at lunch time, and once the driver bounced up onto the sidewalk right outside the aerobics studio, she had to race inside to collect her wallet and pay him.

She took a shower there, peeling the spandex off and leaving it in a clump at her feet, cold water pelting her back and neck as she pressed her palms on the wall tile, exorcising the tension from her body. It was the first opportunity today to really reflect on things.

Her boss, murdered on the street. Sherry, without a career.

Somehow, these were the least of her problems.

Her Volkswagen was parked across the street, meter expired, and with a twenty-dollar fine tucked beneath her windshield wiper. Sherry grabbed the ticket and balled it up, tossing it into her backseat, amazed because that would've shaken her only yesterday. A young nobody from Lincoln, Nebraska, seemed so insignificant when measured against the day's events.

Sherry drove to Westwood. To Marci Howe's house, a one bedroom on the corner of a cross street. Sherry didn't know her all that well, they'd gone to lunch a handful of times while working together, but thought she deserved to know about Ed.

Marci Howe was the only other person in Sherry's life who knew about Ed at all. And that was the issue, Sherry realized. Edward Amberdine was already forgotten. His legacy, swallowed whole. A disturbing notion, that you could cease to exist with the immediacy of a finger snap.

Sherry trotted across the grass, finding regret once more in her failure to pursue that internship with NCS while in college. Norton Cyber Systems. Always the grooviest table at career fair, and with by far the best swag. Had she gone that route, like her advisor suggested, she wouldn't be trespassing in a stranger's yard right now.

A stranger who might not be home. There was no car in the driveway, though two windows were lifted and there was an almost deafening silence inside, like the house itself was petrified and preventing itself from creaking.

"Marci, it's Sherry."

Marci was a year or two older, a struggling actress who favored temp work because she needed to be able to walk away from any and all gigs at a moment's notice whenever Hollywood called.

Which, judging from the closet that Marci lived in, wasn't often, though it wasn't Sherry's place to judge career choices. Look at where hers had led.

She knocked on Marci's door and realized it was off its jamb. A simple brush of her fingers sent it inward. "Marci?" she called, events of the day turning her stomach sour. She took a few cautious shuffles inside.

Marci was laying on her living room couch, sprawled out, one arm and one leg touching the floor, her nightgown open, ruffling in a slight breeze. Unblinking eyes stared up at the whirring ceiling fan, face permanently astonished. Her skin painted the color of violence.

Sherry thought of the Tan Man who had been sitting beside her on the ride downtown this morning, lecturing her on the benefits of compliance. He'd been so tightly wound and ready to snap.

And she knew that when he came here, he did exactly that.

CHAPTER
SEVEN

T ed barely slept last night.

Each time he closed his eyes, the Writer would produce new pages, daring Ted to read them. Monstrous scenarios he refused to admit were real.

Too late for that, he thought, tossing and turning from inside the mind of Janie Richter's killer where every impulse was to tear that girl to shreds. The Writer depicted it over and over. Ted saw her anguished face, his own fingers wiggling threateningly in front of it. In this scenario, his hands were inhuman, tipped with grisly nails closer to talons. The hands of the murderer.

Ted wasn't a monster, literally or figuratively. He merely understood what it felt like to be one. And when those private insistences stopped working, as they inevitably would, he'd go searching for therapy at the bottom of a whiskey bottle. The soggy off-switch. Drink enough to put the Writer to sleep so that Ted's consciousness could snap back to normal, forgetting all about the madmen he invited into his mind.

Madmen, or mad monsters?

Empathy. What it felt like to be a bad guy. Share a stranger's thoughts. Strangers who spent every waking moment thinking about murder.

Because of this, Ted spent a disproportionate amount of his life thinking about death. Every page the Writer typed had him prowling Janie Richter's driveway, studying the scantily clad co-ed through each window. Something about the killer's ritual that night suggested indecision. A moment where the evening could've gone one of two ways. Kill the girl or—

"Or what?" Ted wondered.

In his mind, the Writer's page was blank.

The working theory here made Ted certifiable. He understood that. All he needed was to share his conclusion with Lou and this would be over. Lou would realize his old pal was broken beyond repair. That "The Scent" had done a real number.

Ted could do that today and be free of this.

But he couldn't. He couldn't push away his conclusion any easier than he could mold it into something more easily consumable for the bureaucrats. Whatever was out there tearing Angelinos apart was unlike anything he'd ever known.

And that was the other thing about The Scent. It was never wrong.

Ted tossed and turned until the sun edged into the spaces around the drawn curtains of his bedroom. He took a quick shower and wiped steam off the bathroom mirror to glimpse himself, confirmation that he was still human. For once he turned the Writer loose and the pages added up, such a simple and obvious conclusion was no longer a given.

He dressed and hurried down to his Mazda and drove to his office where he was grateful to disappear into *Red Tide*. The only time the Writer willingly stopped hammering out pages was when Ted sat down in front of the keyboard to do some of the work himself.

And as much as Ted hated to admit it, the schlocky worlds his fingertips conjured provided an escape. Thinking about killer cuttlefish meant he wasn't thinking about Janie Richter. Or the creature that murdered her.

His fingertips blazed across the keys. The click-clacking of his machine satisfying as he plucked each completed page from the paper bail and turned them face-down, atop the rest of the manuscript.

The Writer helped, feeding images that Ted translated to the page. Cuttlefish chewing through the backs of unsuspecting swimmers, amputating limbs. A scene where one of those annoying metal detector guys thinks he's discovered buried treasure in the shallows but is instead buzzing on the fillings inside a severed head moments before his feet are eaten off.

Act three was close. Ted raised the stakes in the form of an approaching hurricane. A way to flood the town and get the fish out of the lake, into people's basements. A subplot where a mother and baby would be trapped inside a Volvo that would become adrift, floating through city streets while the fish got hungry enough to try eating through metal.

Could they? He wasn't sure. Yet.

His mind raced on ahead. Ted reached for his yellow notepad and scribbled down these ideas. An epilogue where the fish could win because they're able to reach a cement drainage pipe, which winds up carrying a small school of them to the ocean, and once they reach the anonymity of the sea…

"Anonymity," Ted said, sitting back in his chair. It was almost noon and the first day in forever that he could knock off while feeling productive. He'd have to go back through the first two-thirds of the book to properly set up the hurricane and drainage subplots that would now be critical to the story. And as he chewed this over, he realized it hadn't been an accident. The Writer had been trying to reach him all morning.

"Drainage," he said.

Then he was driving across Burbank to the Department of Public Works where the parking lot was an exodus. Employees fleeing on their lunch hour. The row of visitor spaces was empty. Ted parked in the spot closest to the door and went inside.

"Well, if it ain't Lonergan." A familiar voice announced from behind the desk, dripping with disdain. Rob Murray rolled up his sleeves as if looking to settle a long-held score.

"Murray," Ted said, "you're looking well."

"Let me guess. Research for another of your masterworks?"

"Don't pretend you don't read me, Murray."

"Yeah," Murray sneered, "got 'em all." He shifted behind the counter as Ted approached, his drinker's nose flaring. The center of his face was cherry-tinged, whatever ailment permanently activated by a daily diet of scotch and sodas.

Murray was ex-homicide. Developed a debilitating limp in the line of duty when he caught a wad of buckshot so severe it should've amputated his leg. Scarred his wife so badly she insisted he leave the force, take another job with the state. But that was the thing with cops. Most were born for a singular pursuit. Taking their badges was like taking away a dog's balls.

Murray despised Ted because, unlike Murray, Ted's body remained willing and able. Was his spirit that got broken and busted. Murray should've been cop enough to understand that watching your partner die was the sort of thing that made a man's soul sick, but that level of introspection didn't cut it with most guys on the force.

"Wife tried to read you once, you know," Murray told him. "Said she read better fiction on bathroom walls."

"You're saying you've got a book back there you'd like me to sign?"

"What the hell do you want, Lonergan?"

"I'll give you one guess."

"You know, you got off real easy."

Ted was so used to hearing these things, he glanced away. "Thank you for weighing in."

"I asked what you want. I was just about to go to lunch."

"Copies of sewer and drainage plans."

"For where?"

Ted shrugged. "The whole city?"

"Oh, is that all?"

"Thought I'd make it easy on you."

"I can get you Burbank. Copy all those streets… gonna take some time. You want the whole of Los Angeles, you're gonna have to visit every DPW. Make the request in person."

"Can you at least call ahead and—"

"Sorry, Lonergan, everyone's on lunch." Murray leaned close and forced a shit-eating smile. Wanted Ted to know he was responsible for the miserable afternoon he was about to endure. A story he could tell his peers over scotch and sodas for the rest of his life.

"Okay, you blame me for what happened with Lyle. Not nearly as much as I blame myself. I'm not here today to do research for my books. This is for… something else."

Murray had already tuned out. No interest in meeting Ted halfway or anywhere at all. In Murray's mind, he was being a team player. Problem was, most of the force had decided long ago that Ted played for the visiting team.

"Give me a few minutes," Murray said and then limped off behind the frosted glass partition.

"I assume the plans indicate street access?" Ted called after him.

"Oh, go to hell."

"I'm going to be spending my afternoon touring every DPW in Los Angeles, Murray. That's exactly where I am."

"Have a seat," Murray called, his voice faded and distant.

Ted resisted that order for a while, pacing the empty room. As Murray's absence extended, he grabbed last month's issue of *Time* off the counter. An illustration of Boeing Chairman T.A. Wilson with the company's various products swirling through the air around him. The headline read "FLYING HIGH" and the subhead beneath it said, "$4 billion for the Cruise Missile."

Murray returned ninety minutes later with a mustard stain on his collar that hadn't been there before. He dropped a hard cylindrical tube on the counter. "Here's the bird's eye view…

you need maps of each street, that's a special request and it's gonna take all summer to—"

"This works."

"Fifteen-dollar processing fee, Lonergan. And I'm obligated by law to tell you that these plans are for city workers only and—"

"Yeah, you're a real stickler for rules, Murray." Ted slapped three fives down and took the plans. "Go out and get another hot dog."

He spent the rest of the day kiting around Los Angeles, collecting similar blueprints from every public works department in the city, where every other processing fee was two dollars. The word "drainage" was ringing through his mind as the Mazda was stuffed with more cardboard tubes.

As he drove back to his office through the grid-like neighborhoods of Pasadena, where life was normal and the air smelled of fresh-cut grass, he remembered there was a monster lurking in this city, even as his common sense fought this proclamation.

That's what he struggled with. Being nuts. Ted Lonergan, a sci-fi nerd who earned a wage as a writer of schlock. If this wasn't a case of his day job interfering with The Scent, then he was at a loss.

Problem was, nothing ever interfered with The Scent.

He juggled multiple caseloads during his decade in law enforcement. The lines never got blurred. The Writer could produce a dozen pages surrounding a half dozen different cases, no problem. But The Scent had no instruction manual. And no warranty. Maybe it didn't last. Or perhaps it was as broken as Ted was.

"Or maybe it's working fine," he said, parking in front of his building. That's what really bothered him. It was his responsibility to find what had mutilated Janie Richter and all those others. No one else's problem, no matter what they believed.

Ted trotted up the stairs with a bunch of poster tubes in his arms, finding a handwritten note taped to his door.

> *I changed my mind. A woman's prerogative.*
> *Will you have dinner? On me.*
> *Eight-ish.*
> *I'll pick you up here.*
> *Jennifer*

Ted grinned and slipped the note inside his pocket as he unlocked the door.

His phone was ringing. Ted let the blueprint tubes scatter across his floor as he hot-stepped around them, racing for the receiver he couldn't immediately find. The phone was buried beneath pages of hand-written notes – all the genius of *Red Tide's* third act he'd scribbled out earlier today.

"Yellow?" Ted answered.

"The people have spoken." He'd been expecting Lou, but it was Victor, starting in like a sprung trap. "Everybody hates *Dark Neighborhood.*"

"Does this mean the press tour is cancelled?"

"I should stuff you in every bookstore up and down the coast for the rest of this year. Make you see the disappointment on the faces of your readers."

"My readers love me." Ted's eyes landed on another handwritten letter, this one pinned to his corkboard from a Christian fundamentalist in Tennessee who promised Ted would burn in hell for the climactic orgy set piece of his second novel, *The Allotriophagy*, or as Ted had called it right up until publication, *Chasing Bill Blatty's Dimes.*

"Readers have short memories for guys like you, Ted. Ask Jack Younger."

"Who?"

"*Satan Sublets… Curse of the Pharaohs…*"

"English, Victor."

"Exactly my point!"

"Victor, I'm not sure what you want me to say. People will like *Dark Neighborhood* fine. It has three chapters from the dog's point of view…"

"I can't even get a blurb."

"Should've gone with my idea of putting a naked woman on the cover, underneath a die-cut flap? Then you wouldn't be in the position of having to make one up."

"Goddammit, Ted. Your next book better set the world on fire."

Ted glanced at his typewriter, the paper curling back on a scene in *Red Tide* where a lifeguard is castrated by hungry fish. "It's my best work, Victor."

An exasperated sigh. "I'll be in touch."

And then Victor was gone, and that was just fine with Ted, who began scooping the tubes off the floor, pinning up sewer plans around his office.

Once they were posted, Ted took another look through Lou's files, placing a thumb tack into each of the places where someone had been murdered. Then he stood back with his arms folded, staring, asking the Writer to summon a pattern.

The victims were not confined to a single area of town but spread out across the city in a way that suggested transportation was easy for the killer. Ted's eyes zipped from one pinned tack to the next, recalling his feet passing over a sewer grate on Janie Richter's street. In fact, sewer access was close by at every crime scene.

"Why didn't anybody check this?" he wondered. Because the sewers were foul and not even the homeless wanted to spend time in them. The EPA was consistently concerned about the city's water quality and had been since Ted was on the force. They claimed city water was impacted by pathogens and other contaminants from untreated human waste, which reinforced Ted's theory. It wasn't a man they hunted.

It's why there were never any eyewitnesses. Why their perpetrator had racked up a body count but continued to be a ghost. Ted nodded along to this realization, adrenaline surging through him. Nothing was more empowering than a breakthrough.

This wasn't the end, of course, but the beginning of the next stage. How they were going to catch their killer.

"You're using the sewers to get around the city unseen, aren't you, my man?"

He picked up the phone and dialed Lou.

CHAPTER
EIGHT

S herry had phoned the police from inside Marci's house, then went outside and waited on the sidewalk for them to arrive. There was enough afternoon bustle, foot traffic and blaring horns from the nearby intersection, that she felt relatively safe, even as she looked over her shoulder, keeping an eye out for this morning's sedan.

For the Tan Man that she kept expecting to see moving through the steadily amassing crowd.

They wouldn't kill her, she hoped, because in their minds they believed she could still be of service to them. That had been the purpose behind today's demonstration, after all.

What did you get me into, Ed?

The police arrived first. The ambulance, a few minutes behind it. By then, the entire street was gathered on the sidewalk, whispered voices guessing at what happened, everybody trying to figure out who even lived here. Nobody knew.

A uniformed patrolman asked Sherry to take a seat in the back of his cruiser. Nothing would be worse than sitting with her knees cramped, staring out from behind a wired cage, so she declined the offer, preferring instead to lean right up against the vehicle with her arms folded.

The patrolman kept glancing over, as if Sherry might decide to run away. She resented his suspicion.

She was the victim here. One of them. Maybe a callous thing to think while poor Marci was lying dead inside the house, an eggplant-colored bruise around her throat. Still, Sherry couldn't help the way she felt. This was a problem and would only get worse.

Two detectives showed up an hour later. They disappeared inside the house and Sherry grew increasingly nervous as she waited, trying to decide just how much information she should share. The greatest temptation being to spill everything and get back to life.

Except... Sherry no longer had a life to get back to. Amberdine Research was no more. And no matter what she ended up telling the police, the men from this morning weren't going away.

At last, one of the detectives re-emerged and adjusted his sport coat as he swapped a couple words with the first officer on the scene. They turned toward Sherry in unison and their expressions matched. Accusatory eyes that made her feel guilty. Then the detective started over.

"Miss Carpenter," he said. "I'm Detective Millbank." He was tall, curly hair that wasn't exactly brown, but wasn't red, either. His moustache darker, a more confident amber color that matched his department store suit. His face, weary in a way that suggested he was overworked, and that this was all some annoyance. Not a hint of empathy for what Sherry had seen in that house.

"Hello... detective."

"What happened here?" He leaned against the car, arm resting along the roof. The other on his hip, a gesture which brushed aside the flap of his coat to reveal the golden badge clipped to his belt, as well as a holstered revolver. His pose felt designed to intimidate, and Sherry resented that too, her body chemistry boiling.

"I, uh, I don't know?"

"Why did you stop by today?"

"I was checking up on Marci and—"

"Why did Marci need to be checked up on?" Nothing about Millbank suggested safety or concern. Certainly not the tone in which he spoke. Inquisitive, as Sherry supposed a detective should be, but with a constantly shifting face that insinuated disbelief at everything Sherry had to say.

"I guess it's easier if I start at the beginning."

"The beginning," he said in a patronizing way. "Yeah. Good idea. Why don't you start at the beginning?"

Sherry couldn't help it. She was desperate and vulnerable. And after everything that had happened today, scared. She could've asked to speak to someone else, someone more assuring, although detectives weren't bank tellers. And even now, she was too polite to rock the boat like that.

She started the story from the top, beginning with aerobics. She told Millbank about the men who had driven her across town. About Mr. Umm and the mastermind, Big Boss, with the cigar.

"Who were these men?" the detective asked, face twisted in constipation.

"If I knew who they were—"

"Just… guess."

"Government," Sherry said. "I don't know." She described how all roads ended at Edward Amberdine's secret laboratory — a place she'd never been. Didn't know existed. "And that's why Marci's dead."

The detective's moustache flapped as he exhaled through his nose, annoyed. No one but him was qualified to make any kind of conclusion, apparently. "You're saying that Marci Howe is dead… because of a secret laboratory? Which is where, exactly?"

"If I knew where, I would've said."

The detective's eyes narrowed into thin, suspicious slits. "Is that true?"

"Do you have to act like you don't believe a word I say?"

"I am a detective, Miss Carpenter."

"Yeah, but what happened to innocent, until proven guilty."

"That's for the courts."

"Oh. Yeah."

"So, is it true?"

"What?"

"The location of the…" Millbank tossed up air quotes. "Secret laboratory."

"I really have no idea."

"Professional estimation."

"Anything's possible, sure. I mean… I don't have any stake in this, detective." And that was true. Ed's research was non-transferable. There was no through line back to Sherry. Ed might've promised her more, but that future died the moment he did. The men she'd meant today, the ones bankrolling the show, could do with it as they pleased.

If they found it.

"What kind of research did Dr. Amberdine do?" the detective asked.

"Genetic research."

"Like… gene sequencing?"

"Yeah," Sherry said. "Very good guess." Too good. He asked it in a hazy way, hinting that he wasn't sure what *gene sequencing* meant, but the quickness with which he offered such a specific example intimated that he had it on standby.

He asked a few more questions, nothing of consequence, and concluded by telling her to stay in town – the second time today somebody had given her this directive.

Now, she only wanted to leave.

Once released, Sherry hurried to her Volkswagen and drove home, fighting off a gnawing feeling. "You did it, Ed." Her words, barely a whisper. But it was the only explanation. He'd gotten past the embryonic stage. As unlikely as it seemed, nothing else could've disrupted her life in such a dramatic, irrevocable way.

When she arrived home to her apartment, she turned on all the lights and checked every nook and cranny. Then she sat at the kitchen table, reminding herself again and again that those men wouldn't hurt her.

Yet.

Her anxiety surged in a way that felt permanent. She paced every room. Bent over the television and flipped the dial, clicking through each channel. Nothing caught her attention, so she unfolded the ironing board in the living room and draped her best dress down over it just to have something to do.

"Where were you hiding it, Ed?" she wondered. If there were any clues at the office, the men would've already had the location. And Sherry had never come across any other address. Of that she was certain.

Total dead end.

She thought back over all her conversations with Ed. The future of human evolution and how Amberdine Research was going to impact that course.

She remembered expecting Ed to come on to her. How those first couple of weeks were hell, waiting for that shoe to drop. Except Ed hadn't so much as looked at her like anything other than an employee, not even once, and Sherry could hardly believe her luck. In all of Los Angeles, she'd landed in the one place that wanted her brain. And nothing more.

Tears streaked down her face. In all the misery, she hadn't had so much as a moment to mourn. Ed had been dead for ten days. She took a deep breath and refocused her thoughts, trying to force herself to remember whether Ed had ever mentioned any family. None that she could recall.

She cried harder as her feelings turned inward, tabling the altruism, all the *"we were going to change the world"* mawkishness. She'd lost a friend. An emotional connection that was suddenly, jarringly, broken.

Next week they were going to drive out to that medical supply warehouse and —

"Oh my God," Sherry said, and then stayed silent just in case her apartment might be bugged. There was one thread to pull on, and she found it. Capitol Lab Supply. Ed had mentioned more than once that he bought all his equipment there. But off-book, meaning there was no paper trail. He went through an employee named Scott, who was always letting things go "at cost," meaning he conveniently left them off inventory and pocketed the money directly, then reported the equipment as "missing." Never received.

Unethical, but necessary. Ed was a one-man operation, not Norton Cyber Systems, whose presence was so large they owned a piece of the Los Angeles skyline with their downtown real estate. Ed had to remain competitive, needed to save all the money he could in order to do it.

This was precisely why the men from this morning had left Sherry alive. She did know how to find the lab. And now that she remembered something useful, there were two ways this could go. Tell them or do nothing. Forget today ever happened. Let the memory of Edward Amberdine fade into obscurity and concentrate on finding another job. Eventually those men would lose interest and—

"—and kill you," she said.

Sherry glanced at the television, where a news broadcast showed a dead-end street, a reporter in a blue blazer standing beneath a sign that read END, a two-story house behind him.

"Here on this quiet little street in North Glendale," the reporter said. "A college coed, twenty-two-year-old Janie Richter became victim number eleven in a series of brutal slayings over the past few weeks."

The hairs on Sherry's neck rose.

"The coroner's office issued a report this morning that Miss

Richter's body had been found beaten, apparently her neck had been broken and her left leg ripped from her body."

Sherry pressed a hand against her mouth. This was so much worse than anyone realized.

"Los Angeles Police Chief Dennis Warren stated today that the killer will be caught and that the police department is working around the clock to bring the killer to justice. Informed sources say, however, that the police department has no real clues and such statements by Chief Warren are 'wishful thinking.' This is Alex Waverly in North Glendale—"

Sherry clicked off the television. "You're not responsible," she told herself, as if that mattered.

She took another lap around the apartment, making sure it was locked and secure. As she was checking her windows, she watched a car slow to a stop at the corner and bank a right. The silhouettes inside it might've had their heads craned in her direction. It might've been the sedan from this morning.

Or it might've been her paranoia ramping up to an eleven.

Sherry couldn't live this way, though there was a third option announcing itself. She could find the lab on her own. Use whatever was there as leverage. That's what Ed would've wanted.

And Scott from Capitol Lab Supply was the only person on Earth who could make that happen.

CHAPTER
NINE

A quiet knock on Ted's door. "It's Jennifer."

"It's open!" Ted looked himself over in the mirror. Not bad, all things considered. His baby blue polo was tucked inside darker blue jeans — a look that edged right up against Canadian Tuxedo. A risk, sure, but it would work in the dim dinner light of whatever place they were headed. "Be out in a minute."

Beyond the door, the sound of Jennifer's clicking heels as she carefully navigated the crowded office space. He'd tidied up but had no place to stash all the blueprint tubes he'd acquired today. They were still rolling around on the floor like a gameshow obstacle course.

Ted took the dusty bottle of Old Spice off the shelf and splashed a couple drops onto his fingers. He tapped those against his neck and his reflection frowned. A judgmental glare, as if he needed to be reminded of what happened the last time he went out on a date.

She wound up dead.

"I found a great restaurant," Jennifer was saying, voice sparking like an excited child. "It's in Century City. They've got their own wine cellar and the food is supposedly fantastic."

Her enthusiasm was so infectious that even the haunted face in the mirror began to smile. Ted opened the door to his office and was knocked flat by the sight before him. Jennifer, dressed not only for a night out, but for a night out with Warren Beatty. Green eyes sparkled beneath dark blue eye shadow that highlighted her stunning features: tanned skin and chiseled cheekbones. A face framed by crimped blond hair. She wore a loose white blazer over her black evening dress, a low v-cut that revealed a liberal amount of skin.

She stood at his desk, holding the photo of Ted and Lyle and her eyes widened at the sight of Ted's eveningwear, managing to catch her reaction in her throat so that a stutter was all that escaped.

"Something wrong?" Ted asked.

"Hi," Jennifer said, collecting herself. Starting over. She placed the photo down and her beaming smile cleansed the awkwardness. "No. Of course not. I was only just thinking… it's Friday. The restaurant is probably going to be very crowded, and I didn't have time to get reservations."

This damn shirt, Ted thought. *Maybe it's the jeans. Maybe I should buy another pair of pants someday.*

"So, here's what I'm thinking instead," Jennifer continued, "why don't we go to my place? I've got some steaks. It'll be quiet. We can talk. And you, uh…" her eyes went down his length and there was a giggle in her throat. "Well, you won't have to dress up."

Ted admired this tactfulness. Jennifer Stanton, skilled persuader and part time supermodel, so far beyond his means it was comical. Here she was, trying to spare his feelings when most women would be running out the door.

"Do you mind?" she asked, studying his face for signs that she might've offended him, her eyes indicating real concern over this possibility.

"No," Ted said. He reached for his cream-colored Members Only blazer. "Let me just get my dinner jacket here…"

Jennifer gestured to the sewer blueprints hanging up around the office. "Redecorating? Or are you taking up civil engineering?"

"Research," he said, pulling open the door and ushering her into the hall.

They walked downstairs and out into a breezy, early summer night. Jennifer's Jaguar parked against the curb. "Fresh out of the shop," she beamed. "Thanks to you. And… no thanks to you."

"You called my guy?"

"Mentioned your name and he got it done this morning."

"Good to know someone still likes me," Ted said. "Some people take an hour lunch and leave me waiting at the window."

"Huh?"

"Just glad you're happy. Is that why you left the note?"

"You're an interesting man. That counts for a lot in this city."

They drove to her place in Santa Monica by way of the 405, Ted staring out the window, transfixed by the blood red sunset. An ominous portent for the evening. The Writer in his mind slotted a fresh page, already typing. Ted had no desire to read a single word. Just wanted a normal night.

He turned toward Jennifer in need of a distraction, admiring her profile. Her strong and angular jawline pulsed as she drove, turning up the radio to Michael Martin Murphey's "Wildfire," singing along. In this moment, it was exactly what Ted needed.

Not even the Writer could hurt him, even as those pages clacked and kept clacking. It was, after all, a big city and somewhere out there, somebody was about to be murdered by that… *thing* tonight.

Stop it, Ted thought. He couldn't prevent anything himself. What he'd done just before Jennifer's arrival was pass his theory along to Lou. That the murderer was using the sewers. Because he'd wanted Lou to hear him out and muster up the manpower necessary to patrol the tunnels, Ted neglected to mention the part about their culprit being an inhuman monster.

While Ted had been part of the force, the hardest thing was knowing that sometimes the only way to catch your man was to sit around and wait for him to kill again. Hope you could access an even fresher crime scene. Hope that maybe the killer would make a critical mistake. Leave some evidence behind in a panic, get spotted by an eyewitness…

For a detective, hope arose from the remnants of someone's shattered life. Just the way it was. Not an easy thing to process.

Jennifer's apartment was cozy. Running shoes in on a mat in the hallway. Muddy soles. A portable massage table folded and leaning against the entry jamb. She gave Ted a quick tour before they popped a bottle of wine and got to cooking. Jennifer, drizzling the rib eyes in oil, coating them in pepper with just a sprinkle of kosher salt, then cooking them quickly over high heat.

Ted chopped broccoli and tossed it in garlic and oil, then roasted the dish in the oven. Less than twenty minutes later, they were eating ravenously.

"Nice sear on this steak," Ted told her when finished. "Did you have to look in Betty Crocker or…?"

"Actually, it's pretty basic know-how."

"Yeah, but it was very good. I enjoyed it very much."

Jennifer cleared her throat. Her face, surprisingly flush off one glass of wine. By comparison, Ted had taken several refills. The bottle between them empty. She gathered the plates and took a deep breath before standing. Wobbling, one hand clamping down on the chair in order to steady herself. "Oh. I'm, uh, feeling a little bit of that wine."

"That's good," Ted said. "Life is meant to be enjoyed with a buzz."

"I wouldn't know. I rarely drink."

"Always time to start."

"Are you always this glib?" she asked this from the next room, the sound of plates clacking together in the sink.

"Only when I drink."

"Well in that case..." Jennifer strode back out with a smile. "Would you like some more?"

"Yes, I would."

"Good. Grab a fresh bottle off the rack over there." She pointed to a metal frame nestled into an alcove across the room, beneath a photo of the San Diego skyline.

"How about some music?" Ted asked.

"Sure. Any requests?"

He bent over the wine rack, browsing labels. "Rovel's 'Boléro?'"

"Huh?"

"Never mind."

Jennifer had a Captain & Tennille record on the turntable and spun it up. Ted retrieved a bottle of Zinfandel dated 1966 and brought it back to the table, fumbling with the cork. Jennifer looped an arm around his neck as she glided past and slid into her seat, the grin on her face looking mischievous in a way that got Ted's heart pounding harder than it had in years.

He was almost alive again.

Her interest had him feeling like a person again, rather than some cast off.

"Here," Jennifer said, noting his struggle to pop the cork. She reached for the bottle. "Let me." Her fingers brushed against his wrist as he handed it over. "What you need is a woman's touch." She popped the cork without issue and refilled his glass to the brim.

"Thank you. I like a girl with commitment."

Jennifer was red-faced and smiling, lurid suggestions taking take shape in her mind. She leaned over to touch Ted's arm and allowed an intentional glimpse of her cleavage as she did it. Playfulness that ignited a pang of lust inside of Ted.

"And I like a guy who doesn't care what anyone else

thinks," Jennifer said. She poured her own glass, just a third of the way up, and sat back, smelling the Zinfandel. Watching the way Ted watched her. Smiling, because she had him on the hook.

"Ah-ha," Ted said. "I'm the antidote."

"To what?"

"Dating woes."

"That's generally how it works. You find someone interesting, and then you take a chance."

Ted sipped his wine, contemplating this.

"Am I wrong?" she pressed.

"No. You're just... very funny."

"Let me guess." Jennifer sipped her wine, green eyes narrowing. "Is this the part of the evening where you say, 'So Ms. Stanton, tell me a little bit about yourself.'"

"Oh, that was earlier. Over dinner. You might not remember because of the wine."

She kicked him beneath the table.

"I don't have to ask," Ted told her. "I already know."

Her eyebrow cocked up as the wine went down. Bemused curiosity on her face as she reached for the bottle. "So, tell me what you know."

"You were born September 20, 1950, in Boston, Massachusetts."

Jennifer wrinkled her brow.

"What?"

"Nothing. It's just... Are you a palm reader or a detective?"

Ted flattened his hand out over the table, waving it back and forth. Half and half.

"You talked to your cop friend," Jennifer clucked with disappointment. "What'd you do? Run a background check on me? Is that the thing with badges? A boys club where you watch each other's backs?"

"Absolutely not." Ted melted beneath the scrutiny of her gaze. "A little."

"You son of a—"

"Allow me continue past that. To what I have deduced. That okay?"

Jennifer sipped her wine noisily.

"You had a very happy childhood."

"What a guess!"

"You graduated from Radcliffe with a 3.6 in Economics. Your father owned a tool and die company."

She was giggling now, tipping the glass all the way back. Another one drained.

"And then there was some tragedy, so—"

"What tragedy?" Her expression hardened for a moment.

"No," Ted said, bullish. "I shouldn't."

She flicked her wrist, sweeping away his reservations, granting permission to continue.

"Your parents were killed," Ted added, unable to resist showing off. "Probably in an automobile accident, considering their ages. And probably sometime during these last five years."

Jennifer forced a smile. Humor, nowhere else to be found but on the upticks of her mouth. A pointless attempt to disguise the heartbreak Ted had summoned to her eyes.

"You inherited the Jaguar," he said, much softer. "It's one of the few things you've got left of them." It all fit, Jennifer had mentioned the car had great sentimental value to her, though Ted's *gift* had cast a pall over the evening, as it always did. He shifted in his seat. "I'm sorry."

"No, it's fine. And you're right."

Except that it wasn't fine. The *gift* wasn't the parlor trick some treated it as. It was the ability to hone deduction and pattern based on human understanding. It's what made him a good cop, a middling writer, and a terrible date.

In that order.

"Look," he told her. "I'm not around people much. This is why."

"I sort of pressed you. And you didn't know."

"I should've."

"Yeah, you are a private *dick*."

"Touché," Ted agreed. "I *was* a detective. And a cop before that."

"So, Mr. Lonergan, tell me a little bit about yourself." Jennifer giggled, restoring playfulness to the evening once again.

"You want to know why I'm not a cop anymore."

"I'm very curious about you."

"When you came by my office yesterday, the guy who was there…"

"Your former partner?"

"No, my old partner is the guy in the photo you were looking at tonight. Lyle Stanfill. We worked cases together for five years. Could finish each other's sentences."

"So, one of you is Karl Malden? The other, Michael Douglas?"

"I could swap my pop rocks for a lollipop and call myself Telly Savalas. But that's a different show."

"Go on, Kojak."

"Lyle and I worked homicide and there was this guy, *Ramrod*, is what we called him—"

"*Ramrod*? I don't think I want to ask."

"Don't. He was running around, slashing up prostitutes. Every couple of weeks, a new body would be found floating in the aqueduct. His handy work. We hunted him for six months and those poor women out there on Hollywood Boulevard… well, they knew they were fish in a barrel, but kept working those streets anyway. Bills to pay and all that."

Jennifer pushed her glass aside, tensing.

"There was so much… *frustration* in Ramrod's work that it didn't take much to build his profile. He was punishing his victims. But for what? Well, eyewitnesses helped us to fill in the blanks. Speech pattern first. Nasally. Barely five-one. For some guys… Get dealt a hand like that and maybe you develop a real inferiority complex. You might take it out on others. And if you were going to do that, well, maybe you had a history of assault and battery as you worked up the nerve to… go all the way."

"How does that narrow it down?"

"It doesn't. There were other things…" He tapered off, hesitant to continue.

"You don't have to, it's alright."

Ted took a moment to collect himself. "Our man turned out to be a failed screenwriter and office manager who was carving up prostitutes that he pretended were the Hollywood starlets he believed the world was denying him. He wasn't just killing them. He was destroying them for everyone else."

"I never even heard of this." Jennifer crossed her arms, shivering.

"Los Angeles has so many serial killers you probably haven't heard about most." That was more dismissive than intended. Ted tuned out the headlines where he could, but if you read the paper at all, you couldn't isolate yourself from the constant bloodshed gripping this city.

"I know about the freeway killer," She sounded defensive, didn't want Ted to think she was some bimbo.

"What about the doomsday cult?" Ted asked.

She shook her head.

"Wackos calling themselves *The Obviate*. Began somewhere in Nevada but have reached Skid Row. Sacrificing homeless people to, well, I'm not sure, exactly, prevent the end of the world."

"You're not joking."

"I'm funnier than that."

"Yeah."

"There's also a string of home invasions up in the Hills. But only when the residence's teenage kids are home alone and that's when—" Ted stopped, noting Jennifer's distress. "Anyway, those are just off the top of my head."

Thing was, Ted felt lighter than he had in years. And it

wasn't the boozing. It was talking about Lyle that felt good, and he realized now this was the only time he'd ever spoken about that day. It had come flooding out of him in ways that were surprising and restorative.

"Very comforting," Jennifer said. "I'm a sitting duck in my own city."

"So aren't we all."

"What happened with *Ramrod*?"

"Lyle and I were catching up. Working with vice. A week in cover alongside those women. Living out of some fleabag hotel, sleeping on a cot that had more stains than a wooden deck. I was wearing my junkie uniform, wandering up and down the boulevard when I spotted a Porsche parked on the sidewalk."

Jennifer stared, blinking.

"A Porsche," Ted said. "Real status symbol. Most johns don't park theirs on the boulevard. See, they're all married. Got careers and reputations to protect. But our guy, our *Ramrod*... He was only pretending at being in the game."

"The Porsche was him? And you just knew it?"

"I went rushing back toward the strip, radioing Lyle. He thought we should stay behind because we had his car. He was dead to rights. Well, I..." Ted took a deep breath, desperate to have Jennifer understand this next part. "We had been working this case for six months. Knew some of those girls better than I know my family. And the thought of him getting to kill one more before the buzzer..." He shook his head. "There's a calculus to this job I never could stand."

"You're right," Jennifer said. "To Protect and to Serve..."

"Lyle staked out the Porsche. And what we didn't know is that Ramrod hung back, wanted to see who was onto him. A cornered animal. Lyle, he, um, caught a blade through the side of his head. Gone instantly. And it was all because I couldn't wait for back-up. All because I was thinking I could, uh, save a life. Wound up losing my best friend's instead."

Jennifer touched Ted's arm. Soft fingers forged a connection that shocked his system. Her concern seemed to solidify in the wake of this confession. "That wasn't your fault."

"Well, I'm afraid you're in the minority with that conclusion."

"We keep tripping each other up tonight, don't we?"

"That's alright, I feel... kind of great."

"And now," she said. "You write books."

"Guilty."

"Like Benchley or Michener?"

"No, not quite. Though my publisher would like to get me there."

"You mean on the bestseller list?"

"I usually wind up in department store twenty-nine cent bins, right next to Bobby Rydell's 'Greatest Hits.'"

Jennifer lifted a small paper bag off the seat beside her. "Funny that you mention that. I stopped by Woolworth's today and..." She slid from it a slightly tattered copy of Ted's first novel, *Brotherhood of Horns* — about a cabal of backwoods pagans hunting a busload of stranded Christian parishioners in West Virginia.

"Fifty cents. You overpaid."

"I can't wait to read, although I do scare easy."

"That won't be a problem. Let me ask you this, Jennifer. Why did you ask me to dinner? Or whatever it is we're doing here."

"Do I need a reason?"

"Everybody needs a reason."

"You're kind of cute... when you're not insecure. And, um, you do have quite a way about you."

Ted still didn't understand, though maybe that was okay. Nobody wanted to spend their time convincing their partner they were genuinely interested.

"I haven't really been with anyone for a long time," Jennifer said.

"Can't be for the lack of opportunity."

"It's just easier with you. You don't come on like a bulldozer. And while you are incredibly odd, more like a con man than an author—"

"Same difference."

"I understand you now. And now that we've scratched the surface, I'm feeling pretty good about my decision to leave that note."

"Don't mistake my being comatose for any sort of style." Ted gestured to the massage table leaning on the jamb. "What's it like being a physical therapist?"

"Physical." Jennifer's tone was flat and carried with it a kind of insinuating gaze, daring him to do something.

Ted remembered now what all of this was like. Was drunk enough to reach out and pull her close. "Come here."

"What?"

"I want to tell you something."

Jennifer bent forward over the table, giving Ted another glimpse of her full cleavage. She grinned as his eyes dipped down, a smirk that suggested everything was going according to her plan.

Two lonely people, connecting.

Ted pushed in, kissing her, soft at first, emboldened by her reception. The quiet moans in her throat, the gentle, wine-tinged breath on his face. They lifted from their chairs in unison, Jennifer tugging at his baby blue Polo, pulling it up over his head and flinging it, running her fingers up his hairy chest, leaving streaks of white-hot relief whenever they went.

Ted pulled Jennifer closer, right up against him, and they tumbled together toward the bedroom, kissing and touching. Once through the bedroom door, Jennifer slid her dress off her shoulders, stepping from it.

Ted cupped her breasts with a gentle squeeze and went to kiss them, but she shoved him across the empty floor space instead, to where the backs of his ankles hit the mattress. His knees buckled and the bed broke his fall as he dropped onto it.

Now, they were more than connecting. They were connected.

Ted watched Jennifer reach for a bottle of oil on her dresser. She poured it across her breasts, down the valley between them to the muscle of her flat stomach. She never broke eye contact, strutting toward the bed and mounting him. As helpless as he felt, as grateful for this moment, he met her with confidence, returning to her mouth with forceful kisses that antagonized her.

He felt better than he had in years, even as the Writer clacked out half a novel about what was happening beneath the city tonight. A creature of unknown origin prowling for flesh.

Jennifer pressed against Ted and the oil was soothing as their bodies rubbed together, his hands roving her body. Jennifer's fumbling with his belt buckle.

Someone's about to die, Ted thought. But he couldn't know that for sure. And he could do even less.

Ted closed his eyes, trying to give himself over to Jennifer entirely. He ignored the Writer and tried even harder not to think about the last woman he'd gotten involved with.

The woman he'd gotten killed.

CHAPTER
TEN

"The Syngenor is—"
The creature heard that voice, had come to think of as Father. His looping and ghostly tenor resonating in concert with the rest of the wanton noise and disruption that defined this world.

The creature lived in discomfort because of these assaults on its senses. All the smells and sounds, equally intrusive. One reason why it embraced the damp gloom of these tunnels. There was only so much to see down here, rats skirting the edges of rancid, oily water, and it preferred wading through human filth to being around the humans themselves.

"The Syngenor is—"

What am I? it wondered.

Above ground, the blaring horn off the top of an eighteen-wheeler forced the creature to stop and collect itself, shaking its head to expel the echo.

What am I? it wondered again, challenging Father's declaration. There were more words than, *"The Syngenor is—"* but the creature did not understand them.

Though it was learning. The Syngenor learned fast.

It continued to be haunted by the girl it killed last night. Her voice, so friendly and carefree. How, then, could she have become so hostile during its moment of need? The opportunity it had been so willing to provide. The Syngenor knew something about human emotion, what it had intuited as fear.

Earlier this evening, it learned that it could process bits of symbolic language because it had followed an echo through these stone-laid corridors to a soot-faced man with heavy eyelids and tattered clothes who barely seemed to notice the Syngenor at all. His breath stunk of the poison many so willingly poured into their bodies, and the man gave a desperate growl as the Syngenor approached, begging the creature to stay back.

It understood this, but did not care, dragging the barely conscious man back toward Father's voice, those same three words echoing.

"The Syngenor is—"

It began to recognize object names. The stone rungs bolted into sections of the wall were called "ladders." Ladders led to "manholes" that were connected to "streets." The more it listened to humans, the more it absorbed. The more it knew.

The Syngenor was always learning.

It understood basic segments of human grammar, though there were variations. Short, English sentences were easy to grasp, but other tongues were beginning to take shape in his mind as well. What had likely taken years of a human's lifecycle to learn, the Syngenor had processed in a matter of days.

That's what the Syngenor was. Superior.

It moved away from Father's voice, traveling beneath the city where throngs of men hunted it, flashlight beams eradicating the gloom. Voices boomed with pronounced cynicism — disbelief that anyone was moving around down here. Their presence created a vulnerability that it resented. Somehow, the humans knew to look for it beneath the city.

Which meant it was only going to get worse from here.

The Syngenor was careful to avoid them, crawling through

the muck on its stomach. In other corridors, it would ascend to the stone rafters. Its movements were measured and patient, and it eventually progressed beyond the constricting dragnet, finding a competitive pride growing inside of it.

Overhead, the sound of distant voices beyond the manhole.

It lifted its head from the muck and a trickle dribbled off the crown of its elongated head. Rivulets of water crossed its silver eyes, streaking the creature's vision like rainwater on a windshield. It made no motion to wipe them. Comfort, a meaningless gesture.

The voices were closer and the Syngenor hoisted itself out of the water, standing to greet them with a reflexive growl rolling off its tongue.

"I don't get it, Virg," one of the voices said, just over the manhole now, on the street above. "How come anytime somethin' goes wrong in the middle of the night, the super always says, 'call Tindall!'"

"Because you're an asshole," Virg said.

"Maybe I am. But what's that say about you?"

"That they're punishing my ass for being your friend."

"It's just what they do. 'Oh sure, Tindall won't mind getting out of bed at three in the morning to bend pipes and wade in shit. Call Tindall! Tin… Dall… Tin… Dall…!"

"Maybe he just likes your smile, Howard."

The Syngenor grew baffled as it listened. The familiarity in their voices suggested good-natured fellowship. Now, the creature understood that too. It watched the manhole cover slide away, scraping along the pavement above. Ambient city sounds sluiced down, reverberating through the confined space. A tangle of blaring horns and distant voices. Disruptions that enraged the creature, turned its claws into fists.

A sickly beam of sodium light swooped down from the opening, illuminating the ladder rungs.

A man appeared there, bent and descending. He stopped halfway and looked back up at a man with darker skin leaning over the hole. "I'm just sayin', man, do you know what I was doing when he called?"

"Lemme guess," Virg gave a reliable laugh. "Valerie?"

"Yeah," Howard said. "I'm trying to bake that potato for the third time tonight and the goddamn phone starts ringing off the hook." He glanced down and surveyed the area, not noticing the Syngenor watching from the shadows.

Harold smiled fondly at the memory of *baking the potato*. "Tellin' ya, Virg, she's a midnight train around the world."

"Would you just go down there so we can get this done. You want to *bake that potato* so badly, you wouldn't be this chatty."

Howard dropped off the ladder and splashed down. The Syngenor waited just outside his cone of light, body tensed and ready. Father's words ever-looping: *"The Syngenor is – "*

"She was all, *oh yeah, oh yeah, oh yeah…*"

"I get the picture, Howard. Really, man."

"Alright," Howard laughed. "Alright. But, hey, I will teach you to score. Load the clown into the cannon. Know what I'm saying?"

"Spare me, man."

And then Howard fell quiet, taking a harder look at his surroundings, sensing that something was wrong. He took a few steps, then shifted his weight and went in another direction, wading deeper into the muck. Shivering. "Jesus. It's cold down here."

The creature seized a large bundle of cross pipes above, lifting onto them, keeping its body squatted, watching Howard spin in circles, frantically checking for whatever had made such a noise.

"You hear that?" Howard's voice was limp. The first sign of weakness when it came to humans. This was going to be easy. "Sounded like a goddamn crocodile!"

"Nah, man. That ain't really happen."

Howard's flashlight searched the water, suspicious of each ripple, flinching against the scurrying rats that brushed past his ankles. He looked everywhere but above. Probably because in his experience, nothing in the sewer ever came from above.

An excited growl passed the Syngenor's mouth, reverberating off the walls.

"Virgil, I'm serious. There's something down here." Howard's panic was thick enough to taste. The Syngenor watched his eyes widen. That strange, pulsing organ at the center of his chest beating against his bones with fury.

The creature moved along the cross pipe until Howard was directly beneath it, shivering in the evaporating humidity.

Howard looked up with a clenched face, spotting the Syngenor. Its silver eyes regarded him with nature's judgment.

Above them both, Virgil's voice continued to filter down.

The Syngenor was no longer listening. It snatched Howard by the throat, hoisting him into the air with all the effort of lifting an empty cardboard box.

Howard screamed. The Syngenor studied his aged face, realizing it could not locate a partner's scent anywhere on him. No trace of companionship. This one did little to advance the survival of his species.

Its tongue lashed out, slipping into Howard's mouth like a lover, as much *baking the potato* as he would ever do again. The man's eyes puffed-up as the creature's tongue stabbed the back of his throat, piercing the soft pink flesh there, his swaying uvula scraping against the intrusive organ.

The Syngenor sucked sweet, sticky fluid back into its own body.

"The Syngenor is —"

The creature had the sense that Father's looping spiel was in praise of its superiority, and it liked knowing that someone out there regarded it with a sense of awe.

Howard went limp, the creature taking just enough fluid to be sated. It yanked the unconscious body up onto the pipes, stashing him face down.

"Hey man," Virgil called out, his throat cracking. "What's going on down there? Valerie come back for more?"

The Syngenor looked up, seeing Virgil's head slide into the empty space.

"This is why I don't buy your shit."

The Syngenor gave Howard's body a tap, prompting a barely conscious-but-protracted groan, blood spilling down, dripping into the muck.

"Hey, Howard, that sounded pretty good." Virgil squinted down into the darkness. "Howard, hey, Howard, I suppose you're waitin' for me to go down there and play some game with you. If you are, you're a bigger asshole than I thought."

The Syngenor eyed Howard again, tempted to drink a little more from him.

"Howard?" Virgil sounded genuinely concerned. "Hey, man, what gives? Oh, come on."

Now Virgil was coming down the manhole, too.

"You're buying a few rounds for this, asshole. Making me go down when your ass pulled the short straw."

The Syngenor's fingers were gnarled and ready.

Virgil came down a few rungs and glanced around. "Please, man, you know I scare easily." He hung there, scanning the landing beneath him, eyes finding the Syngenor's.

The panic on Virgil's face empowered it to drop down off the pipe, displaying its full size to the cowering man. It stalked toward the ladder, claws scraping against the stone wall, summoning sparks of hellfire as its hardened nails left deep rivulets behind.

"Oh, shit, no!" Virgil cried. He scurried up the rungs, scrambling toward safety. His motions were so graceless that his hard hat fell off and plunked down against the Syngenor's feet. The creature glanced at it and somehow understood the blue lettering above the brim read SKYLAB.

It was learning faster now, adapting to this world. Above its head, the bottoms of Virgil's work boots kicked back and forth as his arms dragged his torso along the pavement, struggling to clear the hole, whining as his motions became more desperate.

The creature took the first rung, then the second, following Virgil up.

The manhole cover dropped against the Syngenor's face. Beyond the plate, Virgil was sucking air.

This creature slammed its forearm against the cast iron cover, launching it into the sky with a single push. The manhole spun into the night like a discus and Virgil shrieked. It reached for his leg, nails sinking into his flesh just below the knee, then sliding down to the ankle, cleaving away not only his pant leg, but the flesh beneath it.

"The Syngenor is—" Father's voice echoed.

The creature released its hold on the ladder, gravity tugging it back toward the sewer floor. Virgil slid along too, the Syngenor still holding onto his mangled and jutting bone. The man's other, still-functioning leg went flat across the open manhole cover, but the creature was too heavy. The man's good leg, the one stretched all the way across the hole, bent in half, cracking like thunder. Just before Virgil went vertical, into the hole, his broken leg swung up against his chest, his own foot kicking him up upside the head.

Then Virgil tumbled down, splashing headfirst into sewer water, body going slack. The creature reached up and took Howard's dangling leg, yanking him down off the pipe. Both friends, immobilized. Faint consciousness haunted their frivolous gestures.

The Syngenor hauled both men off by their legs, knowing they'd be reported missing soon. That more men would come down here looking. It didn't matter. The creature was smarter than any of them now.

And Father, it was certain, would agree with this conclusion as more of his words solidified inside the creature's mind.

"The Syngenor is… an abomination… that must be destroyed."

The creature sensed that this new word, *abomination*,

intended disgust. To the Syngenor, this world was the abomination. How could Father believe otherwise?

Surprise and disappointment manifested. Father had hated it as much as it had hated him.

It no longer mattered.

All the Syngenor cared about now was survival.

CHAPTER
ELEVEN

"Capitol Lab Supply."

"Uh, is this Scott?" Sherry asked.

"No."

"Sounds like Scott."

"Got a cold."

"We met a few months ago. I was with Ed Amberdine. We—"

"Can't talk now."

"When?"

"Never. Tell Ed—"

"I can always drive out there and see you."

A sigh through the receiver. Sherry stared out through the open phone booth. The Linden University quad was empty, save for some maintenance staffers repairing a patch of damaged lawn. Her eyes clocked the visitor parking lot just outside the admissions building where her Volkswagen was the only car.

She hadn't seen that sedan since last night. If she had seen it last night.

"Don't come here," Scott told her. "Where are you?"

"Linden University, right off the 405 just outside of Beverly Hill—"

"You're a damn college girl?"

"Meet me in the lobby of the science building."

"This is really messing up my morning."

"It's Saturday," she told him. "How many businesses are buying science supplies today?"

Another sigh, then, "See you in forty." The line clicked dead.

Sherry smoothed the ruffles from her blue skirt and caught herself in the phone booth's reflection, bangs all the way down to the large wire frames covering her face. She wore a gray top and, as stressed as she was, noted how close she'd come to channeling Sarah Jane Smith this morning. A real "Genesis of the Daleks" look without intending it. It brought a fleeting smile to her face. A small assurance this nightmare might eventually pass.

Three students came off the quad, talking and laughing. The dark-skinned boy in university colors checked her out as they passed, turning back for one last glance. *A nice smile*, Sherry thought, though any attention made her uncomfortable right now. She envied their carefree giggles and took an extra moment to watch as they walked toward the pizza joint at the end of the sidewalk.

It felt odd being back here as a "civilian." But safe, too. She had the feeling Scott would be skittish about meeting at all and needed some place benign. Throughout her tenure here, Sherry had never felt safer, and she'd come today hoping that might still be the case.

She cut between the dorms as she crossed the quad in a hurry.

She'd barely slept last night, jumping at every sound, wincing at every shadow. The world before yesterday felt like another life. She'd gone from laboratory research assistant to paranoid conspiracy nut in twenty-four hours, always looking over her shoulder for strange men in sunglasses who committed one murder and wouldn't hesitate to commit another.

In her most hypochondriacal moments, she thought she could feel her raven hair turning grey. It seemed obvious that stress affected the stem cells responsible for regenerating hair pigment and, given everything, she'd be looking like an old maid by next weekend.

"What did you do, Ed?" she asked herself while walking. "*How* did you do it?" The scientist in her was provoked. And while she felt occasional fury at Ed for keeping her at such an arm's length so to never understand the danger just around the corner, she wondered if Ed's secrecy hadn't been intended for her own good.

The science building smelled the same as she stepped inside, musty, as though the whole of it had been built from the opened pages of old books. She stood in the foyer, eyeing a display case of taxidermized wildlife, a honey badger with varnished buck teeth looking out at her, its hunger preserved forever across its enduring features.

While here, she had to check on Professor Lawson. Her office was just upstairs and down the hall. Sherry found the thin, wooden door with the words RITA LAWSON chiseled across a placard. It was locked. The first time in her life the professor wasn't around when she needed her.

There's a message in that, she thought, too tired, too frazzled to parse it.

Instead, she returned to the foyer and bought a Coca-Cola out of the vending machine. Then took a seat on one of the ugly brown cushions that lined the far wall, paranoia insisting that Sherry provide herself plenty of escape avenues should the men in the sedan decide to show up.

On her last day as a student, Sherry had visited Rita Lawson in her office to get her opinion on a couple of job offers, Ed's among them. The professor sat reading through an open binder titled, "The commercial uses of Recombinant DNA."

"Trying to steer our corporate overlords into more... beneficial waters," Rita had said. "Recombinant DNA was our Moon Landing. It can revolutionize everything if we allow it: agriculture, pollution reduction, curing of cancer."

And that's just the start, Sherry remembered thinking. She'd already interviewed with Ed and found his enthusiasm infectious. Rita, on the other land, liked NCS, persuading that Sherry would have all the money she could ever need within five years. And a corner office.

With Ed, though, the possibilities felt endless, and he'd spent much of the interview pitching to Sherry, eager for her to join up.

Recombinant DNA technology meant gathering bits of DNA from different species and placing all those "parts" inside one organism, such as bacteria or yeast, and growing it from there. Sherry had seen some of Ed's labor. Splotches in a petri dish, mostly, but he was adamant as far back as that interview that he was onto something.

Countless studies predicted these new bacteria would inevitably escape their lab settings and create havoc in the outside world. As such, the bacteria were engineered so that they couldn't survive outside their lab environment.

Of course Ed had a secondary lab, Sherry thought. It seemed so obvious now. He wouldn't have risked a breach.

The thing that had killed Ed, that "devil," shouldn't be able to last either. But would Ed have maintained his oath while faced with a breakthrough?

She sipped her soft drink as she considered that.

Ed had shown her some photographs a month back. Innocuous pictures that had progressed beyond a petri dish. Polaroids of a new "lifeform" in embryonic stage. According to Ed, at least.

To Sherry, it looked more like an oversized larval crustacean that some fishermen had found gnawing on whale carcass while somewhere at sea. "You have that here?" she'd asked, looking around the office, eager to see it with her own eyes.

"No," Ed replied, spooked by her curiosity. And then that was it. No more photos. Or discussion. He dropped the topic cold. She had sought too much information, too soon.

But who could blame her?

Once, as a child, Sherry's family stopped at some Tennessee roadside attraction that claimed to have the skeleton of a mermaid on display, which in hindsight made about as much sense as sneakers on dinosaurs, given that Tennessee was nowhere near any significant bodies of water and how in the hell did they get it? And the display was conveniently behind a tank of dirty glass so that you couldn't verify the authenticity of the oversized fish fin attached somehow to the torso of a human skeleton.

The foyer door opened and Scott eased inside, sighing as he spotted Sherry. "Now I remember you."

"Nice to see you again," she said, finishing the drink and discarding it in the nearby trash. "I'll get right to it."

"Where's Ed?"

"Dead."

Scott spun on his heels and started out the door.

Sherry charged across the foyer and grabbed him by the elbow.

"Forget it," he said. "I'm not messing with—"

"If you don't talk to me, I'll let Capitol Lab Supply know exactly how you line your pockets."

Scott looked at her, trying to determine how much she knew. Unfortunately for him, Ed had been so proud of saving a few bucks, that he bragged about the arrangement whenever someone complimented any of their high-end office equipment.

"Hey," Sherry said, forcing a smile that she hoped might put a valve on the escalating tension between them. "I don't care about your hustle, alright? I've got a question about Ed. That's all."

"Fine."

"Ed told me he purchased several anaerobic incubation chambers from you."

Scott shrugged.

"Thing is, we don't have them at our office. Ed had another building where he did most of his work. I need to find it."

"Are you serious?"

Sherry shifted her weight from one foot to the other, indicating that it was her time being wasted now. People always mistook her timidity for insignificance, and Scott was no exception. "You could just tell me. That way you get back to your life and I—"

"Downtown."

"That narrows it down."

"I don't know the address, alright? I don't keep records on this stuff. It's all under the table. Know what that means? Or don't they teach that in this sacred citadel of education?"

"Which street?"

Scott searched the sky above Sherry's head, thinking hard about something, then finding it. "Mahoney Ave."

"Mahoney Ave," Sherry repeated. "Downtown." Good old Ed, hiding out right under their noses. The idea of those goons tearing the city apart while their promised land was within walking distance. There was a miserable sort of humor in it.

"Warehouse district," Scott said. "Underbelly of the whole city."

"Okay," Sherry said. "Thank you."

Scott started back out, pulling open the outer door, and then he stopped. "Actually, your drink made me remember something. Building used to be a cola factory. You know, before they went under? Anyway, signage is still up."

"Thank you," Sherry said. Scott brushed that away with his hand and stepped onto the sidewalk. As the doors swung shut he said, "Don't call me again." And then he hurried off.

"Mahoney Ave," Sherry said and followed Scott outside,

banking a left, the opposite way of his direction, back across campus. She felt a stranger's gaze bolted to her, spinning as she walked, searching everywhere. She gravitated toward pockets of students and wove through several buildings, instinctively realizing this was how to throw off a tail.

A question arose: *What are you going to do once you find the laboratory?* The men who toppled foreign governments and bragged loudly about it would eventually find out. And leave her strangled on her living room floor. That had been Marci's role in this. A sacrifice. Meant to force Sherry's cooperation. Terrify her into compliance.

Why then had it inspired in her the opposite reaction?

Sherry left the English building and jogged toward the dorms, rushing for the door marked Health Services. Inside, a student sat perched behind the reception desk. He didn't bother looking up as Sherry hurried past. Visitor parking was on the other side of this building, announced by a glowing red exit sign.

From the door she saw that her Volkswagen wasn't the only car in the lot. A familiar sedan idled a few spots down.

"Shit!" Sherry threw herself back inside the Health Services suite and rushed back the way she came, turning and checking the door.

Nobody came through. They hadn't noticed her yet.

"Oh God," she said, shaken by the realization of how bad this was. She'd been so careful in getting here this morning. Using side streets. Doubling back. Pulling over. Everything designed to spot a tail. They found her anyway.

"Can I use your phone?" Sherry asked the student worker, who lifted the whole thing off his desk without making eye contact. He placed it on the counter and slid it toward her while ogling the Sports Illustrated Swimsuit Issue from earlier this year, Christie Brinkley in a white string bikini grinning on the cover without a care in the world.

Sherry had the homicide detective's card in her pocket. She dialed him with trembling fingers.

"Detective Millbank."

"Detective, hi. It's Sherry Carpenter. Marci Howe—"

"I know who you are, Miss Carpenter. Got something else to tell me?"

"The men who murdered Marci are after me now."

The boy behind the desk got up and disappeared into an office marked EMPLOYEES ONLY. From there, a single click locked that door into place.

"What?" the detective asked.

"I'm at Linden University and, well, I don't think I'll be getting out of here without your help. Please, detective."

"Slow down, Miss Carpenter. Are you in a public place?"

"Sort of. I'm in the Health Services department."

"And the men... They're the ones who brought you downtown yesterday?"

Sherry didn't know that for sure. She hadn't seen them. "It's the same car, sitting right in Visitor Parking. Please, detective. Hurry!"

"Okay," his voice was tinged with urgency. "Can you get to a more public place?"

"Yes." She didn't want to stay in here. The boy watching from behind locked glass wouldn't help defend Sherry from a squirrel.

"I'll meet you down at the athletics field," she told the detective. "It's all the way across campus and there's always something going on, even in May. Just... meet me there as soon as you can."

"On my way." The detective clicked off and Sherry was alone.

She rushed back the way she came, waiting for that small group of maintenance workers to pass by. Sherry rushed out and moved with them, away from the parking lot. They pushed an equipment cart to the library and disappeared inside. Sherry snatched a small utility knife off it and broke away, moving once more through each of the buildings — better cover— until she was on the long and winding trail to the athletics field.

Getting far away from campus.

It being May, there were no team practices or scrimmages, but the field had been a great way to kill a Saturday. Students tossed a football around. Others down field kicked a soccer ball. Some people jogged laps. The glorious safety of innocuous strangers.

All she needed was to stay around them until Detective Millbank arrived.

She took a seat in the bleachers and watching the students exercise felt strange. The lives of these people... none of it had been that long ago for Sherry. Another world now, but until yesterday, it hadn't been.

A student leapt up to intercept a pass while someone on the other team grabbed his torso and knocked him out of the air, the two of them tumbling to the ground while the football bounced to Sherry's feet.

She smiled, her eyes drifting toward the parking lot beyond the field where she watched for the detective's car, trying to figure how long it had taken her to get across campus — almost fifteen minutes, she guessed. It shouldn't take Millbank much longer.

One of the boys running laps flashed Sherry a smile as he huffed past and she felt safe enough to return the gesture, watching him dart off in short Nike shorts and a sleeveless Puma tee. By the time he looped around the far side of the field, he was looking at her again, flashing an even wider smile. And then a wave.

Sherry waved back, giggling, a nervous crinkle of energy announcing itself. If the jogger wanted to try his luck as she waited for the police, she would more than welcome the company.

As the runner came around the bend, the confidence drained

off his face. He turned so his head was in profile, looking straight ahead, and simply jogged off. Behind Sherry, the sun shifted with the sudden presence of someone standing there.

"You're starting to give us a hard time."

Sherry turned and looked up at the silhouette. The man sat down, revealing himself as he came out of the sun. The same shark's grin she'd seen in the rearview mirror yesterday morning. The Driver.

She started to move away.

"No, no, no," he said. The same way a parent might try and deter a toddler from swallowing a toy. "Make me chase you any further and this gets worse."

"What could you possibly want with me?"

"What are you doing here?" the Driver asked.

The jogger was on the far side of the track now, refusing to even look. "Thinking."

"I'm supposed to bring you back."

"I'm not going anywhere." Sherry's words were clipped on account of her heart rising into her throat.

"You're under the impression you have a say," The Driver growled, noticing the jogger, waiting for him to pass by. Once he did, the Driver lifted his sport coat to reveal a holstered pistol. "Let's go."

"You're not going to shoot me."

"Not if you move your ass."

Sherry weighed this carefully, watching the parking lot for Millbank. She was slow to rise and the Driver matched her movements, the two of them stepping down the bleachers together, looping around toward the trail that went back to campus. "I don't know anything else."

"If we didn't think you were telling the truth, you wouldn't have made it out of there yesterday."

"And now?" Sherry looked behind her. The parking lot was as quiet as ever. The detective wasn't coming.

"Now, the people I work for have decided to cut you in."

"A job?"

"You need one, right? Or are you wearing that getup because you were down at the temp agency this morning?"

"I, uh, I need one."

"Beggars can't be choosers."

"Right."

"It's not so bad, they even let you get a few hours of sunlight each week."

"Sounds like prison."

"Well, beggars can't be choosers," he repeated, the two of them walking the wooded corridor.

Sherry pulled the knife from her bag, uncertain then of what she intended to do with it. Desperate indecision, every cell in her body screaming out in unison to just get the hell away. She only knew she wasn't going with him. If she did, she'd end up with a purple stain on her neck same as Marci.

The Driver's eyes popped with surprise and his wrist pushed aside his blazer, going for the handgun.

"No!" Sherry chirped, plunging the blade into his side. The Driver howled and went spinning around, reaching for his gun.

With a shriek, Sherry stuck him again, twisting the blade while the Driver dropped his pistol to the dirt. He went stumbling into the trees, blood gushing from his side as he collapsed among the tall grass.

Sherry watched him sputter like that until his lights clicked off behind his eyes. Her days were stranger now, a reality she no longer recognized now that she was a murderer. And a fugitive. Wasn't any different from the way her day had started, actually. Healthy doses of paranoia sprinkled with intermittent panic.

She spun around and examined her surroundings. The trail was empty.

She reached down and took the Driver's gun, stuffed it inside her bag. No idea how to use one, had never so much as held one. She was going to have to start, though.

The Driver stared up at Sherry in permanent disbelief, taken out by a mousy little science nerd. If that had been his final thought, then good. She felt an odd swell of satisfaction for it.

She sprinted back to her car as if trying to outrun the trouble she was in. It was so much worse than she thought. Detective Millbank had known where to find her, and then so magically had the Driver.

"He ratted me out."

The shadow men controlled the police. Meaning she could not depend on them at all. Could not call them again. And as soon as they found out what happened here, they'd turn her into a fugitive. For real. Nice and official.

The absurdity made Sherry laugh. It was time to run. Only she couldn't. There was one way to save herself. By finding Ed's lab.

Get the information contained therein. And then decide what to do with it.

The handgun was like a brick in her bag as she reached her car, thinking she was going to have to learn how to fire it before this was all over.

CHAPTER
TWELVE

Ted awoke to curtains billowing like ghosts in the coastal Santa Monica breeze. The bedroom windows were open and the crash of ocean waves were distant and soothing.

The curve of Jennifer's back greeted him as his eyes came into focus and the particulars of last night solidified. For a moment, there was no anxiety in his chest or stress in his veins.

Beneath the covers, Jennifer's feet brushed against his thigh, her big toe tracing the round of his glute, contented sighs escaping into her pillow. The kind of peace he hadn't felt in years.

In Ted's mind, a stack of fresh-typed pages waited. The Writer had worked through the night and Ted scanned them. Scenes of baffled police officers wading through sewer water, wondering whose intel was responsible for them having to trawl knee-deep filth.

The next few pages described the creature's lumbering footsteps. It looked up through a sewer grate, transfixed by the Los Angeles skyline beyond it. The Writer attempting to internalize its thoughts, failing to articulate them...

What was clear, however, was that something beyond curiosity was beginning to announce itself inside the creature's mind. A change was taking place. A self-awareness that it hadn't possessed even a few days earlier while murdering Janie Richter.

A resentment, Ted realized. We lived above the ground while the creature hid beneath it like some bastard stray. It had taken so many lives, so easily, and night-after-night without even the slightest resistance. How could it conclude anything, save for its own superiority?

Ted was fully awake. He sat up and watched Jennifer roll onto her back, envying her rhythmic and contented breathing. Then he stood naked and gathered his clothes from the floor. He slipped into the hall and took one last look at Jennifer, whose arm was draped over her head, resting on the headboard. A beautiful and peaceful pose. A serene image he'd tuck away into the back of his mind for when the world got too dark.

Because it was going to get dark.

He dressed and considered calling Lou, but then shook that idea away. Lou would tell him in great detail how last night went. Or didn't go, based on the Writer's conclusions. That information would further entrench Ted in this manhunt. And he was already in too deep, the Writer, in danger of consuming his thoughts entirely.

"You knew this would happen, Lou, you son of a bitch."

More murders had undoubtedly occurred over the last two nights. Lou would tell him about those, too. And next would come the guilt for trying to live any semblance of a normal life. Time with Jennifer, provided he didn't screw it up first, was about to become *verboten* where the Writer was concerned.

Keep hunting, the Writer suggested. That's all you're good at. The Writer despised the way Ted toiled over a typewriter, churning out cheap thrills and distractions. The Writer wanted Ted to put his *gift* to good work, no matter the toll. And the Writer was stronger, on the verge of taking over. If Ted kept at this game any longer, the Writer would win.

He walked down to the donut shop on the corner and

ordered two black coffees. Didn't know how Jennifer took hers, and this was the safest guess. He bought a paper off the newsstand along with two packages of Atomic Rocks, then thumbed straight to the crime section, scanning for the creature's latest work.

Death, the Writer taunted. *While you were holed up inside, having a nice night.*

In sports, writer Richard Hoffer was still gloating over the Phillies blowing a 9-0 lead to the Dodgers a couple of weeks back. In politics, speculation over how George Bush was about to end his bid for the presidency after blowing sixteen million dollars and two years of campaigning. Kevin Thomas panned the new Stanley Kubrick picture *The Shining*, which he described as "A Freudian's Picnic." And in local news, Silver Lake residents were up in arms over the planned construction of a fifty-lot condominium.

If the creature had killed last night, it wasn't being reported.

Call Lou, the Writer urged. *There's only one reason why you wouldn't.*

The *reason* was sitting at the kitchen table in her bathrobe when Ted returned. He placed a coffee down in front of Jennifer and she smiled at the gesture. Closed her eyes and yawned.

"Admit it," Ted said, taking a seat across from her. "You thought I ran out."

She took a cautious sip, then smirked. Confirmation that Ted had been correct in his guess. Coffee. Blacker than a moonless night. "Wow," she told him. "It's like you… know everything."

"Is that your way of asking me to stick around?"

They were flirting again. Only without wine, and both of their defenses down. Jennifer proposed spending the day together. Ted felt that he shouldn't, that there was too much to do, but recognized that he needed the distraction. All he'd done these last few years was write.

This was a change of pace.

They drank coffee, discussed plans, and Jennifer chided Ted over his opinion that "Solitary Man" was Neil Diamond's best song. Then Jennifer announced she was going to take a shower and Ted, with a surge of boldness, suggested he join her.

The look on Jennifer's face, chewing the inside of her cheek, maybe to suppress a naughty smile, was blindingly erotic. Her reserved demeanor giving way to a host of dirty images flickering through her mind.

She stood, rosé cheeks illustrating her shyness. Despite them, she allowed her robe to fall and become a fabric pool on the floor. She sauntered down the hall, tossing a single glance back over her shoulder. Mouth playfully propped.

Ted followed, tugging at his sorry excuse for a polo shirt, flinging it off. Jennifer was in the bathroom now, the eager spray from the shower nozzle spurting off as he fumbled for his pants, shimmying them down his thighs and doing an awkward potato sack hop to the door, where shower steam already seeped out into the hall like a sauna.

Jennifer was posed in the shower, palms pressed against tile, head dipped down between her shoulders. The spray broke around her neck, prompting beads of water to fall across the length of her back, past the small of it, to the round of her ass.

Ted had nothing to say. He just slipped in and pressed against her. She moaned and lifted her head, turning it halfway. Their lips touched. Their tongues followed.

They drove out to San Pedro that afternoon, Dobie Gray's "Drift Away" on the radio as they rolled into the marina parking lot.

"You have a boat?" Ted asked.

"I wish." Jennifer stared out at the placid pacific water, humid and crystalline, a hundred small white boats bobbing on it like bath toys. "My father used to talk about getting one in his retirement." Her jaw tightened as she remembered something, then cracked the door and got out.

They walked along the waterfront, shoulder-to-shoulder. A light breeze ghosted in off the ocean, adding to the calm and comfort that existed between them. "Worked this place a lot in my years as a private investigator," Ted said.

"Let me guess. Cheating husbands."

"Having a faithful partner who belongs to a yacht club is about as likely as being able to tickle yourself."

She giggled. A sweet and kind of innocent sound. Another reminder that life could be simple and good. Worth fighting for. And yet, even now, the Writer battled that conclusion, typing up pages of destruction and despair as if in response.

"Why'd you give up that life?"

"I think we've had enough *tell me about yourself* for one weekend."

"Whoa, hold on." Her fingers curled around Ted's elbow, easing him to a halt. "I want to see if I have the *gift*."

"It's not a party trick."

"Like you don't ever use it to impress people."

"Actually—"

"Actually, *nothing*. You did it last night."

Her smile, as wide and as beaming as ever — that same movie star buoyancy she seemed to naturally possess — distracted him. As did her amethyst purple jeans made of lustrous cotton sateen and the way she hooked her thumbs into the two front scoop pockets before checking him with her hip made Ted realize he'd do anything for her in this moment.

"Be my guest," he said.

"A girl." Her words were reflexive, like they'd been loaded for a while.

"You'll have to be more specific than that."

Jennifer looked at him, then her eyes lifted toward a string of clouds that hovered over the ocean and she searched for answers there. "What did you do? Fall for someone's wife?"

"Why'd I give it up? I guess I just wanted something that allowed me to be around people even less."

"Oh, come on."

"Yeah. Those long stakeouts in my car were nice, not quite lonesome enough."

"A real anti-social, huh?"

"You've seen the way I dress."

"Speaking of which," Jennifer said, looking him over. "We really ought to… Do something about that."

"You want to take me Back-to-School shopping?"

Another hip check, Ted wobbling along the marina's edge.

They headed for the tiki bar called "Ron's" at the end of the pier. They ordered whiskey sours and drank them while constantly shooing off California gulls who would come swooping down for the complimentary popcorn crumbs.

Jennifer explained her therapeutic massage practice in full. Exclusive appointments all over Los Angeles, mostly in Beverly Hills, Westwood, and Pacific Palisades. Her client roster included actors, professional athletes, "And even a few authors," she added with a playful wink.

"Don't think I could afford your services," Ted quipped, a ribald implication that got him a slap on the arm.

Turned out she was so good, so successful, that her schedule was booked solid the rest of the year, and already into 1981. Her plans were to channel this demand into something larger, opening an actual spa by the end of '81, early '82 at the latest.

Ted shuddered to think about the sheer number of junk novels he'd have put into the world by early 1982.

Doesn't have to be that way, the Writer argued. Keys clack, clack, clacking away in the darkest recesses of Ted's mind.

"Now that you mention it," Jennifer said. "I am a little insulted." A playful smirk broke around the straw that was pursed between her lips.

"About?"

"You've known that I'm a masseuse for twenty-four hours now, and you haven't asked for a massage."

"People say I'm beyond therapy."

"It's usually the first thing a man asks after finding out what I do."

"I'm happy to keep on insulting you."

"You know, you play it down, but I think it's impressive that you earn a living writing."

"Not that impressive."

"It's fascinating. Most people have to do something tactile to earn a living. You… well, it all starts in that wonderfully weird brain of yours."

"It's cynical. That's what it is."

"How so?"

"Well, first, you're pitching your editor. Gotta find the right subject before you can write a word. Only problem is that editors are never interested in the idea that really speaks to you. Somehow, that one is never sellable. 'Unmarketable,' they say, right before they remind you that you gotta stay competitive. That this is a business… Like you ever have a chance to forget that."

"I just thought you wrote whatever you want."

"Think I'd write the crap I do by choice?"

"I read twenty pages this morning. It's good."

"Anyway," Ted swerved, "if you're a real hack, then you're always chasing the success of someone else's book. Sometimes, that's the way your publisher wants it. Or it's the way you do things because you've fooled yourself into believing your work is different. You're the talented one."

Only that was never true in publishing. It was all trends. Blatty and Seltzer had left the devil behind long ago, for example, but nobody in the industry seemed to notice, just kept churning out devil books.

"I think it's the author who makes their story unique," Jennifer said. "The details they choose to include. That's what creates style. And style is more important than story. It's what I remember."

"Can you be my editor?" For Ted, the job was more workmanlike. It had to be, because his life was one mad sprint to stay ahead of deadlines. Who could afford to worry about prose? Just get it to market!

Victor's mantra.

Ted wasn't always so mercenary. He began with a bit more pride in his work. His earliest books, more literary in design. It's just that he'd abandoned that practice rather quickly once the rigors of his contract became clear. And it didn't matter anyway. Ted found that his readers considered him an "acquired taste" even on his best day. Worse authors had greater success.

With their drinks done, Jennifer suggested a trip back to Ted's office.

"So you can drop me off?" he joked, half expecting that to be the truth.

"On the contrary, I want to see all your books."

That musty dive was the last place Ted wanted to be today. But Jennifer insisted and Ted was warming to her interest, her persuasion impossible to resist.

So they went.

And he watched Jennifer sit in front of his paperback shelf, taking down each of his works, turning them over in her hand. Thumbing through each one. She was especially interested in *Lance*, the story of an adopted boy who turned out to be a shape-shifting leopard creature. "I really need to get your whole library."

"You don't."

"Oh my gosh, would you stop?" She slotted the book and got back to her feet, coughing at the cloud of dust she'd kicked up. "Ted… I can think of one really good reason you don't like being here."

"What's that?"

She gestured to the dust floating back down to earth, blanketing everything. "It's sort of a mess? We could get it cleaned up."

"You've had too many whiskey sours."

"I haven't," Jennifer said, wrinkling her brow as she considered that. "Okay, I have. And I do clean when I'm drunk. But you know what? This place is neglected, Ted, and it doesn't have to be. When's the last time you even opened those blinds?"

Ted turned to the slotted shades and had to think about that question. "I guess I forgot they were here."

"I'm going to help you get this place ship-shape. And then you're going to love coming to work. You'll see."

"I really doubt that."

Her smile instilled confidence. "Let me run across the street for supplies. I'll be right back."

She was gone before Ted could protest.

He sat down at his desk to reread the last few paragraphs of *Red Tide* and had no desire to keep writing. Not when people in this city were dying at the hand of something that should've been relegated to these pages.

The door swung open. Ted didn't bother looking up.

"You've been ducking my calls," Lou said.

"I didn't go home last night."

"You weren't sleeping here. I came by."

"No, I wasn't."

Lou grinned at the insinuation. "That lady who was here the other day?"

Ted's shrug answered, *what can I say?*

"That's great, man. That's exactly what you need."

Ted glanced at Lyle, encased in a silver frame. The only photograph of he and his former partner together. "I don't know about that," he said.

"It was a long time ago, man."

"Doesn't make it any easier," Ted said. "And whatever

you're going to tell me, Lou… I'm not so sure I want to hear it."

"Then you have been ducking me."

"I don't know. Maybe."

Lou came in, kicking aside a few plan tubes as he glanced at the sewer maps on the walls. He sat across from Ted and stared. Scrutiny that made Ted reach instinctively for the whiskey bottle in his desk.

"I'm good," Lou said. "You don't need that shit either, man. Just hear me out."

Ted took a defiant swig and Lou's eyes shimmered with disappointment.

"We've worked some real offbeat cases together, man. But this one… real strange. And getting stranger…"

Ted took a couple more swigs. Anything to stem the tide of information the Writer had been bracing him for since this morning.

"It's worse than it looks," Lou continued. "The cases I gave you… those are the reported ones. Turns out, we've got more than few disappearances that we're beginning to attribute to our man. People in this city are dropping like flies."

"It's in the sewers, Lou."

"Hell you mean, *it*?"

Ted glanced at the curled page swaying in the typewriter's carriage. Held his gaze there until Lou made the connection.

"Man, you're so drunk you're living in a dream."

"*He's* in the sewers, Lou."

"We'll get to the sewers. But first… I'm talking to my newspaper contacts, right? Feeding them some info because I want less people on the streets at night. And this kind of thing should be enough to scare 'em, don't you think?"

"Sure."

"Turns out the papers won't run it. You believe that?"

"I'm the wrong guy to ask. Never has been a free and fair press."

"They're still a business, ain't they? 'If it bleeds, it leads' and all that shit? I've got enough blood to fill a fuckin' swimming pool and those assholes are talking about summer fashion trends."

"Someone's pulling the strings. Someone always is."

"That's your prerogative, man."

"Everyone is under control, Lou. Sooner you realize that—"

"Maybe you're right. But that's exactly why I'm gonna catch this psycho."

"Well, he's not here."

"These are my streets. The bureaucrats and the media don't have to care what happens on them. I do. I took an oath. Every person who dies out there is a loss in my column. But, damn, man, there ain't even a pattern—"

"There's always a pattern."

"Not to this," Lou said. "Whoever this guy is, he's stronger and bolder and more cunning than any other lunatic cruising this city. Two nights ago, he pulled a door completely off a car before tearing his victim to shreds. And he's doing it night after night like some kind of fuckin' machine."

Ted took another swig, slammed the bottle down. His heart, close to exploding. The Writer's theory, proven. Something inhuman prowled the city. What troubled Ted now was that this went beyond the creature. The media was in on the blackout because somebody out there didn't want the world to know.

"Hey," Lou said. "You don't believe me, come down to the station. I'll show you the car. I'll show you the body…"

"I believe you. That's the problem."

"Ted… I've spoken to the chief and he's willing to bring you in on this."

"Nope. No way."

"He'll give you anything you want."

"Have a nice day, Lou."

"You were right about the sewers. Two DPW men went missing last night. Patrolman found their truck near a manhole and there's blood all over the place."

"It's exactly what I said."

"And I'm saying that you need this, man. I can see it in your eyes. You're still running."

"I appreciate what you're trying to do here, but this isn't it, okay? I don't need any half-assed therapy, nor do I want it. You asked for my opinion, I gave it to you. I brought you right to its doorstop."

"I'm here 'cause we need help. I need help. The people of this city need help. And I don't seem to be able to give it to them. You pegged the sewers, man, yes you did. Now I need to you look a little deeper."

"You know what you're asking me to do."

"It grinds your brain into pulp. I get it. You think I'd be here if I wasn't desperate?"

Jennifer reappeared in the doorway, announcing herself by crumpling the paper bag in her arms. From her scowl, she'd been out in the hall a minute, absorbing this spirited discussion. All the joy that had been present in her face today was gone, replaced by something graven.

She glared at the back of Lou's head with revulsion.

Lou turned and noted her hostility, then swung back around. "You're our best shot, Ted."

"And I believe he just gave you his answer." Jennifer's words sounded firm and final. She slammed the bag down on the desk and placed her hands on her hips, daring Lou to say something more.

Lou winced beneath this scrutiny, but kept his eyes glued to Ted, his jaw swiveling.

"I'm sorry, Lou," Ted told him. "I'm just not ready to do that."

Lou took a deep breath, then pushed out of his chair. "I'm sorry, too. See you around."

He didn't acknowledge Jennifer as he exited. She stood looking at Ted, saying nothing. She had located his inner struggle and moved around to the back of the desk where she placed her hands on his shoulders, exorcising tension with an immediacy that Ted could only rationalize as sorcery.

"Forget him," she whispered.

"I would just like to note that I still didn't ask."

Jennifer leaned into his ear. "That's why you're getting it." She gave a playful slap to the back of his head where, inside, the Writer had slotted a fresh page based on Lou's intel and was beginning to type.

Only now, Ted couldn't resist the words. He read them as soon as they appeared.

This chapter was all about Jennifer. She glided through a darkened alley, oblivious to the danger coiled in the shadows up ahead.

The Writer was in a groove, clacking keys conjuring words faster than Ted could interpret them. The Writer described the creature rising out of the night, a shadow arranging itself into a monstrous threat.

The Writer described the creature's powerful footfalls. Jennifer stopping, turning, seeing the shadows disappear off the creature as it strode into slatted light coming down off a nearby vent shaft. The Writer had chosen not to describe the creature, a decision Ted found maddening.

What in the hell is it?

"So, let's get this place cleaned up," Jennifer suggested, her voice snapping Ted back to reality while the Writer clacked away in isolation, confident that Ted would be returning to read the rest.

It might never be Jennifer, Ted realized, though the Writer's point was clear. Someone in this city was going to die tonight, as had happened every night. Murdered lovers and friends. Dead fathers and daughters.

Ted had every right to preserve his own sanity, of course, but could he? The longer this continued? That was the bigger question gnawing at him. Those in charge were content to allow this madness to keep happening. And Ted didn't think he could ignore it any longer.

"There's always a pattern." That's what he'd told Lou. Problem was, not everybody could see it. He might be the only guy who can.

Which was why he was going to have to go hunting.

CHAPTER
THIRTEEN

T ed waited until he was alone and then unlocked the gun cabinet.

His attention was on the collection of handguns, each of them hanging by their trigger guards. He went for the Browning Hi-Power because it was easy enough to conceal and didn't feel like being hassled by the city's finest, should they interfere with his down-low investigation.

He left a message for Lou, both at home and at the station, and then while he waited for him to call back, loaded 9mm bullets into each of the Browning's five magazines splayed out across his desk. Each time he slotted a new bullet, pushing it deeper inside the mag, he felt more like his old self.

And that made him think of Jennifer, who hadn't been too happy about going home early tonight, but who also appreciated Ted's responsibility. "It must not be an easy thing to turn off," she'd said. He told her there was a rash of murders the detectives couldn't solve, and she'd left without so much as a sigh, so long as he promised to call her tomorrow, even slipping him a spare key, in case he wrapped up early tonight.

Once Lou returned the call, Ted kept it short. "Just tell me where the girl died. The one whose car door was torn off."

"Thank you."

"Don't thank me. I'm just checking something out."

Lou provided the information as Ted slid a holster over his belt, placing the pistol inside of it, then concealing the weapon beneath an oversized Dodgers sweatshirt.

He drove out to where it happened. Parked in the spot where the girl's car had been found destroyed. Ted slipped past the tree line, his flashlight beam sweeping over dirt, searching for anything the detectives might've missed.

The dry ground became damp, his shoes making suction sounds as the trail ended at the mouth of an open runoff drain. A large pipe that disappeared into the hillside, its darkened maw providing entry to the sewers.

"That's how you got here," Ted said. He shined his light inward. The glow barely dented the cylindrical darkness.

Back through the trees, a string of houses dotted the hillside like Christmas lights. The creature had been looking at this view two nights ago. Ted closed his eyes and asked the Writer to tell him what the monster had been thinking.

"You saw these lights, realized you could bring a few of them back with you. That you didn't have far to travel."

On the road, a car rounded the bend coming down out of the hills. It slowed, the vehicle's headlights briefly igniting the forest like stage lights, swerving to avoid Ted's parked car as it passed.

The girl who was murdered here had attracted the creature in exactly this way. By distracting it. This area was appealing because of the cover it provided. And given that two sewer workers were now missing, the killer's profile had become even clearer. It was through taking unnecessary risks, was instead using its environment to its advantage.

"You heard her voice," Ted said. "Distant but alluring." He moved toward the road, staring at the hillside lights, his free hand gnarling into a claw as the creature's thoughts folded into his own. He imagined hearing those echoes, the voices that had provoked it. Drunken laughter. "It attracted you at first. That's why you hung back. You wanted her, specifically."

He tilted his head as he considered this.

The houses spaced out over the terrain above had been the lure. But it decided to take a bigger risk that had been fruitless, resulting in a car door being torn off its hinge.

The monster had been careful until two nights ago when its attack pattern became more impulsive. And now the missing sewer workers suggested it was back to being vigilant again.

So why the risk?

Ted considered his own impulsivity that same day. His chance meeting with Jennifer. His unexplainable pursuit of her. His risk had been putting his neck out, bracing for the rejection he was sure would come.

But never did.

In a short time, Jennifer had changed Ted in unexpected ways. Given him what he needed. Her warmth and humanity becoming the connection that brought him out here tonight, determined to protect the woman he cared for, as well as the millions of other love stories unfolding around them.

It hadn't worked out that way for the creature, who'd torn away a car door in a display of rage.

"Did you fall in love, my man?" Ted asked, laughing at the absurdity of the suggestion. Laughing, but unable to eliminate the possibility. "I suppose the question is what would *love* mean to you?"

He stepped onto the pavement. The trail was cold. The monster, long gone. And it wasn't coming back. It had noticed the influx of men combing the sewers and understood their purpose.

"Shit," Ted grumbled, realizing they might've been jumping the gun. In their haste to catch this thing, they tipped themselves off and forced the creature's hand.

It was going to stay a lot closer to home.

"And where is that?" Ted wondered. "Where is home?"

He walked back to his car and drove to the nearest payphone, dialing Lou, who again, had been waiting for a ring.

"Tell me you've got something."

"The sewer workers were no accident."

"I know that."

"What I'm saying is, our psycho knows that we're looking for him."

"I got officers out there, an army of volunteers combing the underground. If he's hiding—"

"I don't think he is. He's not hiding at all. Just using the sewers to his advantage."

The Writer typed hard and fast, crafting a passage where the creature stood on a cement slab near the manhole cover that it had climbed from. Its surrounding environment was cardboard boxes, a dilapidated workbench, old seasonal decorations, and broken furniture.

"It's changing its strategy," Ted said. "Pay attention to any reports of burglar activity – especially in old apartment buildings that could have derelict sewer access. That's how it'll attack from here on out."

Silence from the other line.

"You get that?"

"This is the second time you've called this guy an *it*."

"You've known me a while and—"

"So spit it out, man."

"It isn't a man at all."

An even longer spell of silence this time.

The Writer's pages described the creature prowling through a basement, toward an open door where rows of laundry machines lined the walls. A staircase leading to apartment suites. Rows of tenants lined up for slaughter.

Not unlike the homes in the hills, just more cloistered. The same principles applied.

"I know you think I'm headed out to pasture," Ted said. "But I saw that haunted look in your eyes today, Lou. You know none of this adds up."

"Smells so bad my damn dog won't sniff it. You sure about the apartments?"

"Start checking and let me work." Ted slammed the phone down on its cradle and ran back to his Mazda, the Browning Hi-Power slotted against his hip, helping to calm his anxiety as waves of it crested through him.

He fumbled with the sewer plans stacked on the passenger seat. Maybe he was right that there was always a pattern, though he struggled to find it.

Buildings rarely had sewer access. The department of public works relocated these hubs whenever new or changing real estate demanded it. As such, these "retired points" were indicated across each map as a red circle with a line through it. And there were a lot of them.

He scanned through each map with his flashlight, finger racing along all the relevant openings, falling back on a decade of law enforcement to visualize as many locales as he'd visited, trying to eliminate the ones the creature wouldn't use.

It was useless. The pattern, too wide.

He hurried to the phone and dialed Lou back.

"Got a possibility," Lou said. "Reports of a junkie squatting in a laundry room."

"Where?"

"Miracle Mile." He gave the address and Ted sprinted back to the Mazda, fumbling to find the right sewer plan. The apartment was located above a large junction chamber.

"That's where you are, aren't you?"

Ted pushed the map off his knees and flicked the ignition, speeding off across town, racing through red lights, skidding around corners, driving like a madman while the Writer described tight, constricted hallways, terrified faces staring up, shrieking...

Maybe the creature wasn't being careful after all. Perhaps it was getting desperate.

The Mazda flew like a bullet down a one-way street. The city outside Ted's windshield, a blur of lights. He'd traversed half of it in record time, breaking in front of the apartment and hopping out.

Nobody on the scene.

"Figures."

Ted unholstered his gun and jogged toward the entrance, a glass vestibule framed on either side of double doors by two potted palm plants.

The lobby was sparsely decorated and almost silent. A woman standing at her mailbox gasped at the sight of the handgun, throwing her back to the wall.

"Police," Ted said. "In fact, go call them." He proceeded inside while the whimpering woman pushed out into the night, the clop clop of her heels receding into silence.

Ted lifted his gun. Tightened his fingers around the grip. He clicked his flashlight on and held the beam in this free hand, beneath the gun barrel. He could go upstairs, but the Writer didn't think the creature would risk getting trapped up there. Too many eyes.

Instead, he banked a left and shouldered through a door marked LAUNDRY. The air shifted as soon as he was on the landing. Cold, close to freezing, as if all the humidity had evaporated. Ted shivered and descended, moving along the cement wall, gun trained on the blanketing darkness below.

The city above dialed down to nothing. No sounds. No signs of life. Ted's reality became the flashlight beam, the world it revealed: faded signage reiterating the building's rules, scattered laundry on the last few steps, and an overturned plastic basket on the floor.

At the bottom of the stairs, the basement was one large room with rows of laundry machines lining one side. The Writer had described it to almost the exact letter. Beyond them, a set of dented double doors, a crooked placard bolted to one side that read: EMPLOYEES ONLY.

Ted walked across the laundry room, finger resting against the curled iron trigger. The slab floor beneath his feet was pocked with blood. Small and indiscriminate droplets that formed a breadcrumb trail through the double doors.

The Writer typed with a speed Ted had never experienced, page after page set inside this building. Ted scanned the chapter, which seemed to chronicle the truth of what had just occurred.

The first man was killed with his back to the creature. Too distracted by his wash, the clattering machine's noisy whir. On Ted's right, one washer was popped open, revealing a load of whites in a damp tangle. The blood splatters began directly beneath it.

The creature had incapacitated him quickly before going on the move. It stalked into the building proper and caught its next victim coming downstairs, spilling laundry everywhere, which is when somebody else had phoned the police, reiterating what they thought had happened.

The building was quiet on this Saturday evening because its residents were terrified. They were terrified because of the awful, screeching noises that had come from the basement.

The creature had pulled two tenants beyond the EMPLOYEES ONLY door, and the Writer described a twinge of pride for how well it was adapting. There didn't seem to be anybody in the city that could stop it.

The Writer described the creature's decision to feed on the laundry woman, its desire to drain her entirely because it had been deprived of this satisfaction yesterday. A guess, given that the missing sewer workers were serving an as-of-yet-unknown purpose.

The laundry woman tensed as the creature's tongue pierced the back of her throat, drawing nourishment that made it feel calm and centered.

"What the hell?" Ted mumbled. The Writer had given him new information, which was difficult to process. The creature wasn't eating its victims, so the Writer had deduced something else. What bothered Ted is that it somehow felt right.

Ted shook his head clear as he approached the double doors. Every vein in his body pulsed, blood pushing through like molasses. The creature at the end of this nightmare was waiting for him just beyond.

Life as he knew it was about to change.

The doors burst open before Ted could touch them. They clipped the side of his face, sending him tumbling as a woman rushed through, her hand around her throat, blood pumping through the spaces between her fingers.

She collapsed.

The ground became a puddle of slow-spreading blood. Ted got on his knees and watched her pupils dilate in his flashlight beam.

You weren't fast enough, the Writer said in a way that was almost mocking.

Now that the doors were open, Ted's light spotted a stash of holiday decorations in the room beyond. A tree stand, a star tree topper, silvery tinsel, all of it glinting off his beam.

His light crept along, revealing new seasonal décor. A box of bulbs. Two smaller silver orbs sitting on a shelf by themselves. The beam glided past, and the Writer forced Ted to slide the beam back over them.

They weren't silver bulbs, but eyes. Watching him, widening on sight.

The Writer continued typing, describing Ted as he took a few steps forward and pointed the gun. The Writer telling him that the creature had no real knowledge of firearms and so the weapon was about as threatening to it as a child with a water pistol.

The creature eyed him with interest. A man that seemed

ready to face it head on. Almost as if Ted had been expecting to find it.

Ted wasn't going to give it time to act. He straightened his arm and fired.

CHAPTER
FOURTEEN

The burst of pain both surprised and disturbed the Syngenor. Discomfort moved through its hand, up its shoulder as the creature leapt into the hole, splashing down into putrid water.

Two of its fingers were missing and the man who shot it rushed to the manhole, sweeping his light around, trying to locate where the Syngenor had gone.

The broken body the creature had thrown down earlier was just a lump of depleted flesh now. The Syngenor looked at it, the slashes in his back still trickling blood, although the faint gasp in his throat had at last quieted.

From here, the Syngenor eyed the manhole, making sure the curious flashlight beam above stayed exactly that. Curious. Too scared to come down.

It could not take this body back, because the man overhead would be coming, and transporting it would make the creature too easy to follow. The man who'd shot him was a complication. They had exchanged one simple look, and there had been nothing distinguishing there as far as the Syngenor concerned.

Just another piece of cattle.

Except the pain it suffered said otherwise. The pain complicated things even further. It had shaken the Syngenor in ways it had never been shaken, fresh notions of doubt announcing themselves.

The man had succeeded in hurting it. For the first time, the creature had experienced failure. And in this moment, Father's words returned in full.

"The Syngenor is... an abomination..."

It retreated through the tunnels, confident at least that the men couldn't track it down here with any more accuracy than they'd displayed. Too many other smells to blur one's senses: human waste, rotten food, and in some cases, dead men.

The Syngenor stared as its palm, its blood oozing from the jagged nubs where its fingers had been.

Abomination?

Impossible, the Syngenor thought. The pain in its hand was already subsiding as it raced for its nest, relieved to discover that the man who'd shot it had not permanently injured it.

Its thoughts continued to dwell on that man, his haunted eyes, something approaching validation — as if the Syngenor had been the very thing he was expecting to find as he raced into that basement.

How could he know?

The Syngenor hesitated to call it respect, though there was at least a driving curiosity in this man that it found deeply unsettling. As was the fact that it would see him again. That was a hassle it did not need.

Something else began to happen. Something that made the Syngenor even more curious. A sensation in its palm. It stared dumbly at its damaged hand, growling in admiration.

"The Syngenor is... an abomination..."

It did not know about that.

Father didn't mean it, either. It understood this now. That people often said things they did not mean, and that the truth was better confined to tone. Maybe Father had realized the danger the Syngenor represented, his looping words laced with a certain amount of fear, after all. Fear and a little shame.

But nothing about the Syngenor could be described as abominable because now tiny stubs inched out from where its fingers had been blown only an hour ago.

New appendages sprouting up right before its silver eyes to replace his missing ones.

In the dark, the creature purred with relief, knowing now it could not so easily be taken from this world.

CHAPTER
FIFTEEN

The street was sectioned off on both ends by LAPD-branded sawhorses. Red and blue lights strobed and projected exaggerated shadows onto the sides of surrounding buildings.

The apartment complex was evacuated. Its tenants stood around in small pockets on the sidewalk, speculating on might've driven them from their homes. Most seemed certain it was drugs, though one older woman talked loudly about that satanic cult from the desert that everyone seemed to agree was recruiting off the homeless.

Ted felt their collective energy and all of it was negative. He stood in the middle of the street surrounded by squad cars. A carousel of sour eyes squinted in his direction no matter which way he turned. Every tenant seemed determined to blame him for this inconvenience, for all they really knew was that Ted had come into their home and fired off a couple of shots.

He didn't think they wanted to know any more than that.

Next to Ted, Lou's arms were folded, looking at his old buddy as if he were a stranger. One eyebrow cocked, scrutinizing every word out of Ted's mouth. "So you were down there," he said, "spotted him in the shadows, fired three shots at the man you knew was there... and you're telling me you didn't *really* see him?"

"That's right."

Lou glanced over his shoulder to ensure no one else was in ear shot. "Is that the truth?" His voice ticked down to a nervous whisper. "Or are you telling me what you think I want to hear?"

Ted forced a humorless smile. His story was that he hadn't seen what the killer looked like. That was still the truth. He'd only seen eyes. They were attached to something big and inhuman, sure, but it was dark down there. If he bent his report any further in either direction, he was interfering with the investigation or lining himself up for a straitjacket.

"I didn't see anything else, Lou. I'm lucky I realized he was down there with me."

"Yeah. Well... I'm glad you're okay, but shit. We were close."

"We still are. We know where he went."

"It's a *he* now?"

"It's... beyond the scope of things."

"Goddammit, Ted—"

"What can I say? You asked me to come aboard. Remember?"

"Rawlings isn't going to let me patrol the damn sewer night after night."

Ted pointed to the swarm of tenants, to that one lady still going on about the cult she swore was everywhere in this city. "Just listen to her," he said. "Tell the chief that some crazy zealots have set up shop down there, proselytizing in the shit."

Lou laughed, turning to answer a uniformed officer's question.

Ted thought of those terrible silver eyes. He remembered life before the force as an awkward teenager, devouring science fiction paperbacks while floating stoned in Amy Nelson's pool, smelling of suntan lotion and weed, and watching the sky blacken into an infinite starfield overhead. At that earlier point in his life, Ted dreamt of traveling to other worlds, encountering alien civilizations. Imagining the awe that would come along with it.

"Life never happens in a straight line," he mumbled. His illusory encounter with a strange lifeform hadn't occurred at the edge of the universe the way those stoned daydreams had envisioned.

Tonight, the basement had been devoid of all wonder and astonishment, presenting instead a codified image of terror that would be forever documented on those curled typewriter pages inside Ted's mind. The Writer, going on and on about those silver discs, cold and hateful, yet possessing a wicked intelligence. That gaze, eternally flickering and leering.

He'd never forget it.

And even now, Ted felt terrified. His body agitated. Adrenalized, yet shaken, like in the aftermath of any brush with death — a freeway pileup or being held at gunpoint. Only this was worse because one of the darkest secrets the world had ever known had revealed itself, had looked Ted square in the eye tonight. Every unexplained mystery had come alive down there in that moment. And even if Ted never saw that creature again, its face, what little of it he'd glimpsed, would still be forever frozen in his mind.

His own burden to bear. Lou could never know. Lou would never believe.

"Hey, Lou." A detective with a crimson moustache emerged from the tangle of police cruisers. "I gotta to talk to you." Lou moved to the rear of his car to meet the man and the two of them exchanged words that were lost to the ambient chatter on the street.

None of it interested Ted, who was contemplating whether it was too late to stop off and visit Jennifer. But then Lou glanced up, looking directly at Ted as the other detective continued talking in his ear. Ted mouthed "no." This was the end of his involvement.

Then Lou tapped the other detective's elbow and they started toward Ted together. "Hey man... you gotta hear this."

"Have a nice night, Lou." Ted was at the nearest sawhorse when Lou caught him, placed a hand on his shoulder.

"Ted, meet Detective Millbank."

"Don't be in such a rush, Lonergan," the detective grinned.

"I have a quiche in the oven," Ted replied. "Burned it last time. Crispy edges. Real bad."

Millbank smirked, the hollow grin somehow enhancing his disdain. "Not every day you get to meet somebody famous."

"In this city?" Ted said. "The famous are like cockroaches."

Millbank extended his hand. Ted shook it, deciding he didn't like the man at all. Dismissive and arrogant. Probably a shitty detective.

"This case has taken a turn," Lou said.

"I really have to be going."

"Just hang on... I need your take on this."

From inside Lou's cruiser, the radio barked and both detectives snapped toward it as though it were a whip crack. A familiar voice bled through as static. "— hell's going on down there? I gotta go on TV and address the city and you haven't told me —"

Captain Rawlings.

The detectives converged on the cruiser as Lou reached in and lifted the receiver. Ted hung back where he could eavesdrop, morbid curiosity for what his former superior had to say about tonight.

He spotted another man in a tan suit weaving through the crowd, overdressed for this neighborhood. It could've been another detective, maybe even Millbank's partner, though Ted didn't think so. There was too much entitlement in his gait, and he headed toward the apartment's entrance, turning back to survey the sawhorses once he was close. Looking to make sure he wasn't noticed.

"Who the hell are you?" Ted wondered.

Ted in his Dodgers sweatshirt was as transient-looking as ever, and probably passed as a local. He could move with anonymity through these crowds. The tan suit was checking for uniforms. Other suits. Not beach bums.

Ted passed some tenants who were loudly asking when they would be let back into their homes. He pointed to Millbank, hovering over Lou's shoulder. "That's Detective Millbank, capital M-I-L—" he spelled the name out. "It's his authority, so make sure you ask him. And be persuasive!"

Then he hurried to catch the suit who ducked beneath the ticker tape. A man whose head was shaved down to a scuzz, save for one small patch of pink flesh in the shape of a T.

Ted knew exactly where he was going, down the cement staircase. He followed him inside and waited until the other man's footsteps had reached the landing below before descending. He took light steps down the treads, as nimble as he could, hoping it was enough to avoid detection.

The suit waited for him at the bottom, arms folded expectantly.

"Just need to get my delicates out of the washer," Ted said.

"You're about to be thrown off the case." The man did not remove his sunglasses, despite the piss yellow lighting that was so weak it defied any real utilitarian function. He glanced over his shoulder, unfazed by the body bag lying in a puddle of black blood that had spread halfway across the floor. "You got too close, Lonergan."

"To?"

"That is the real question. Isn't it?"

"I didn't see anything."

"I don't think that's true. You're a capable man."

"Thank you for the confidence."

"You might play a headcase, but you're not going to discharge your weapon without a good goddamn reason."

"I don't think we've been introduced."

"Go home, Lonergan. Back to your life. Back to your keyboard."

"Alphabet branch," Ted said. The man's over-encompassing knowledge confirmed that suspicion. "Should've known."

"We're going to take it from here." He turned his back on Ted, looking through the double doorway at the end of the laundry room. The doors were still open, revealing the storage space beyond it. The open sewer cover on the ground, the stench of Los Angeles' liquefied filth beneath it wafting up.

Ted visualized those silver eyes rising out of the hole and shook his head in order to chase that thought away.

The suit stood his ground. He wasn't intimidating Ted, though. He simply refused to go any further into the room, fear keeping him anchored in place. The suit knew more about the creature than he would say, and he worked for the kind of people who could keep such information out of the papers.

And the suit's hesitation to go any further also suggested that nobody wanted to go after it.

Least of all Ted, who had something to lose now.

"I'm glad to go home," he said. "I am tired." The operative had given him healthy advice. Go home to his keyboard, armed with the knowledge that monsters were real. Somehow, he was supposed to pretend he could get back to normal from here.

He'd gotten his man, so to speak. The government goons could take it from here.

And fuck it up like they always did.

"Have a nice evening," Ted told him and started back up the stairs, where Lou and Detective Millbank stood in the lobby, the curly-haired detective in a huff.

"This guy ever stop playing games?"

"My last one," Ted said. "I've got a book to finish."

"We're working alongside the G-men now," Lou said. "Can you believe it? They got me looking for some girl."

"What girl?" Ted asked.

"Sherry Carpenter. Apparently, she's a person of interest in these murders."

"That's ridiculous," Ted said. "They know exactly what's going on. You're on the hunt for more than some girl."

"We got her house staked out," Millbank said. "She hasn't been seen since this morning."

Ted sighed. This was getting less interesting by the second. He wanted to see Jennifer. This day had started as magic, the best shower of his life followed by drinks on the pier. And it had ended with him facing down an alien creature in a filthy storage cellar.

"Ted, man, she's a twenty-three-year-old scientist…"

"And a murderer," Millbank added.

"I have complete faith in you, Lou," Ted said. He noticed the eager residents beginning to gather right outside the foyer. He opened the door and he turned back to Millbank. "And let these people back into their homes, okay? Stop being drunk on power."

This got a rise out of the crowd, who were angrily shouting Millbank's name, threatening to phone his supervisor.

Lou fought a smile, had nothing else to say.

Just let Ted go.

CHAPTER
SIXTEEN

Sherry showered quickly and with the bathroom door wide
open so she could hear if anyone tried to get into her motel
room.

Once she was finished, she stepped shivering onto the cold
tile floor and told herself the uncontrollable shakes were due to
temperature. She wrapped a towel around her body and cleared
a streak of fog off the mirror with the palm of her hand. Her
reflection was enough to re-ignite the panic spreading through
her body.

"You're okay," she told herself, weak and wobbly words
balking at the absurdity of that assurance. She wasn't okay. She
was a murderer. On the run.

Sherry went to the window and peered out from the behind
the drawn curtain. This motel was in the middle of nowhere, a
few miles outside of Palm Springs and surrounded on all sides
by the desert.

The guy behind the front desk had told her that people only
stayed here once all the popular places were booked up, and
that she had her pick of rooms this weekend because it was still
technically "off season."

She figured at first that being alone in a motel would make

her feel better. Safer, because there were no other tenants to worry about. Now, though, she realized it was so much worse. If those men somehow came out this way, the office manager would be well-aware of the one woman staying here. He'd point them right along.

In the parking lot, an old Chevrolet Bel Air sat beneath the glow of the motel light. One other pick up was parked in the shadows. Both had been there since she checked in, so things were clear. For now.

Sherry tossed the towel at her feet and changed into the attire she'd picked up a few hours ago at the gas station down the road. Touristy things she'd never otherwise wear, a pair of red Dolphin shorts with an embroidered LOS ANGELES logo right where the hem ended and a baby blue tee shirt emblazoned with the words, CALIFORNIA — DREAM BIG.

If anyone asked, she was just off the bus for the summer, eager to see the sights — especially Palm Springs. And that she was staying with a cousin in Redondo Beach but had to get out for the night on account of *Cuz* wanting to spend some sack time with her boyfriend.

If only Mom and Dad could see me now, Sherry thought. She needed to get a message to them. The driver's body had surely been discovered, which meant the police were putting the pieces together.

Detective Millbank would assume Sherry's next logical move would be to rush back home.

She picked up the phone and started to dial, glimpsing herself in the mirror across the room, a stranger in tacky clothes. A long way from Sarah Jane Smith in "Genesis of the Daleks." The large-frame glasses contradicted her attire, but Sherry was adamant that she keep them on. She already felt like too much of a stranger and couldn't lose the one thing she still recognized about herself.

She dropped the phone back onto its cradle. If she had to call Mom and Dad, it couldn't be from here. Wouldn't that create a phone record? She was a wanted woman and had to think about these things.

"What am I doing?" she groaned and then crossed the room to check the parking lot again. The same scene as earlier.

The vacuous lot didn't make her feel any better, though. The men who wanted her would stop at nothing to recover Ed's secret. No matter how many people had to die. Sherry had grown up believing those who worked in such citadels of power were supposed to be the good guys.

Except that today, the "good guys" had tried to murder her.

She had to get moving. Put on her sneakers and went out into the night, keeping to the shadows as she headed for the street, turning right and walking down the road, toward the gas station lights in the distance.

A black Trans-Am slowed as it passed her, "Dreaming" by Blondie on blast. Behind the wheel, a silhouette turned and watched Sherry in the second it took for the car to roll past. Then it was gone, Debbie Harry's voice becoming unmoored and echoing across the flat desert night like a ghost.

Sherry quickened her pace to the gas station. Behind her, the song refused to fade from earshot. It was coming back up to full volume while the light at her back began to shift, making her shadow grow large and unwieldy across the tarmac – a result of the backlight.

The Trans-Am had turned around, slowing to a crawl beside her.

Sherry braced and reached for the key ring in her purse. It wasn't much, but if the driver tried anything, she was going to jab his eye out just for the bother. She had blood on her hands now.

"Hey," the soft voice said in a casual drawl.

Sherry turned and the boy behind the wheel was blond, younger than her, probably sixteen or seventeen.

"It's late," he said.

"No kidding," Sherry called over the grumbling engine. Up ahead, the lights of the all-night gas station were a beacon.

"Hey, I just mean... You shouldn't be out here alone."

"Neither should you," she said. "Don't you have curfew?"

The boy laughed, his elbow dangling out the open window frame where his palm slapped against his door. The Trans-Am swerved even closer. "You're funny."

"Have a nice night." Sherry started to speed walk toward the gas station, the faded sign PALM SPRINGS FILL 'ER UP morphing out of the darkness. Beyond the lights, a store clerk was perched on a stool behind the register, a shadow framed perfectly in the windowfront.

"Hey," the kid continued. "I just want to ask you something."

Sherry stopped, hands on her hips. Did she really have to do this? Now?

The boy, perhaps reading the frustration on her face, noting the anger he'd inadvertently teed up, stepped on the breaks and cracked the door. He got out and lifted his hands into a surrender position. "I'm out here at my aunt's house for the weekend. Got the whole place to myself." He gestured to the darkened horizon behind them. "Just a few miles back there. We could—"

"How exciting for you." Sherry was already moving toward the gas station again. Without turning around, she heard the slam of the car door and then, the Trans-Am beginning to prowl forward.

She was close enough to the fill 'er up that she broke into a soft jog, racing for the lights, a bee-line for the convenience store part of the station.

Behind her, the Trans-Am rolled into the lot and sat idling at the edge of it.

"Do you have a phone?" Sherry asked as soon as she walked through the door. The clerk behind the counter was about as useful as the boy at Student Health Services today, gesturing to the restroom hallway. He took a swig of Tab and checked out her legs as Sherry moved down an aisle.

In the lot, the Trans-Am wasn't moving. Its headlights seemed to be tracking Sherry as she walked the length of the store. All she wanted was to be back at work. Anonymous and forgotten. Helping to realize Ed's vision of the future.

A new lifeform. He'd actually done it.

Which is why you're in this mess, she thought, and then picked up the phone, dialing home.

"Hello?" Dad asked with more than a bit of breathlessness in his throat.

"Dad, it's Sherry."

"Hank, is it her?" Mom asked from just beside him.

"Sherry, where are you?"

The question gave her pause. It wasn't "Are you okay?" or "What happened?" The speed with which he answered her call, coupled with Mom's frantic, nails-in-his-shoulder questioning, suggested that someone else was close by, had already spoken with them, let them know there was only one question that needed asking.

"Sherry, where are you?"

On this, Sherry happened to glance out across the store's back aisle, the Trans-Am sitting just off the road beyond the glass windowfront. Just behind that car, lit against the teenager's red break lights, a sedan zipped past.

"Oh no," she said.

Something about its presence caused Sherry to leave the receiver dangling. She glided across the main aisle, gravitating toward the front window where the dummy in the Trans-Am was now flashing his high beams as if she might otherwise miss him.

She didn't care about him, was instead interested in the car that had just sped by. She was sure she'd been inside of it two days ago.

Further down the road, that sedan's headlights swung sharp into the motel parking lot.

Sherry rushed back to the phone, puzzle pieces clicking together. Somehow, the men had found her vehicle — the one thing she hadn't been able to ditch. "Dad, I'm fine," she said. "Talk soon. Love to Mom."

Click.

She was already running through the store, outside, rushing straight for the Trans-Am, realizing her dumb luck as she stared in the direction of the motel. The sedan had missed her by minutes and this place would be the first one they checked once they realized she wasn't there.

"Hey, uh…" the driver said with a stupid grin as Sherry got into the passenger's seat and slunk all the way down.

"Take me to your aunt's place," she ordered. "As fast as you can."

"All right!" the driver threw the car into reverse, cranked the radio – something by Boz Scaggs – and smashed the gas. The Trans-Am burned a trail of rubber across the pavement as the car swung all the way around and launched itself at the open road.

Sherry placed a hand on the driver's arm, holding her breath as they whizzed by the motel. The dark sedan was in front of the office. Sherry saw one man walking along the second-floor balcony in her room's general direction. Then she was staring at the rearview, half expecting to see those headlights come charging out of the motel lot in hot pursuit.

Only that never happened.

Sherry was, for the briefest of moments, safe. Detective Millbank must've had people calling around to every motel in the city, asking each office to check their parking lots for the make / model of Sherry's Volkswagen.

She couldn't afford to be that stupid again.

"Just so you're aware," Sherry said, looking at the driver

with the brightest smile she could muster. "This isn't what you think."

"Whatever you say." The driver just sounded happy to have the company. "I'm easy."

"Yeah," Sherry told him. "That's what scares me."

CHAPTER
SEVENTEEN

Jennifer was still awake when Ted dropped by, using her spare key to go inside. He found her in bed, propped against the headboard, nose buried in one of Ted's earliest novels, *Demon Bells*, about a strange church in Duluth, Georgia that slowly turns its parishioners into sex-crazed demons.

On most nights, Ted would've felt embarrassed to see this, a book he barely remembered writing over the span of three months in the fall of 1978, but he'd stopped off for a few drinks on the way to Jennifer's, hoping the alcohol would've forced the Writer to take a few hours off. To quit hammering those pages into his brain.

It hadn't worked. The Writer was past the mid-point of the story now, on a creative jag. Typing, typing, typing.

Always typing.

Jennifer smiled at Ted's appearance in the doorway and placed the book beside her. When she did, one of her nightgown straps slid off her shoulder. She left it hanging there, a suggestive smile on her face widening, but only for a second. Replaced by worry. Her nose caught a whiff of whiskey, that smell beginning to spread through the room.

"You went out drinking?"

Ted flung his clothes off and fell onto the bed, groaning into his pillow. "I thought it'd help." He turned halfway so he could see Jennifer. "Surprised you're not sauced yourself, reading that."

She placed a hand on Ted's bare shoulder. Her touch was gentle, finger pads brushing along his back, enough of a sensation to startle the Writer, clacking keys going on mute. "You know how to keep the pages turning," she told him. "That's a gift unto itself."

"Tell it to Victor."

"I'd rather you tell me why you stopped off for a few drinks. Alone."

He laughed. What was he supposed to say? The truth? That the failed detective turned failed author just so happened to discover an alien being in the basement of some dive apartment? And that he was certain he'd injured it, but then along came a helpful government operative, whose presence alone was evidence that Ted wasn't crazy?

He could've told Jennifer how each time he closed his eyes, the creature's silver orbs were there, staining his consciousness. But how would that make him sound?

Whoever had said *"the truth will set you free"* was an asshole, because in this case the truth would cost Ted the only two relationships in his measly life.

He closed his eyes. The creature was there, watching. A shimmer of curiosity moving through those orbs, as if they were tuned to a live broadcast. The animated way in which its eyes narrowed, searching, trying to understand the brain it haunted.

It was more than a mental Polaroid. The projected eyes studied Ted from inside his own skull, access to all his thoughts. And Ted worried that the creature was somehow looking out of his eyes, into Jennifer's bedroom. Studying Jennifer while she studied Ted, fingers brushing against his cheek. This filled him with an almost violent anxiety because now it had taken an interest in Ted Lonergan.

Nobody else had ever managed to hurt it.

But if he admitted any of this to Jennifer, he'd never see this bedroom again. Would be deprived of her company. Of that confident smile that made him feel like there was at least a chance to become whole again. Her warm fingers on his flesh, melting the tension from his muscles. He needed to protect this relationship, even if that meant keeping those horrible, silver eyes to himself.

Jennifer, on the other hand, was getting curious. She rearranged herself, rising above him on the bed, her bare thighs closing around his hips as she mounted him. Her fingers did gentle zigzags along his back and she realized just how rigid his body felt in this moment. "Jeez, you weren't like this earlier today."

"You may be surprised to hear, Ms. Stanton, that I have some issues."

"Don't we all? Living despite them is what matters."

"I like that."

"Yeah, you could stand to hear a little optimism each day."

"See, if I could get this kind of pep talk over corn flakes, I might be able to get my head right in ten years. Eleven tops."

"I work a lot faster than that." Jennifer's hands did too, loosening the knots on his back, inching down the length of his spine, kneading the tightest patches of skin. Her aroma was sandalwood and Ted puffed his nostrils to absorb a little more of it, finding that it calmed him down.

He stared at the tent-folded *Demon Bells* paperback propped on the bedsheet beside them. He didn't want to close his eyes again and risk seeing those silver dollars, so he stared at the back cover blurb from Robert Bloch. Effusive praise announcing Ted as "a major talent of the macabre."

The author of *Psycho*, ladies and gentlemen. It was difficult for Ted to believe that Victor had been able to get that quote, but at an earlier point in Ted's career, the publisher had been banking on his ability to escape the mid-list. And Ted still wanted to. Settle in and find a nice crime series. Maybe create a wonderfully complicated woman criminal character to balance out all those Richard Stark *Parker* novels.

Only Victor wasn't having it. *"Once you are where you are, you stay where you are."* A worldview Ted didn't believe was especially productive for writers or readers. People evolved all the time. And for a multitude of reasons.

"You're not even going to tell me what's wrong?" Jennifer asked, tsking her tongue. "I mean, I am working on my day off here."

"I've been doing some advising for Lou."

"I know that."

"It got a little too personal tonight." Ted didn't have to close his eyes to see those silver orbs now. They were in the bedroom, transposed over everything like a dream so eager to claw its way from his subconscious. And when Ted finally blinked, his vision going dark for a split second, he flashed on an empty desk. The typewriter sitting atop it.

The Writer's post, abandoned.

"Personal?" Jennifer wondered. "How?"

"Failure has a way of following me. You're halfway through *Demon Bells*, so you might've already guessed that."

She gave him a gentle slap across his head.

The silver eyes remained focused on her. Somewhere out there, the creature was more than curious. It wanted to know everything about the man that had hurt it. It was fixing to hurt him back.

Ted was desperate to tell Jennifer what scared him. But after the way Lou had looked at him tonight, with quiet judgment and encroaching disappointment, he knew that he couldn't. It hurt bad enough, watching Lou try and mask those thoughts, wondering what in the hell had happened to his old pal, Ted.

He couldn't live with seeing that disappointment on Jennifer's face.

"Be serious, Ted."

"I'm just worried that the person I am is going to prevent me from becoming somebody else. Someone happier."

Jennifer slid the other flap off her nightgown and the silk fell to her waist, her topless silhouette reflected in the bedroom windows. She said nothing, kissing Ted's neck while her breasts pressed against his back, a soft sensation that conjured in him a couple of moans. "This isn't making you happy?"

"This is the happiest I've been in a long time."

Ted flipped himself around and Jennifer forced her mouth to his. His hands explored her curves while she ran her fingers along his chest. They moaned into each other's mouths as their tongues danced, connectivity driving them onward to hard and forceful sex — as aggressive as Ted had ever done it. He thrusted up into her, transfixed by the way her face responded to each sensation. And when he got close, he rolled their tangled limbs over, positioning Jennifer onto her back, her legs spread wide while her palms slid around his ass, pushing him deeper, moaning turning to screaming.

The silver orbs saw this intimacy. Didn't matter whether Ted's eyes were open or shut. The creature watched, taking great interest in Jennifer's lacquered body. Interest in Ted licking the beaded moisture off her glossy shoulders. Interest in the overall ritual, the way their bodies joined together.

And then the Writer sat back down at his desk, typing out a revelation, recalling Janie Richter in her house on that quiet, dead-end street. Harkening then to the next night's girl, whose door the creature had torn off in frustrated pursuit. That was the key, the Writer suggested. *Frustration*. Both young women had died more brutally than the rest, the creature quite literally tearing them to pieces.

Why?

Because it hadn't set out to murder either one of them.

It was more than simply food. The Writer had explained earlier that the creature was somehow nourishing itself off our internal organs, using its tongue to get what it needed from our bodies. Ted didn't understand how the Writer had intuited that knowledge, though now he had no trouble imagining a slithering tongue along with those silver eyes and knew the deduction was correct.

And still, there was more to it.

Ted and Jennifer climaxed together, bodies tensing, hers arching all the way back, whining at the ceiling before loosening her muscles and splaying across the sheets, spent and placated by the calming sense that only deep satisfaction could deliver.

This ritual had attracted the creature's interest because it had plans for some of its victims. In that moment, rolling off Jennifer and sucking air, Ted understood the creature even better than he realized.

It was trying to reproduce.

And when he closed his eyes, searching for sleep, those silver orbs were there. Glaring at him, for now he knew too much.

CHAPTER
EIGHTEEN

"My Mom doesn't like me coming out here alone," the kid driving the Trans-Am said, speaking out one side of his mouth, annunciating that surfer drawl. "She says this place is, like, the Hamptons of Los Angeles and that I need to be careful about who I talk to out here." He cocked his head and threw Sherry a dorky smile. "Do I have to be careful of you?"

"Oh, I'm not from around here."

He swung the Trans-Am into a darkened driveway and shifted into park. "That's not what I asked."

"I, uh, I don't —" Sherry craned her neck toward the road. Every house was in shadow, lights off. There hadn't been a single pair of headlights to disrupt the gloom of this neighborhood anywhere on these last few streets. It was difficult to believe Sherry could be so lucky as to make a clean getaway, but that sedan was nowhere to be found. "I think you probably do."

She placed her hands on the dashboard and pressed her fingers down — an exercise to steady her trembling arms. She sat like that a moment, attempting to calm herself with deep breaths.

"Well, I'm not scared," the boy chuckled. He popped his

door and the interior light came on, and his eyes roved Sherry's bare thighs, which were on full display beneath the hem of her tourist shorts. Her legs were beginning to stubble, but the teenage boy didn't seem to notice or care. It had been days since she'd last shaved them and had never once in her life considered slipping into a pair of dolphin shorts.

Life this week was unexpected in so many ways.

"Hey," Sherry said, "what did we talk about?"

"I know, I know." The boy averted his gaze. "Whatever happens is cool with me, dude."

"Nothing," Sherry said. "Nothing will happen."

"Yeah, um, what I mean is, you wanna smoke a little and then lock yourself in the spare bedroom, be my guest. Just glad to have some company is all."

Sherry looked at the house. There was safety in numbers, sure, but this poor boy wasn't going to be much help should the assassins decide to come door-to-door. If they were determined to sever all loose ends, wouldn't they go that far?

Further.

Except, you're not a loose end. That was important to remember. Nobody else knew the location of Ed's laboratory. And as soon as Sherry could safely ditch the tail, she'd go there, acquire all the leverage needed to —

To, what? What exactly was the play? Sherry didn't know. Just that she felt a responsibility to Ed's legacy. He would've preferred her making the final decision as to the experiment. Certainly in lieu of rogue government killers who were probably looking to unleash the species in some foreign country.

"Anyway…" The boy climbed out and started toward the front porch.

Sherry followed him inside. The décor was strangely old world, 19th century farmhouse or something. Exposed wood beams ran across the ceiling, a butcher block counter in the kitchen, along with an apron sink to reinforce the home's rustic quality, and wicker decorations for each shelf and corner.

"We even got a pool out back," the boy said, clicking on a few house lights and then checking out Sherry's legs again. "If you, uh, wanted to take a swim."

"I don't have a suit."

The boy only grinned.

"Oh, shut up," she said and went wandering the house, trying to dislodge her thoughts. Figure out what she was going to do once she reached the laboratory. The boy followed, and Sherry felt his eyes glued to her butt, and she hated these stupid shorts and the unwanted attention they invited.

"Hey, uh…" the boy cleared his throat. "I don't even know your name, dude."

"Janey," Sherry told him.

"Janey. Cool. Janey. Yeah. I'm Lane."

"Hi, Lane."

Lane's face ignited with hopefulness — this might be a pleasant evening after all. He snapped his finger as if remembering something. "Oh, refreshments, right?" Then he went rushing off before Sherry could respond, and that was fine. She collapsed on a nearby wicker chair overlooking the back patio, a row of terra cotta vases lining one side of the crimson brick.

"You wanted to create a new form of human life," Sherry whispered, reflecting on Ed's ambitions. His idealism had swayed her toward employment when every other bone in her body thought Norton Cyber Systems was the play. Not that any of that mattered anymore. "You failed."

Ed's primary interest was genes. As a species, human beings had roughly twenty thousand of them and science knew precious little about the functions of each. Ed begrudgingly admitted how naïve their field was when it came to the very basics of biology, and that had served as the basis for his experiments.

Which genes were essential to life? Ed had suspected fewer than his peers hypothesized. He intended to prove it by shaving down the genome of various bacteria in order to find the barest set of genetic instructions that would produce life. He'd shown Sherry various synthetic genetic bacteria with fewer than a thousand genes, certain they could get even lower and still have a functioning lifeform.

One afternoon, Ed had come storming from his rear lab in the Hollywood office, screaming for Sherry. He cornered her at the paper cutter, eyes blazing with scorching curiosity — his mad scientist moment. And all he wanted then was her input on one specific question. "We know now that we can take genes away. But… What do you suppose would happen if we added the DNA of another species to our own?"

The Polaroid that Ed had shown her weeks later suggested he'd managed to do it. The curiosity Sherry felt in looking at that photograph had energized her in ways she'd never felt. She wanted to pick Ed's brain, sit back and soak up every word. Learn exactly how he'd done it. But he responded to her curiosity by turning off that spigot of information, never to speak of it again, terrified and ashamed of his own progress.

That was Sherry's guess, at least.

She suspected that Ed had managed to insert arthropod DNA into some part of a human organism, potentially a zygote for as effective has the result had been. And she knew now that that reason she was in this mess wasn't simply because Ed had effectively created a new organism, but that he had successfully incubated it. Grew it.

And now it was running around Los Angeles, completely out of control.

"You have to stop it," Sherry mumbled, looping back to her earlier question. What to do once she reached the lab? A chill moved through her. "In order to do that, you need to understand it."

A few rooms over, Lane rummaged through the

refrigerator, loudly questioning his own decisions, deciding against bringing a bag of chips along with the drinks. And then his footsteps began winding back through the house, his reflection appearing in the window a few moments later. He had two beer cans in his arms and danced from one foot to the other.

"You seem so nervous, dude."

"So do you," Sherry said.

He handed Sherry a can of Olympia, then peeled his open. "I, uh, kinda get nervous around girls," he said, more than a little ashamed. "When I saw you walking back there, I thought, *'she seems nice.'* Oh, and don't worry. No funny stuff, like you said. I get it."

"It's a little stalker-y," Sherry said. "Following me to the gas station. Only it turns out you sorta saved my butt so..." She raised a finger to emphasize this being an isolated incident. "You probably shouldn't try that again."

Sherry pulled the tab on the beer and winced at the thought of drinking it. In all her life, she'd never actually finished one of these things.

Lane came a little closer and tapped his can against hers, a toast to... whatever. And then they drank, and it was crisp and refreshing and she hadn't eaten anything at all today, so the buzz kicked right in, good-natured light-headedness that dissolved the pressures simmering inside her.

"This is good," she said.

"Your cheeks are turning red."

"Hey—"

"I know," Lane said, annoyance rising. Slight offense over Sherry's constant guardedness. This made her giggle and calmed her down. He was so skittish, she knew she could trust him, and that was nice.

"How come you're out here all alone?" she asked.

"I like to come out here and think."

"Think about what?"

"Everything," he said. "Sometimes, I feel like it's the only place where I can just take a minute, you know?"

"I do."

"I mean… I got friends back in the city who are, like, turning this summer into their own soap opera, you know? So every week, someone's mad at someone else and we all gotta talk about it, help sort it out."

"You're out here to get away," she said.

Lane seemed surprised that anyone understood, and because Sherry understood better than anyone, a small bond formed between them. "All this drama and…" he looked at Sherry, helpless, his original expectations for tonight drifting out to sea. "I just thought it'd be cool to talk to you." And then he looked away, getting so much quieter before adding, "You're so pretty."

Sherry laughed. Not at the boy, but at the situation.

"My bowl's, um, in the other room. I think I kinda need it."

They went to the living room, turning off every light in the house, pulling all the curtains closed. And then they were on opposite ends of the couch, lit only by the blueish tint of the television.

"So," Lane said, once he'd finished packing his bong. "Are you, like hiding from someone or…?"

"You bailed me out of a tough spot."

"Just my luck," Lane said, lips closing around the mouthpiece while flicking his lighter over the bowl.

"Yeah," Sherry said. "Sorry about that." She went to the window and looked out on the quiet street. All was as it had been, except for a car parked in front of a house a few lots down. Just sitting against the curb. It hadn't been there when they first arrived.

"It's fine," Lane said. "We're safe out here."

Sherry didn't feel safe anywhere anymore. Her heart drummed as she searched every angle through the window, expecting to spot a shadow creeping around the backs of the houses. But the area was oppressively dark, and she'd never see it, even if it was there. "How many ways in does this house have?"

Behind her, the watery the crackle of Lane's bong. Smoke wafting toward the ceiling beams. "Just two," he coughed.

Sherry walked to another window. The night was unassuming from every vantage. She didn't trust it. "Ever have any trouble while you're out here?"

"Sure," Lane said, smoke chuffing past his lips. "Burglars, mostly. You know? Most of the people who live in this neighborhood aren't out here year-round, so the bad guys are always trying their luck."

Sherry went to the couch and pulled the driver's pistol from her handbag, its presence augmenting her sense of security. "Just in case someone tries their luck tonight…"

The teenager had no reaction to this. He just eyed the steel, a smirk spreading over his mouth. "That's cool," he said. "What do you carry? Looks like a Colt 1911."

"Uh…" Sherry turned the gun onto its side, searching for some type of identifying logo.

Lane arranged himself into a sitting position, more animated now. "How much trouble are you in?"

"Gonna kick me out?" The question was more playful than Sherry intended, and as soon as she'd asked it, a groaning noise, like bending wood, from somewhere in the house. They looked at each other with matching paranoia.

"No," Lane said. "I want to help."

"You know guns?"

"Sure." He noticed the way Sherry was holding it. Like it was a bomb about to go off. "Do you?"

"No," she said. Until now, the very thought of holding a gun filled Sherry with existential dread. But she'd been forced to murder a man in self-defense. Couldn't trust the police, the government, or her parents. Her only friend, as of this moment, was a horny stoner. "Now let's make sure we're still alone in this house."

They swept through it and everything was as it should've been, save for a continued creaking that was always coming from somewhere else. Lane didn't know the building well enough to confirm them as "settling noises," but it didn't matter. Sherry wasn't going to be able relax tonight.

"Hey," Lane said as they looped back to the living room. "You shouldn't keep your finger around the trigger like that. Not unless you're ready to shoot."

"I am."

"Well, hopefully not me."

"No, Lane. Not you."

"You, um, sure you know how to use it? Because I can show you."

She handed it over. "I've never touched one."

"They're a total cinch." He took it. "My dad takes me to the range every Saturday." He showed her the slide and explained the chamber and magazine, which was fully loaded with what Lane theorized were hollow-point rounds. He popped the mag out, made sure the chamber was clear, and let Sherry do some dry firing just so she could get comfortable with the process.

That's when there was a knock from the front door. Trouble had a way of finding her.

"I'll get it," Lane whispered.

"No, please—"

"I can send him away. He doesn't know you're here. And if that doesn't work, you shoot."

Sherry eyed the Colt in her first. She could do that.

They crept toward the front of the house, Sherry on her tip toes to avoid the sound of footsteps. The knock came again, more impatient this time. Sherry braced herself against the wall in the adjacent room, gun raised. Lane opened the door a hair, peering through the crack.

"Are you in the house alone?"

"Yeah, dude, my mom's in editing back in the city—"

"Saw some lights on. Only one on the street."

"I'm watching television."

"With who?"

"Uh, I'm in the house alone, dude."

"Mind if I come in? Palm Springs PD."

Sherry's fingers closed around the pistol grip.

"Hey, dude, I mind. It's late and I'm stoned. What do you want?"

"I'm the police."

"That's great, dude. My dad donates a few thousand to you guys each year. I'll tell him you said hey."

A long spell of silence. Sixty seconds. Maybe more. The same familiar intimidation Sherry had experienced two days ago in the corner office of that downtown building.

"Have a nice night," the voice said, and in a moment, footsteps shuffling on pavement.

The voice sounded familiar because it was familiar. Big Boss. Sherry glanced out the window and saw the stocky shadow strolling across the lawn, stopping indiscriminately to scrutinize some shadows and sounds along the way.

Sherry and Lane stood in silence, too afraid to move for the longest time. And then the engine surged and the car rolled off down the road.

"I don't think he knew anything," Lane said. "Dude looked tired and desperate."

Sherry imagined Big Boss cruising around Palm Springs, prowling back yards, looking desperately through windows. She'd managed to become a needle in this desert resort haystack and wrapped her arms around Lane, squeezing. "You did great."

"I need a bowl."

They went back to the living room and Lane dropped onto the couch. Sherry stood at the television, flipping through the distractions until she spotted that reporter, Alex Waverly, in a mustard sport coat, standing in front of an apartment building.

"The City Killer strikes again," the reporter announced, "this time in the basement of an apartment complex in Miracle Mile. There are confirmed reports of gunfire on the scene, and at least one person is dead tonight in the wake of another senseless attack. Almost two weeks of this…"

"Oh, Ed…" Sherry cupped a hand over her mouth. Behind her, Lane took the biggest hit of his life. Determined to reach contentment.

"While the police have disclosed very few details about the incident," the reporter said, "we were able to ascertain the identity of the shooter."

On screen, the picture shifted to a black and white photo of a man flashing an awkward smile. He wore a V-neck sweater and looked as though he'd rather be doing anything else.

Waverly's narration continued over the headshot. "Disgraced LAPD detective turned author, Ted Lonergan, who was unable to be reached for comment."

"Ted Lonergan," Sherry said, turning over that name so not to forget it.

"However," Waverly continued, "embattled Police Chief Dennis Warren was quick to state Lonergan is not acting on behalf of the Los Angeles Police Department and may in fact be prosecuted for his unauthorized discharge of a firearm."

Lonergan's headshot remained on screen for a second longer than it should've, and Sherry trusted the man's hardened eyes. "If the police don't like you, then maybe I will," she said. "Maybe you're who I need to talk to."

From the couch, Lane snored. Sherry placed a thin blanket over him, then sat in a recliner across the way, listening to him breathe. His personal dramas, what he hid from out here, was on the cusp of evaporating, and he had no idea. High school felt so immediate and severe, and nobody really tells you that it's basically just a fleeting dream you wake from the moment you graduate.

After that, your real problems begin.

Once it was closer to dawn, Sherry crept into the kitchen and scribbled out a note to him.

Lane, I am in trouble. I need to borrow your car. You were nice enough to get me out of a bad spot last night and, believe me, this is the easiest way for me to repay the favor. I promise to return it when I am done. -
Janey

She hurried out to the driveway with the gun in her hand and hopped into the Trans-Am, starting it up and swinging into the street.

Then she was speeding back toward the city to find the one man who might be able to help her.

CHAPTER
NINETEEN

Ted was up early so he made breakfast, and Jennifer was eventually roused by the smell of crackling bacon in the cast iron, delighted by the spread of eggs, toast, and raspberries that Ted had placed out.

They made dinner plans for that night. Jennifer would swing over to his office in the early evening after her massage therapy sessions, two appointments in the hills that afternoon, and then they'd grab a bite at that steakhouse. The one Ted hadn't been properly dressed for the last time.

"I'll even get a new blazer," he told her.

She bit a piece of bacon in half. "But do I trust you to get a *good* blazer?"

"I'll be the sharpest dressed man in the city."

She giggled. That thought, completely impossible.

"I haven't bought new clothes in about five years, so I can splurge a little."

"Well, how am I supposed to resist that? I'll see you tonight."

He dialed Lou from the phone booth down the block, but his desk just rang. Ted wasn't sure what Lou was going to do with the knowledge the Writer had helped him to gleam last night, but he didn't want to be the sole custodian of it.

He took a slow drive back across town, finding new ways to procrastinate. He ducked into a bookstore on Ventura and signed through all his paperbacks that were in stock, quite a few of them.

When he got back to his office around eleven, he found Lou and Detective Millbank waiting in the upstairs hallway.

"Don't you guys ever work?"

"You seem well-rested, Ted." Lou gave a knowing smile, glad to see his old pal looking happy.

"We are working, Lonergan," Millbank snapped. He seemed even more gaunt in daylight, lots of deep folds tucked into his craggy face, a lifetime of grimaces. Sometimes, people couldn't help but show you who they were.

Off Lou's body language, always turned away from the other detective, Ted could tell that his friend didn't exactly care for Millbank, but a job's a job.

Ted never could hack that mindset.

The thing about Lou though was that he'd always been able to leave the lion's share of bureaucracy at the office at the end of the day. Knew how to compartmentalize himself that way. Enjoy life in the off hours. That was the real gift and Ted would give anything to have it.

"I'd invite you in," Ted told them, "but my publisher is getting ready to keelhaul me if I don't turn in this book."

Lou handed Ted a black and white photograph. A mousy-looking college student with glasses that took up half her face. Brainy and cute. Her whole future ahead of her.

Provided that silver-eyed monster didn't kill her.

"Meet Sherry Carpenter," Lou said.

"Sherry." Ted extended his hand to Detective Millbank, who sighed and crossed his arms.

"Millbank has a witness placing Sherry in Palm Springs as of last night. A motel clerk."

"Oh, guys, Palm Springs is that way." Ted pointed over his shoulder.

"We think she'll come here," Millbank said. "And we'd like to know about it if she tries to make contact with you."

"Why would she do that?"

"You're a writer, aren't you?" Millbank said. "Maybe she's a fan."

"She strikes me as having good taste," Ted said.

"Rawlings gave your picture to the press last night," Lou mumbled.

"Use me as bait, very clever."

"I couldn't stop him, Ted," Lou said.

"Forget it. I'll probably enjoy a surge of book sales this week." He looked at the photo in his hand and wondered, *What did you do, Sherry Carpenter?*

"There's real eagerness to bring her in," Millbank added.

Ted was no longer listening, though he was interested in finding the girl. Probably for very different reasons.

Whatever the thing in the basement was, it had come from somewhere. Sherry Carpenter, he guessed, knew the answer to that question — as well as others. Ted felt those silver orbs scrutinizing him again and knew only of one way to exorcize them from his head. He had to understand what the creature wanted.

"Does that make sense to you, Lonergan?" Millbank asked.

Ted clicked his heels and saluted, then gave Lou a tap on the shoulder as he unlocked his office door. "I'll call you later."

Then the detectives shuffled down the stairwell to the city below.

Neither of the men who came outside and stood beneath the building's awning noticed the idling Trans-Am across the street.

And even if they had, they wouldn't have spotted the driver, who was scrunched down, most of her black hair tucked up inside Lane's mesh Los Angeles Kings hat, the bill drawn down over her forehead.

All Sherry could think in this moment was, *Millbank knows Lonergan. You can't trust him any more than you can trust the police. They're all in this together. Working against you. Working to find you.*

They're going to kill you.

"You don't have a friend in the world," Sherry reminded herself.

Except the black man, another detective, Sherry guessed, glared at Millbank with disdain he couldn't hide. A verbal disagreement happening between them, the men shouting at each other.

That kind of revulsion was the only energy Millbank deserved, and Sherry thought she might be able to trust one of them after all.

The black man glanced up at the building and then the two of them walked off, both annoyed and trying to stay a few steps ahead of the other like a bickering couple.

And when they disappeared from Sherry's rearview, she started up the engine and rolled off.

Ted stared at the blank sheet of typewriter paper. *Red Tide* was getting nowhere.

The photo of Sherry Carpenter that Lou had given him sat on the right side of his desk. His attention kept gravitating to it.

The girl who knew too much.

If he didn't find her today, the men who could keep stories out of newspapers would soon be planting one about her. And then she'd be out of reach.

"What'd you do, Sherry?"

And what did Detective Millbank know?

He picked up the photo and stared, trying to learn a little more, asking the Writer what he knew. In his mind were blank pages. The Writer was more sporadic now, in hiding, because he shared a head with those silver eyes and didn't want them to find him.

"Shit," Ted hissed.

Everything felt wrong. He picked up the phone and dialed.

"Marsha Adams."

"Marsha. Ted Lonergan. How is life these days?"

"What is it, Ted?"

"Are you still tattling on other cops?"

"Fuck you, Ted."

He laughed. "I was wondering if you could look into someone. Off the record, of course."

"Inspiration for your next novel?"

"Something like that."

"I don't know, you're *persona non grata* around here."

"I'll dedicate my next book to you, Marsha. Now how 'bout it?"

"Is it someone I.A. is watching?"

"Maybe."

"Go ahead."

"Millbank." He spelled it out for her.

"Remember that bar where Gregor retired?"

"The White Dove."

"Meet me there in two hours. Buy me a drink."

"You're the greatest, Marsha."

Sherry returned to Lonergan's office late in the afternoon.

She spent the day outfitting herself in a more suitable wardrobe, something that made her stand out less. A white sun dress with a V-neckline and a stretchy fitted bodice that reminded her, at a glance, of Sarah Jane Smith in "Pyramids of

Mars," from *Doctor Who's* thirteenth season, which she'd taken as a sign.

She had to tuck the Colt 1911 into her handbag like some kind of secret agent. Sherry had never been big on James Bond, but had gone to see *Moonraker* with friends in college and it was pretty alright.

The dress, coupled with her knowledge of how to defend herself, thank you, Lane, meant Sherry was confident in a way she hadn't previously been.

A trial by fire can leave sparkling diamonds in its wake.

She jogged across the street and hurried under the awning of Lonergan's building. Ted's name was on the index in the foyer, his office on the second floor. She took the steps carefully, growing nervous as she approached.

Still don't think I can trust him in full. Or at all.

Of course Ted had locked up before leaving. Sherry pulled a slip of paper from her bag and pressed it against the wall, uncapping a BiC and scribbling out a note.

Not exactly *Help me Obi-Wan Kenobi, you're my only hope*, but on that idea.

"Can I help you?"

The unexpected voice startled Sherry into a shriek.

The woman behind her shrieked too, and then they looked at each other, fingers hovering over their mouths, stifling mutual nervous laughter.

The woman in the stairwell was lovely, blond, fit. One of Ted's clients, obviously. Probably a jilted housewife.

"Are you looking for Ted?" the blond wondered, then realized there were no lights on in the office behind the frosted glass. "He's, uh, supposed to be in there."

"Ted." Sherry noted the familiarity with which she spoke of him.

"Yeah, Ted."

"Oh, you're his—"

The blond shook her head, then looked up at the ceiling,

reconsidering. Her gaze becoming more confident. "I suppose I am. Who are you?"

"I'm…" Sherry noticed the words PRIVATE INVESTIGATOR scraped off the door's glass. "I guess I'm out of luck."

The blond came out of the stairwell. Sherry flinched, which made the blond back off. "Are you in trouble?"

"I don't know how to answer that."

"It's… not usually a trick question."

"The police are after me but—"

"The police?"

"I didn't do anything wrong."

"That's why you're looking for Ted."

"I don't… I mean… Can I trust him?"

The blond offered a look of understanding, as if she somehow knew what Sherry had been through. She made no pointless assurances, just smiled and shrugged. "I would say yes, but—"

"Can I trust you instead?"

The blond paused, wondering if that was a trick question.

"I'm running short on trust these days," Sherry told her. "I called the police for help and all they did was sell me out."

"Ted isn't exactly a friend to the force."

"What about this?" Sherry said, a more secure plan announcing itself. "You come to the lab with me—"

"I'm sorry, *lab*?"

"Yeah." Sherry snapped her fingers. "I give *you* the evidence, you bring it back here. To Ted. And then I disappear. The men don't find me, and Ted gets everything he needs to… finish his job."

"I'm sure Ted will be right—"

"Ted's all over the news. They're already watching him. It's better for both of us if we don't connect at this point."

"Who are you?"

"In over my head, trying to do what's best for everyone."

"This relates to the case Ted's been working?"

"Yes," Sherry said. "Look, I know we just met and that I'm asking a lot."

The blond considered this, then nodded slowly. "Tell me where we're going."

"Downtown. The old cola factory on Mahoney Ave. Eight o' clock. Don't write it down and *please* don't tell anyone else. Not even Ted, alright? He can't trust some of the men he's working with."

"Well then maybe I should—"

"You will be saving my life."

"Okay," the blond told her. "I can meet you there. If it helps—"

"It helps. Thank you, um—"

"Jennifer."

"Thank you, Jennifer. I'm Sherry. You're the only friend I have in this world right now."

"Yeah, that's obvious."

Sherry stared at her blankly.

"You're so willing to trust me," Jennifer said. "And you can, but—"

"Desperate, not willing." And then Sherry hurried past her, back to her car. Still one important stop to make before tonight.

CHAPTER
TWENTY

The Syngenor's hand, good as new, fell against the cast iron manhole cover and shoved it aside. The sights, sounds, and smells of the city assailed it in one agonizing rush.

The alleyway where the creature lifted into had two dumpsters and a hatchback car. The Syngenor was not interested in passing beyond these obstructions to reach the distant city street. Instead, it sighted a bundle of wires fixed along the building's length and slashed right through them.

Its hand closed into a fist and wrapped around the large metal door, crumpling the knob like a ball of paper. It clattered to the ground beneath the creature's taloned feet and the heavy door lurched open, enabling the Syngenor to slip inside the parking structure.

The noise in here was aggressive. Reverberating sounds pinballed through the creature's head. The Syngenor grumbled and forced itself forward, cocking its head one way, and then the next, as it homed in on specific noises in the distance. Ghostly pings at the edges of all other echoes.

Pings that became voices floating somewhere above.

"What's taking you guys so long?"

The question was asked from atop the highest level of the

parking structure. The creature moved on instinct toward the ramp, its gait full of caution — the way any predator slinked toward its prey.

Another voice added, "Oh man, one of my wheels came apart."

The Syngenor stopped as the next sound landed. Those wheels striking pavement. Not tires, but small and hardened plastic wheels these humans occasionally wore on the bottoms of their feet.

Fury gave way to eagerness as the creature realized whoever was skating up there was about to come rolling down.

It counted the voices and heartbeats. Four bodies. The creature decided it would remain on the lowest level of the parking structure, where the darkness was thick and unbreakable. The ones on skates would come gliding to their deaths without expecting a thing.

And they would all die easily because every human died easily. Except for the man with the gun, whose own tortured expression haunted the Syngenor. It did not enjoy thinking of him and wiggled its two regenerated fingers in that moment to remind itself that he had not done it any long-term harm.

Though that had been his intent.

That disturbed the creature. The Syngenor was being hunted, which forced in it a grim determination to accomplish all that it needed, for it might very soon be dead. One way or another.

"I've got to go back to the car," one of the girls called out. "Let me have the keys."

"What for, Sandy?"

"God," the other girl said, annoyance rising. "I'm not waiting for any of you. It's gonna get dark in an hour and you're just wasting time."

"Sorry, Kelly, but I forgot my lip gloss."

The boys laughed. Kelly's heartbeat increased. The gang's disinterest in the activity really bothered her.

This is what the Syngenor wanted. One of the unsuspecting, announcing to the others that she intended to come down here on her own.

"Sandy, what are you doing to me?" Kelly asked, the sound of roller-skates striking the pavement, moving around the otherwise immobile group in smooth, confident circles.

"I'm getting my lip gloss. That's what."

"Lip gloss," Kelly said, on the move, extending into a larger skate circle, channeling her frustration into speed. "We're roller-skating, not going to Chasens."

"I hate Chasens," Sandy said. "All that wood paneling. Feels like a ski lodge."

"Chasens," one of the boys said. "There's an idea! Fontaine told me he had dinner two tables away from Cheryl Tiegs last week. He had to put the dinner napkin in his lap to hide his boner." The boys laughed and clapped.

"Besides, Kell, we can skate in here past dark, you know. They turn the lights on at night."

"And it's only five o' clock," the other boy added. "It won't be dark for hours."

"Yeah, fine." Kelly's roller-skates moved closer to the ramp. "I'm gonna take a quick run to the bottom, get this energy out of my system."

"By yourself?"

The Syngenor hoped the boy's question would not make her reconsider. It moved into the darkest space it could find, pressing behind a delivery van, its body mass prompting the vehicle to slide across the pavement. A disruptive noise that seemed to echo everywhere at once.

"What the hell was that?" Sandy called from above.

"Sounds like someone's power steering going out."

Kelly's roller-skates sliced along the pavement, a smooth and hypnotic sound the creature found almost pleasant in its constant, graceful motion. She looped the corner without interruption, tearing down the ramp, looping again, coming ever-closer, oblivious to her demise.

"Why did you let Kelly go by herself? I wanna skate too you know?"

"She's probably at the bottom by now, she'll be right back."

The creature's tongue tap-tapped its tooth in eagerness.

And the skates grew louder as the voices atop the structure became ambient sounds, no more pronounced than the distant chatter on the sidewalk, the Syngenor finally learning it could be blotted out.

Then Kelly zipped past the creature, a blur of bare shoulders, red tank top dangling loosely, thighs flexing as she sped, weaving around cars.

"Whew!" she cried out, energized, looking triumphantly at the cement ceiling as she caught her breath. "Has to be a record." Her voice got smaller. "And you all would've seen it if Little Miss Homecoming didn't have to get her goddamn lip gloss."

Kelly's head tipped to one side, her ears tuning, searching out the source of her sudden discomfort. There was nothing to hear. Just the creature's silent breath, humidity seeping into its exoskeleton, making the ground level colder than it had ever been.

Kelly's palms closed around her shoulders to suppress a shiver. Then she crouched and untied her skates, slipping them off and flinging them over her back, rushing right past the creature's hiding space toward the elevator.

She didn't realize yet that it was no longer functioning or that the power had been clipped.

She pressed the button and repeated the gesture several more times before discovering that it was unresponsive.

"Okay, forget this," she said and rushed back the way she came, keying in on an EXIT sign that would've normally been glowing red.

The Syngenor waited. It listened as the girl reached the door.

Chains rustled. The knob clicked. It was locked and bolted. A panicked gasp. The creature felt a stich of cruel satisfaction there, realizing how much it wanted to hurt this weak and foolish human.

"Shit!" Kelly cried, one last defeated clink of chains as the padlock slammed against the door. More footsteps then. Running alongside the wall toward the ramp she'd come down on. The only way out.

The creature knew that.

And stepped out to greet her, panic detonating across face. She tried to turn but the Syngenor stormed forward and took her by her sweat-slicked shoulders as the air around them became ice.

Kelly screamed and the creature's tongue pounced. Her muscular body went limp in its oversized claws. Her head lolled. Blood pattered across her shoulder blades, dribbling down off her chin. Its tongue anchored to the back of her throat. She gagged on its intrusion. In a moment, the sweet flow of cerebrospinal fluid rushed into its mouth and its large eyes closed with contentment.

"That sounded like Kelly," one of the boys said from high above.

"Cool it, Scott, don't try and scare me."

"You're right," the other boy agreed. "Let's go down there."

"She could be hurt."

Kelly faded, eyelids beginning to slow. The sputtering groan in her throat was like a dying motor.

"Wait a minute," Sandy called from above. "I'm not going down there."

Roller-skates struck the pavement, speeding down, about to provide the Syngenor with all the bodies it would need.

"Hurry up, Sandy!" one of the boys shouted.

"I don't think so! I'm calling the police."

Kelly's mouth popped wide at that, as if trying to scream. Only an excess of spinal liquid gushed past her lips, and the waste instilled a sense of panic in the Syngenor. It disengaged its tongue from the soft of her throat, lapping instead her grimace, cleansing her of the sticky mixture of bodily fluids. None of it could go to waste.

On the ramp, the skates were getting closer.

And so now were the police, apparently. The creature did not fully understand what this meant, thinking again of the man with the gun, knowing there was enough association between the two.

With one final lick of Kelly's face, the Syngenor dropped her to the ground and moved back the way it came. The skaters had landed while Sandy fled to the street in order to flag down the police.

The Syngenor was already in the shadows as the boys skidded to a stop.

"Kelly," one gasped. "What the hell did this, man?"

The other boy didn't answer. Kept trying to skate back up the ramp, falling over and whimpering.

A shame, the Syngenor thought. They would've been so easy to take.

But then it was back outside and moving toward the manhole, a sense of disgrace propelling it underground. It wasn't the boys that had frightened it off, but notions of the police instead.

They would summon the man who'd shot it.

The Syngenor realized that it feared him.

CHAPTER
TWENTY-ONE

Lou rushed across the parking lot and Ted ran to catch him. The detective hadn't spotted Ted, and something about the way he moved suggested that Old Silver Eyes had struck again.

Lou was unlocking the door to his sedan when Ted came jogging up along the passenger side, slamming his fist down on the roof, startling Lou into grabbing for the pistol in his holster.

"Jesus, man!"

"Sorry. I was coming to talk to you."

"Well… Get in."

"There's another one, isn't there?"

"Let's go."

Lou set his red and blues flashing and then tore out of the parking lot, the sedan screaming down Wilshire. Lou weaved in and out of traffic, steering the vehicle into the oncoming lane, and skirting pockets of immobilized commuters.

"Internal Affairs has a file on Millbank," Ted told him.

"Doesn't surprise me."

"They can't do much about it. Guy has lots of friends in high places." Ted couldn't resist throwing a little side-eye. "Seems to have friends everywhere."

"I'm doing what Warren tells me," Lou growled. "Some of us gotta work for a living."

"Don't you think it's odd they've got half the department running down some girl?"

"Two plus two is fuckin' nine these days."

"Well guess what…?"

Lou continued to barrel toward approaching traffic, cars swerving into empty parking spots to escape his path. Bleary horns ignited in the rearview. A pedestrian dove for the safety of the sidewalk. Lou's jaw tightened.

"…Millbank hasn't been looking all that hard for Sherry Carpenter," Ted said.

Lou cried out, "Shit!" and swerved back into their lane to avoid a city bus, smashing the gas, racing through an intersection.

"I called around," Ted said. "Sherry graduated from Linden University this past December. Went to work for a guy called Edward Amberdine. Some whack job scientist who thought he was about to change the world through the regeneration of human limbs… or something like that."

This information was compelling enough to draw Lou's eyes off the road for a split second. He glanced at Ted with something approaching admiration. A validating smile, perhaps. The idea that bringing him in to work this case hadn't been a waste of time.

"Now get this," Ted added. "The good Doctor Amberdine died two weeks ago. And boy did he die."

Lou was back to swerving, the sedan slipping through any opening where the road could accommodate it.

"A homeless man was caught disposing Amberdine's body in Silver Lake. The police questioned him, and he claimed to be following the orders of *'the devil himself'* – which is also who he said slaughtered Amberdine. The devil. Right before his very eyes."

"Shit," Lou said. "He still in custody?"

"Swallowed his tongue during interrogation."

"Shit," Lou repeated. "*The devil himself.*" His eyes were furious. "You were calling our perp an *it* before I called you on it."

"Way I see it, Amberdine's experiment gets out of control, he tries to put it under. Dies for his trouble."

"And some schizoid witnesses the whole thing, interprets it as the devil making him into a messenger."

"About right for the City of Angels, I'd say."

"So, what's the deal with this girl?"

"Oh, I think you already know."

"They want her because…" Lou's words trailed off, though his face was never more animated. The whole puzzle slotting into place. "She knows what that… *thing* is." He added a little nod to the end of his sentence showing Ted that he believed him.

"Who wants her?" Ted asked. "That's the question."

"What'd Internal Affairs say?"

"Only that he's dirty. And not too smart. Because what I dug up on this *Sherry Carpenter*, it's easy to find. Called around to a couple colleges, talked to the bursar's offices. Anyone can do that."

"He's obstructing."

"Like a good alphabet," Ted said. "FBI, CIA, fuck you."

Lou's breathing became labored, even as the streets thinned of traffic. "That girl's in trouble, wherever she is."

"If she's alive."

"Man…" Lou tapered off, letting it sink in. Nothing to say. Ted had gotten it in one.

They rode the rest of the way in silence, pulling to the curb in front of a parking garage. The entrance was adorned with ambulances, fire trucks, and uniformed officers trying to keep the press back. Curious onlookers gathered around sawhorses, trying to glimpse whatever was happening.

Lou and Ted entered on the sloping ramp and followed the

commotion down to a blood-dragged landing where a wide-eyed body stared up at them. A young woman's final moment, pure terror externalized and preserved.

Ted had to look away because he felt the creature's eyes behind his own, admiring the cruelty it had used to destroy her.

"It's beginning to enjoy itself," Ted whispered. "The realization that it can utterly annihilate us with ease."

"There's more," a uniformed officer announced, gesturing for them to come deeper into the basement level. Lantern lights were spaced out across the ground all the way back to the elevators and Ted saw several faces lit in sickly orange glow.

A young woman in roller-skates was hunched on the hood of an AMC Pacer, her distant eyes staring into space. She daubed a hunk of lip gloss over her mouth, rubbing her lips together as if she still had evening plans.

"Can you talk, sweetie?" Lou asked her.

"Name is Sandy Geeson," the officer beside them said.

On the far side of the car, two boys were huddled around another officer. They spoke in whispered tones while each of the kids' parents hovered by the elevator, waiting eagerly to bring their children home.

"Can you tell me your name?" Lou asked. "You're going to be alright, okay? We're here to help."

Sandy forced an empty smile, unassured by Lou's words. If there was any truth to them, the LAPD would've had this creature dead to rights by now. To Ted, her unspoken criticism was warranted. They all deserved this kind of skepticism, and worse for how long they allowed this thing to continue tearing apart their city.

"Nothing's going to happen to you," Lou said, even softer. A wasted effort. "You're perfectly safe. Can you tell me what you saw?"

Sandy's eyes focused for a moment, suddenly aware that somebody was attempting to communicate with her. Her neck craned, looking past Lou's shoulder and her eyes landed on her murdered friend there, still lying at the base of the ramp, eyes still wide as if paused while waking from a nightmare. "Oh God," Sandy screamed. Her voice echoed like a sledgehammer in this confined space. "Kelly!"

"Doc!" Lou called. "Come here."

The medic examining the boys turned and came rushing, clicking on his penlight, swooping it across her eyes. "She is in deep shock. All three of them."

"Will she come around soon?" Lou asked. "I'd like to question her."

"She'll come out of it eventually, but exactly when... that's hard to say."

"Could you, I don't know, give her something to calm her down so that I can ask a few questions?"

"That isn't wise. Let's get her to the hospital and then we'll see."

"And them?" Lou's timbre was rising as he gestured to the boys. This couldn't be the dead end he was beginning to fear it was.

Though Ted had already decided there was nothing here.

"Please," the medic said. "Let's just get them treated. Then you can ask whatever you want."

"Okay," Lou sighed. "Let me know where they're taking them."

Ted wandered back to the dead girl's body. Her shoulders glistened with that same unidentified slime. "You had the chance to kill the others," Ted whispered, glancing around. "You were all alone down here and it made you feel powerful. So why'd you stop?"

"What the hell is he doing here?" The voice was familiar, bringing Ted back to a time when he wore a badge on his belt. "I told you no, Capell! Do not bring that maniac here."

Ted shivered, ashamed of his vulnerability. It had been years since the captain had any sway over him, and yet, that voice could still render him small and insignificant.

"You have radar or what?" Lou said as Chief Warren marched in through the alley exit. He wore a tuxedo, and his hair was slicked back. His evening plans, clearly interrupted.

"I always know," Warren snapped. "That's why I'm the chief, and you're just—"

"The guy who makes you look good?" Ted said. "That's what you should be saying, Dennis."

Warren's look could cut metal. He circled the crime scene, offering empty assurances and condolences to the traumatized children and their families. Then soft-spoken officers guided them away, toward the ambulances on the street level above.

Warren held his temper until they were out of earshot. "This the work of the same creep?"

"Take one guess," Lou said.

Warren pointed at the corpse. "And who's going to notify her parents?" His tone suggested inconvenience, as if asking who was going to clean up a spilled cup of coffee.

"I am," Lou said. "I'm about to go over there in person."

"Then go, goddammit. Jesus Christ, what happens if they figure it out from watching the news?"

Lou nodded, becoming nervous. "Hey Ted, come on, huh?"

"Oh no," Warren added. "Go. I'll deal with Mr. Lonergan."

Lou gave Ted one last apologetic look on his way out. Ted nodded in absolution. "Nice to see you again, Dennis. How's the constipation?"

"A girl dies and he's cracking jokes."

"You're the one waltzing through here like a bull in a china shop, all the compassion of a cold winter's night."

"Go home, Lonergan. You can't do spit here."

"You asked me. I didn't ask you."

"And now I'm telling you to leave."

Ted gestured to the road. "Could I... Bum a ride? My car hit a bison and—"

"Out."

"Could I come to your dinner party?"

"I told Lou you wouldn't be sober long enough to stick your nose into this."

"Aren't we hostile? Why don't you ask him how much further along you are because of me?"

"Further along?" Warren looked at the corpse again. "Tell that girl's family how far along we are."

"You're going to have a lot more girls exactly like this one. You should have an army crawling those sewers. Maybe the CIA can pull some of its stormtroopers out of Guatemala and—"

"I can think of a much simpler solution," Warren growled. "You piss off. And if Lou thinks about looping you in again, his pension will burn up faster than the goddamn Chicago Fires."

Ted started up the ramp, turning back toward his old boss. "One more question, Dennis."

The chief stared up at him with wide, irritated eyes.

"Where is Detective Millbank?"

The chief shook his head.

"You'd think he'd be here." Ted's attention swung down to the body, a white sheet now covering it as coroners lifted it onto a gurney. "Unless they already know what's doing this."

"The hell's that mean?"

"Talk to Lou. He'll let you know that you're no longer in charge. Local chatter is that you need all the help you can get. Trouble with you, Dennis, is that you were never able to find your ass, not even with both hands."

Warren stomped his foot in tantrum. "Get him out of here, now! Before I lock him up and throw away the key!"

Ted walked up the ramp, feeling none of the triumph he wished he could've savored in this moment. Instead, he pitied the young girl whose life was cut short, and he despised the men who were doing nothing to stop it.

CHAPTER
TWENTY-TWO

S herry had done two things after encountering Jennifer
Stanton in the hallway outside of Ted Lonergan's office.

First, she bought a spiral notepad and spent an hour
documenting the events of the last two weeks as she
understood them. She did this from behind the wheel of the
idling Trans-Am, the pistol tucked beneath a newspaper on the
passenger seat beside her. Then she stuffed the notebook into a
manilla envelope and brought it to the post office on Pico where
she opened a P.O. box, paying for a week.

She asked the clerk to please mail the contents of the box in
two days if she didn't return. The package was addressed to
Channel 7 News.

Next, Sherry crossed the street and called her parents from
the payphone there. Once again, her father answered on the first
ring.

"Hello?"

"Dad, it's Sherry."

"Jeez, we thought — is everything okay?"

"Fine, I—"

"Where are you?"

"Arizona."

"Arizona? What's going on? There are men looking for you."

"Don't I know it."

"Come home."

Sherry thought of her tiny bedroom back in Nebraska. The old black and white television on the wobbly brass stand. The hours of *Doctor Who* and *Star Trek* watched while dreaming of her future. And here she was now, on the precipice of a genetic breakthrough. A secret that had put Edward Amberdine into an early grave. She could run, sure. Go home to that bedroom, which would feel a lot closer to a prison cell, and obsess over the future that was denied her.

Or she could fight. She'd come this far, and the truth was, the Sherry Carpenter who had grown up in that tiny bedroom no longer existed. This week had reshaped her into someone else. A stranger who carried those memories and experiences, but who was better equipped to handle this morally dubious world she found herself navigating. There was no more home for her to go back to. Home was here.

"I'll talk to you soon," she told her father. "Love to Mom. Love you both." She slammed down the phone and sprinted across the street.

And then she sped from Century City, away from that phone call and the final vestiges of her old life, using Olympic Boulevard to escape. Unlike most arterial roads in Los Angeles, this one did not connect to any major attractions, making it the best choice when trying to get somewhere quickly.

As she was tonight.

Her heart drummed as she thought about the lab. About how she was going to become the custodian of all that was in there.

The Trans-Am ebbed in sporadic traffic. There was suddenly an especially long jam in front of the 10th Street School while "Vahevala" by Loggins and Messina piped through the speakers, making Sherry nostalgic for that week late last summer when she'd spent four days with Wayne Markle at his parents' house in Venice Beach.

Everything seemed so simple then.

On the street corner up ahead, red and blue lights flashed. Sherry's panic reignited, until she saw two men in robes bent over the hood of a patrol car, the cuffs that were clamped to their wrists glinting off her headlights. She took a right turn and kept on the path toward downtown Los Angeles, passing a brick building, the Hula Club, which had a mural of two figures, a man and woman, dancing in silhouette among palm trees while the skyline behind them was pink, and a billboard was mounted directly above that, reading: FIND OUT WHEN – KNX NEWSRADIO 10.70.

Area traffic turned more infrequent. Shuttered businesses were more common here. Sherry became aware of the sedan in her rearview, taking all of the same turns, as though the two vehicles were hitched together.

High beams clicked on, washing out Sherry's rearview. The tail accelerated right up against her bumper. Sherry stomped the gas. The Trans-Am surely had more juice, could keep its head start. But the sedan was surprisingly competitive, and the two cars were suddenly racing along a darkened patch of city street, mostly desolate and unobstructed, the buildings generating long shadows across the tarmac.

"You son of a bitch!" Sherry growled, slamming her foot to the floor. The Trans-Am bucked and the speedometer needle began to waver.

The sedan made its move. It glided out from behind Sherry's bumper, coming up alongside her, keeping pace with the Trans-Am, forcing the vehicles to trade paint, the friction between them creating a sea of angry sparks.

Two homeless people pushed a cart along the sidewalk. The cars blew past them and once they were far enough behind, and the walkway was clear as far as Sherry's headlights could show, she swerved up onto it and the sedan followed, making the Trans-Am wobble as they drove.

She screamed out as her headlights revealed a parked car ahead. An immobile shadow that seemed to rush toward her, the whole thing lapsing into slow motion.

She attempted to swerve back into the street, but the sedan wouldn't allow it, seeming to push harder, ensuring the Trans-Am remained on its current track. It was unavoidable now. Sherry's eyes popped wide. She braced herself for the inevitability of collision, throwing her hands up over her face, protecting it with her forearms.

The world exploded into glass and a metallic scream roared through her eardrums.

The crash launched Sherry from her seat, headfirst through the windshield of jagged glass. She glided like a missile, her body scraping along the Trans-Am's hood, which had jutting ridges like an accordion, the whole car crumpled up. Pointed metal stung her body as she bounced along and the rush of blood was warm, seemingly everywhere at once. She stopped on a heap of twisted metal, the space where the Trans-Am and the parked car had combined into one entwined mass of indistinguishable manufacturing.

Sherry knew she was dead then and her thoughts were a blur. Just flashes of moments. None of which had anything to do with Ed Amberdine, his experiment, or even the men who had worked so hard to kill her.

In that flash, no more than half a second of reality, but an eternity in Sherry's mind, there was the summer of 1970. A girl of ten, sitting on Mom and Dad's deck, dreaming of how she was going to change the world. Her parents never fed her developing ego with promises of celebrity or fortune, but instead suggested that she focus her future on making a difference. While that house in Nebraska, with its tiny bedroom and even smaller deck, had nurtured her, she truly had evolved into something else. Just hadn't felt it until tonight.

Now, her mouth stung with the bitter taste of blood. And, somewhere in the darkness, a soft voice barked into a radio.

"Cleaning it up now."

Sherry heard this first as indiscriminate sounds, then a couple of errant vowels. But as her consciousness picked itself up off the heap of scrap, the sounds solidified into words.

Sherry's eyes struggled to find focus. Everything was soft and blurry, her field of vision tinged with dotted lights. The sedan, just two red and circular bulbs in the distance as she lifted her head.

The metal heaved with Sherry's every motion and what remained of the shattered glass dislodged itself from the busted windowpanes, tiny pieces plinking into piles.

"She's just going to—" The voice went silent and then came the sound of a creaking door.

Sherry slid down off the wreck, knees like Jell-O, her body completely wobbly, difficult to stand.

"Miss Carpenter." The voice was familiar, urgent, and inspired dread. "Miss Carpenter, you were driving like mad back there."

She took an instinctive stumble toward what remained of the Trans-Am as hurried footsteps rushed across the tarmac. A hand fell on her shoulder and whirled her around.

Detective Millbank smirked, searching her glassy features for signs of consciousness. "Let's take a ride."

"Where?" she asked, as if there was a choice.

"Away from here." The detective looked around, finding only empty sidewalks. His voice grew colder and more confident, realizing they were alone. "You shouldn't have sent another woman to the lab, she led us right to it." He brushed his coat aside, showing the holstered sidearm on his belt. "We don't need you anymore."

"Why?"

Millbank took her by the wrist and dragged her along.

Sherry plucked her arm from his grip and staggered back toward the Trans-Am. "Wait."

"None of this matters anymore."

"Not even my notes?" she asked.

The detective considered this, placed one hand atop his holster to let her know she'd be dead if she tried anything. "Yeah, sure. Get them. Save me the effort of rummaging through the debris."

Sherry staggered back to the car. The door was so twisted, it wouldn't budge. "I have to crawl in through the windshield," she said, getting back up onto the hood once Millbank made no visible objection.

The handgun was no longer on the passenger's seat, and the floor was a pool of endless shadows. She reached down there, glass from the windshield beginning to gnaw at her belly as she stretched her arm and then her fingers, groaning because every part of her was on fire.

"Sorry I crashed your car, Lane," she mumbled as her fingertips brushed against cold steel. The Colt, just out of reach.

"Let's go!" Millbank ordered from the sidewalk. He came around to the driver's door, peering in to check on her.

Sherry's fingers closed around the pistol grip. "Almost... have... it..."

"Now."

Her body was more than halfway into the Trans-Am. Sherry used her free hand to close around the dashboard in order to steady herself and then, with a deep breath, the most painful draw of air she'd ever taken, lifted the gun into the light.

Millbank unholstered his gun the second her Colt came into view.

Sherry rolled onto her side as she brought her right hand up, pointing it at the glass and squeezing the trigger.

The driver window exploded, and Millbank's whole body jerked backward, as if stunned. His footsteps were scuffles, and his own gun went skittering across the sidewalk. Sherry took the time to sight another shot, this time at this stomach, which was the only thing visible in the window frame now.

Blam.

This one caught him in the gut, and the detective flew off his feet, collapsing to the ground.

Sherry kept the gun trained on the window, eyes wide and watery. The severity of the night, of this situation, unable to register. Two of these bastards dead.

How?

She wiggled her way out of the windshield. Then off the crumpled Trans-Am hood and onto the ground, where Millbank's face was locked up in a display of astonishment. Sherry's first bullet had carved a third eye into the center of his forehead.

"Because they keep underestimating you," Sherry said.

She took a moment to catch her breath, then realized she had to meet Jennifer downtown. Because she'd inadvertently gotten her into trouble.

Sherry dragged herself to the still-idling sedan, body aches beginning to manifest as perpetual discomfort. She wondered if she'd be able to keep herself conscious as she drove the rest of the way, and if she could get there in a stolen police vehicle.

CHAPTER
TWENTY-THREE

D owntown at dark. Jennifer wanted to be anywhere else.

She guided her Jaguar through blighted streets of failed businesses, burned-out buildings, small pockets of people who gave territorial stares.

They were in charge down here.

None of this was smart, she knew. But the young woman had been so scared, a child without a friend in the world. How was Jennifer supposed to refuse that?

Ted himself was skeptical of the police and the other powers running this city. It was a world view Jennifer did not share, doubted that she ever would, though she did acknowledge that Ted's experiences were not her own and understood his path might have resulted in different conclusions. It was one of the things she found most interesting about the man.

"Mahoney Ave," Jennifer said and turned at the signage. The Jaguar was crawling along now, Jennifer's eyes peeled for the cola factory that had been closed since before she was born, and yet, somehow, remained a ghost that haunted this part of town.

The throngs of drifters that moved through this district thinned out as she coasted down the street. There were two men on a corner, staring wide-eyed as she glided past, crossing some unspoken threshold, and then the sidewalks were desolate. In the rearview, the men became shrinking silhouettes and after them, there was no one else.

Empty sidewalks lining a forgotten city.

Los Angeles had nearly ten million people, yet here was a street with nobody on it. Statistically, it seemed impossible.

The Jaguar slowed in front of a long-faded sign that read "FITZZ'S COLA – 'LIQUID CANDY.'"

Jennifer ran her tongue along her teeth and suddenly wished she could brush them as she turned right and passed through a wobbling fence, tires crunching over debris. Hard to believe this was where Sherry wanted to meet. Harder to believe that anybody had been beyond this fence in a very long time.

Jennifer rolled to a stop and craned her neck. The surrounding air was dead, couldn't even locate the pulse from Los Angeles proper out here. Just utter silence, as if she'd somehow moved back through time.

Gonna have to remember to give that to Ted for his next novel, she thought, and then cracked the door, curiosity luring her to the front entrance.

Through the glass, the interior seemed relatively clean. A sitting area and unmanned reception desk were visible. This wasn't a run-down cola factory anymore.

Jennifer knocked and got no response. Pulled on the handle, but it was locked.

"Come on, Sherry," Jennifer whined, feeling like something was watching her from an anonymous vantage. She whirled, finding the city block unchanged. Buildings as a bunch of dilapidated silhouettes. No motion of any kind.

Jennifer moved around the side of the building, and then to the back. The dumpster was empty, and it wouldn't have been unless the department of sanitation was still collecting it.

A large door marked "SERVICE ENTRANCE" was back

there, ajar, and with an odd cobweb-like substance stretched over the space that formed the opening.

Jennifer pulled one half of the door toward her and the webbing stretched out like taffy. She pushed the door all the way open, right up against the building, and the web snapped and fell away in a quiet puff.

She walked inside and moved down the double-wide hallway. The floor was lined with patches of that same webbing, and she assumed spiders had seized on this largely abandoned space.

"So why am I in here?" she wondered.

From somewhere deeper inside the building, a voice talked in constant monotone, words becoming clearer as Jennifer got closer.

"The Syngenor is… an abomination…"

The hallway banked left, opening into what had once been the old soda warehouse. The voice boomed out of the walls there, echoing through the wide-open space.

"… that must be destroyed."

There was a large switch positioned on the wall beside the entrance to the room. Jennifer pushed the lever up and the fixtures high overhead clicked on, one-by-one, illuminating the area. Smaller lights awoke next, drawing her attention to laboratory equipment she couldn't identify.

The voice continued unabated, "I realize now that what I have created must be destroyed. There is still too much about this lifeform that I do not know."

"Sherry," Jennifer called, her voice thundering across the canyon of open space. "Are you in here?"

A rancid smell hung in the air. Far worse than the stench of old trash or spoiled food and seemingly everywhere Jennifer walked. She passed rows of empty glass tanks with the back of her hand pressed against her nose, expecting to find a mutilated carcass.

At the center of the room was a metal dais hosting the

largest glass chamber in here, probably designed to control atmospheric conditions for whatever had been inside of it. On the raised floor at Jennifer's hips, an animal's cage with bars thicker than a jail cell, decorated in the same webbing. Discarded bones were piled across the inside, each of them picked clean, much too large to belong to a stray cat or any mice.

Years had passed since Jennifer studied human anatomy, but she recognized a femur among the remains.

"What the hell?"

Water pattered down from the ceiling, droplets splashing across the slab floor. A bundle of shadows came loose from the rest of the darkened rafters and a shape began to move across the beams.

Jennifer's heart pumped so hard her chest began to hurt. The ink-black shadows up there morphed back into a solid sheet of darkness. Nothing but her eyes playing tricks, adjusting to the odd pockets of gloom.

That's what I'm telling myself, she thought and started for the exit. Better to wait for Sherry outside. And if Sherry didn't show, she could always come back here with Ted. In the morning. See what he would make of this.

Where'd you go, Ted? She waited at his office today, but he'd been a no-show. He had broken dinner plans. Wasn't at his house. And Lou was just as difficult to reach.

And her heart was pumping harder.

"If there's anyone else in here…" she started, voice booming as she turned back down the corridor that had led her in from the outside. Only the evening light at the end was blotted now because the door had swung all the way back against the jamb, closing. She would have to walk a quarter mile in the pitch darkness to reach it.

No way.

Jennifer shivered, a ripple of fear moving through her. The

chemicals in her body spinning up the urge to run. Her internal chemistry sounding every alarm that it could.

She would not risk that path. Would not risk running into whatever had closed that door, as it probably waited somewhere inside the gloom there.

She preferred instead to remain in the light of the main floor, even as the shadows overhead began swirling again, provoking her peripheral vision, daring her to look up.

Her shivers intensified. The air in here was colder than it had been a moment ago, and getting even colder, as if she'd wandered into the world's largest walk-in refrigerator.

It was so cold that the rancid stench had thinned out, nowhere near as perceptible now.

Jennifer opened her mouth to speak, but instinctively held the words in the bowels of her throat. She looked past the light fixtures above, steel beams groaning and whining beneath the weight of whatever moved across them.

And that same dry voice continued to speak, talking to anyone whether they listened or not. Jennifer hadn't been, though the ominous words worked now in tandem with the rattling above, making her whimper:

"What began as a way for me to understand the fundamentals of human life has grown into something else entirely, and I fear that I no longer recognize my original pursuits, only what has become my madness…"

Jennifer ran across the floor toward the office space she'd seen from the outside. The main entrance was locked, though she hoped to be able to get out from there.

Adrenaline rocketed her across the main floor, prompting whatever was clinging to the shadows above to pass a startled, inhuman growl. Jennifer shrieked in response, which forced her floodgates open, an onslaught of panic taking hold as she pushed through the door marked "EXIT" and sprinted into the office.

It was two rows of unused desks, new chairs that still had plastic wrap over the backs.

The front door was straight ahead, right past that curved reception desk. Jennifer approached it with such speed there wasn't time to slow. She just lowered her shoulder and slammed against it, pushing on it, finding that it wouldn't move.

"Shit," she cried, pounding on the glass. "Anyone!" she screamed, imagining the throngs of homeless she'd passed by to get here. Realizing why every one of them stayed so far away.

On the warehouse side of the building, something large crashed down onto the slab floor. Patient footsteps lurched forward.

Jennifer turned and spotted it in the doorway. The lights were off behind it, and the air in here froze over. Her breath materialized as though her spirit was desperate to escape the monster's wrath even if her body could not.

I came right to it, she thought. All the warning signs had been there and yet, she couldn't help herself. The young woman today had seemed so desperate, and Jennifer wanted to help. Not only her, but also Ted.

Her attention snapped back to the door, forearms flying against the glass. Then she glanced over her shoulder. The creature was gone, just a couple errant strands of webbing flailing in the doorway where it had stood.

Jennifer picked up the phone at reception. The line was nonexistent. A pair of scissors beside it was all the protection she could get her hands on. She closed them in her fist and went on the move.

There had to be another way out. She kept low and crossed back into the warehouse, moving alongside stacks of boxes for cover. In the air, the creature's growls were in Sensurround, impossible to pinpoint its exact location.

You're going to have to run the gauntlet, Jennifer thought. Reach the long corridor and run like hell.

Two silver eyes grew out of the blackness in front of her, glowing against the distant light that reflected off them. Light from the glass office on the catwalk above that must've been on a different power circuit. It revealed the contours of a misshapen, demonic face. The owner of that terrible growl.

A powerful hand seized Jennifer's throat. Her fingers slipped off its hard-shelled wrist as the monster pulled her close, scrutinizing her in terrible close-up. It's saucer eyes remained inexpressive as it regarded her, suggesting this lifeforce was unreachable, uncommunicable.

What looked to be a jutting spine ran all the way up its forehead along the center of its skull, and what could only be described as smaller ribs were angled off this spine on horizontal lines. Its jutting cheekbones were sharp enough to cut, and below them, a mouth stuffed full of killing teeth.

Those teeth parted and Jennifer's damaged throat could only achieve a rusty groan, pleading and then shrieking as her nose brushed against the protuberance of bone the monster wore at the center of its own face.

Jennifer braced herself for a bite that never came.

Its tongue slithered out from between its teeth, two hardened forks at the end of a prong, pinching against her lips, drawing two tiny trickles of blood that went dribbling down her chin.

It slipped into her mouth, leaving behind trails of sludge that tasted of curdled milk. Jennifer felt a pinch at the back of her throat and then she lost control, her body lapsing into involuntary spasms.

The creature slurped, as if drinking through a straw, fluid beginning to rise through her body, extracted through this thing's hollow tongue. After a moment, the feeding was done. It retracted its tongue and released Jennifer from its grip, stepping back as if to look at her in full.

It growled and there was genuine amusement in the sound.

The world wobbled around Jennifer. She pushed herself to

move steadily in what she knew to be the direction of the long hallway. The creature might decide to kill her before then, but she was too weak to fight, her consciousness fading. She tumbled forward through a void until she was somehow at the cargo door, pushing it open, stumbling into the night.

Then she was staggering around the side of the building toward the Jaguar.

In the distant evening came a rush of excited voices.

Jennifer thought she was saved, the last bits of cognizance slipping away, the abyss sweeping over her.

The Jaguar bled into her unstable vision. Two men standing on one side of it. A sound of shattering glass. The men jumping back, surprised by the scatter of the explosion.

Jennifer lumbered forward, trying to speak, part of her realizing these men would not be her salvation.

They spotted her now, trading panicked words as she reached them.

"Whoa, man," one of them said and Jennifer realized that they weren't men at all, but children.

Small children.

"She looks blasted."

Jennifer's knees buckled, then gave out and she dropped onto them, spotting another vehicle beside her own. Most of it, obscured by shadow. On the ground beside it was a body, a balding head with a face that no longer existed, cleaved away, just a mash of bloody pulp and broken bone fragments where a nose and eyes had once been.

"Told ya they're gonna blame us for this shit!"

The corpse had a handgun tucked into its fist and Jennifer had one final thought before the lights went out. This man was the reason Sherry had asked her to come.

And then Jennifer's eyes rolled back in her head, and everything went black as she hit the ground.

CHAPTER
TWENTY-FOUR

"Jennifer Stanton. Is she here?"

The woman at the hospital's front desk confirmed that she was, then directed Ted to the fourth floor. The neurological intensive care unit. This set off a dozen questions that Ted did not bother to ask, rushing instead to the elevators, cursing himself for thinking he could ever rejoin the world.

It's a disaster each time you do.

And it's your fault.

Jennifer wouldn't be here if not for you.

The elevator doors glided open and a nurse wheeled a patient in head gauze past. Ted ran to the nursing station and found a doctor there, scribbling a note in someone's file. Two nurses stood beside him, having a low-level conversation.

"Jennifer Stanton," Ted said, voice wavering. "I'm here to see her."

"Are you family?" the doctor asked without looking up.

"Yes," Ted lied. "Where is she?"

The doctor eyed Ted's bare knuckles on the counter, clocking the lack of a ring on any of his fingers. He passed the file to one of the nurses and stepped out from behind the desk. "Right this way."

They walked shoulder-to-shoulder to the end of the hall, Ted's frantic questions going unanswered. "Here," the doctor said in front of an open door. He took Ted by the crook of his arm, preventing him from going any further.

Jennifer was just a lump beneath a bedsheet. Her pale face lit against the flicker of the black and white television. On screen, Cheryl Ladd in an episode of *Charlie's Angels*, diving out of her car as a forklift dropped a palette of cinder blocks on top of it.

"Well?" Ted asked.

"We're not sure," the doctor told him.

"Not sure? Not sure?"

"Has Ms. Stanton ever complained of headaches?"

"Not that I'm aware of."

"Abnormality of gait?"

"Gait?" Ted scoffed. "Gait? You're asking me about the way she walks?"

"I'm asking because she was brought in tonight in a terrible way. Badly traumatized, but without any physical trauma. A scrape on her lip. That's about it. She was babbling incoherently, slurring her words and suffering from an irregular heart rate."

"And?"

"And we've run tests. It's still early, you understand, but I'm going to guess a diagnosis. I think Ms. Stanton has a brain tumor."

"Based on what?"

"Muscular degeneration, sensory disturbances…"

"Couldn't that be from the physical trauma?"

"I told you there wasn't any."

"How did she get here?"

"A couple homeless kids found her downtown."

"Where?"

"The warehouse district."

"What the hell was she—?"

"We. Don't. Know," the doctor said, his rising tone imploring Ted to remain calm. "They were breaking into her car when they came across her body. It's hard to believe they called it in. Rough part of town."

Ted didn't find it as difficult to believe. People down there played the part of the upstanding citizen for many reasons. Sometimes it was because the police didn't go there and someone had to keep order. Other times, it was to prevent outsiders from getting hurt. If too many people were mugged or killed, the police would sweep in, turn over every rock, make their lives collectively worse.

Saving Jennifer had been a peace offering.

"Is she going to make it?" Ted winced as he asked this.

The doctor's eyes softened, noting how much she meant to him. "We're doing everything we can, but…"

Ted stepped into the room as the doctor trailed off. His footsteps began to dwindle as he walked back to the nurse's station and Ted crossed to Jennifer's bed.

"How are you, honey?" he asked. Honey. He'd hadn't called her that before. Notions of time and opportunity haunted him, as if he were suddenly out of both. All he wanted was for Jennifer to hear him.

But what if she didn't want that?

This is your fault, the Writer reminded him.

The expression on Jennifer's face was placid, a bit too close to death. Ted's eyes were rimmed with tears. He should have been man enough to leave her alone. Live out his years writing paperbacks, forgetting about trying to belong somewhere. To someone.

His obsessions had always been self-serving, succeeding only in getting others killed. As he stood among the intermittent beeps that belonged to the monitoring machines, he understood at last that he was the curse. *"There's always a pattern,"* he'd told Lou. And that was true for him as well. No such thing as coincidence. His partner. His former lover. And now Jennifer. A pattern that would continue for as long as Ted lived.

"Before I tried my hand at writing," Ted said. "I was a private investigator. I told you that. I didn't know what I was going to do then. My whole life had been law enforcement and when your whole life is one thing, it's all you know. I thought becoming a P.I. would allow me to stay in that world to some extent, take only the cases I wanted, filter out the rest."

Jennifer's eyes moved behind her eyelids. The slightest flicker of attention.

"That worked out well, until I was hired by Lara Schaefer, the wife of Hollywood producer Stephen Schaefer. She wanted me to prove that her husband was... less than faithful. Hard to believe in the movie business, I know."

Jennifer's head lolled slightly to one side. Responsiveness. All Ted needed to continue.

"Lara was a diamond," he said. "One of those starlets who stepped off the bus, right into a film career. Did two movies, one for Roger Corman, another for Avco Embassy, then married Stephen. When she hired me, it was because she wanted to fight for her marriage. A hopeless romantic that way. Unique in this town. Refused to accept the excuse of *'that's show business.'*"

Ted coughed, his throat doing everything in its power to prevent the story from being said aloud.

"She paid me a lot of money to prove her husband was unfaithful. And that was easy. Stephen had *expensive* appetites. Every few days there was another paramour. Men and women, young hopefuls, all. I talked to a dozen of them. And during that time, Lara grew more devastated with each name I gave her. I was the only one to—"

Ted was finding it harder to speak, but Jennifer deserved to hear this. If not a confession, exactly, then an admission of guilt. How desperate he was to be forgiven, even though Jennifer could not grant the absolution he needed.

"I became involved with her. There was real despair in Lara. She died a little each time I revealed to her that Stephen's casting couch was an endless conga line. She liked being around me. And I welcomed her companionship… after what happened with Lyle, I'd forgotten what it was like to be around anyone."

Ted collected himself through a few deep breaths, anything to stave off the emotion trying to escape him.

"The funny thing?" he said. "Stephen had a guy on me. A studio P.I. spying on his wife's P.I., shooting all our hotel room getaways. You can argue cause and causation, but at the end of the day our affair was no different than what Stephen was doing. Except he was in a position of power and didn't have to tolerate it."

Ted wiped a falling tear off his face.

"And his guy was a lot meaner than I was. There was a confrontation. Guns pointed. Threats made. He beat the shit out of me and said if I ever came near Lara again, I'd disappear. Then he gave me twenty-thousand dollars to be silent. I drove it right back to the Schaefer Estate and burned the briefcase on their lawn. Easy come, easy go."

From the bed, the faintest smile passed over Jennifer's face. Gone in flash. Maybe it was just what Ted wanted to see.

"Lara threw herself in the ocean," he said. "They pulled her out a few days later. I think it… It was my fault. I had to try and rescue her soul. Made everything worse. Compounded her anguish until she felt the only release was to take her own life. At twenty-five years old."

Ted ran a hand down Jennifer's arm.

In his mind, The Writer was hard at work on crafting new pages. Ted scanned them. Jennifer in a dark space, crawling on hands and knees, fighting to keep hysterical sobs locked inside. And silver eyes growing out of the void, a malevolent specter about to strike.

This wasn't a brain tumor.

The only question was, how in a city of ten million people did the creature happen to find her?

And why had it allowed her to live?

It's making it personal, Ted realized. *Wants to go another round.* And then the Writer clued him in on why the creature had fled the parking garage tonight, rather than kill the other three kids.

One of them had gone rushing out to phone the police, and the creature was afraid that reinforcements would summon Ted. It was afraid of Ted hurting it for a second time.

Both Ted and the creature had arrived at a mutual terror. Both were eager to finish this. But on the creature's terms.

Jennifer was the message.

"I'm sorry, Jennifer," he said and cupped his palm over her forehead. "The doctor says you're going to pull though. You just have to be strong. Can you do that?"

Ted stopped himself. It was a lie he couldn't sell. The world was uncertain. This room. The streets. His pages. Nothing was guaranteed. He closed his eyes and found the typewriter there, reminding the Writer how to spell 'happy ending.'

But the keys were stuck on strike and had to be pushed back down to try again. And now the ribbon was dry.

"While you're in here," Ted added, "you're in good hands. And I'm going to be back in just a bit, okay? I need to go out and take care of something real fast."

Ted rushed from the room to the elevators, and the beeping of Jennifer's monitoring equipment followed him.

The man with the shaved head sat in the lobby, trying to hide behind an issue of *Time Life* the hospital kept strewn across its hassocks.

Ted spotted him right off by the pink scar on his scalp and felt a swell of anger. "Hello, Uncle Sam." His voice was loud enough to turn every head, more attention than the operative had ever faced. He lowered the magazine, revealing tinted Ray-Bans. An entirely natural accessory for the middle of the night. "Funny how we keep running into each other like this."

The man grinned, a sort of untouchable air about him, then he lifted the magazine back up over his face.

Ted tore it from his hands and threw it across the floor. On the other side of the room, the hospital security guard started toward them. Ted fished his old police badge from his pocket and flashed it. "Besides," he said to the guard who was in the process of backing off. "This one's from the government. He can take care of himself."

The operative shook his head. "You're overstepping, Lonergan."

"That's my life story."

"Every story ends."

Ted knelt against the operative's face. "If anything happens to her," he whispered. "I'm going to find you, and put my revolver down your throat, pull the trigger. Might be the last thing I do, but it'll be worth it."

"Who? Your girlfriend? We don't care about her."

"Then you think that other girl might show up here?"

A wolf's grin stretched to the edges of the operative's face. "Never know. Had a sighting just a few hours ago. She vanished."

"Well, I'm sure you're doing everything you can to find her."

Ted crossed the foyer and motioned for the security guard. He gave him Jennifer's room number and asked if the hospital could please post a guard outside of it. Just until the precinct could get a uniform out here. Then he gave his name as "Lou Capell" and when the guard agreed, Ted walked outside, back to the Mazda.

"Find it," Ted barked to the Writer. "Find that fucking thing, then tell me how to kill it."

The Mazda's engine rumbled to life and when Ted glanced in his rearview, he spotted the operative standing on the sidewalk, still in his Ray-Bans. Ted backed out of the spot and rolled his window down. "They ought to teach you guys how to blend in with the rest of us humans," he said. "It'd be a worthwhile skill to acquire."

Then he gunned it, speeding through empty city streets, and soon, cruising along the Pacific Coast Highway, where the water on his left was dark and placid, and the breeze blowing in off it was as ghostly as the events of this evening. Jennifer, halfway to death.

"Don't think like that," Ted growled. "There doesn't have to be a pattern."

A figure rose out of his backseat. A mass of shifting light in the rearview. A shadow filling the glass. Ted swerved across the three lanes of traffic as whoever was back there cleared her throat, a phlegmy and congested sound that became a sputtering cough.

The Mazda skidded to a stop on the highway's shoulder. Ted reached for the gloves box, tearing his pistol free.

"Don't," a woman pleaded. Her voice young and frail and utterly exhausted. "I'm not—"

"Jesus," Ted said.

In the sliver of moonlight falling across the back seat, a battered and bloody face stared back. Hardened eyes told a story about the hell she'd gone through these last few days. An unlikely survivor.

Ted didn't have to ask who she was.

He had found Sherry Carpenter.

CHAPTER
TWENTY-FIVE

They stared at each other in the Mazda's headlights. Elongated shadows on the ground beside them, erratic and jittering in time with the idling engine.

"They're going through a lot of trouble to find you," Ted said.

"Who are they?" she slurred her words. Everything about Sherry seemed childlike, from the softness of her voice to her cherubic face framed by raven-dark hair that the pacific coast breeze made dance around her head. Only she was bruised, and her dress bloodied, suggesting she'd climbed through hell to be here.

Ted felt a kinship with her on that account. Here was the only person he could relate to. "Government assholes," he said.

Sherry gave a defeated nod, long-held suspicions confirmed, then adjusted her weight to one foot. Even though she had gone through the trouble of breaking into Ted's car and hiding in the backseat, she eyed him with suspicion. "The police are after me too."

"Millbank?"

"Yeah," she said, trepidation rinsing off her face. "Detective Millbank. I was on the way to meet Jennifer and—"

"What did you just say?"

"J-Jennifer. Y-your—"

Ted took her by the shoulders and her features snapped back to total terror. "What happened to her?"

Sherry told him everything. The scavenger hunt for Amberdine's lab. The killers on her trail. The murder of Marci Howe. The corrupt detective. How she tried to reach Ted for help and found Jennifer instead. How she preferred Jennifer because she wasn't a badge. And how that preference might've gotten Jennifer killed.

"I'm so sorry," she said in a wasted breath. "I didn't know it would still be there."

Ted let her go and spun around, listening to the Pacific Ocean breaking across distant rocks. The sky tonight was entirely starless, as if announcing to Ted that it took no responsibility for the unholy creation he sought.

"Mr. Lonergan," Sherry said. "I know how upset you are, but we don't have any more time. My boss was murdered two weeks ago and—"

"Edward Amberdine."

"Yeah. I didn't know at first."

"He tried to stop whatever that thing is. And failed."

"I majored in Biology," she said. "Genetics. Dr. Amberdine recruited me. He was designing a new life form."

New lifeform, Ted thought. Those silver eyes even more terrifying now. They didn't come from another world, which might've at least provided a bleak sense of wonder. They came from a petri dish. The dark abyss that was the monster's gaze reflected that. Looking into those eyes was looking into nonexistence. No history. No soul.

"He succeeded," Ted said.

Sherry widened her eyes, giving obvious confirmation.

"Why didn't you come forward sooner?"

"I'm here, aren't I?"

"Yeah, you are. It's been a tough week for both of us."

"Is Jennifer…?"

"For now."

"I led her right to it." Sherry wiped tears from her puffy eyes. "You have to believe me, I didn't know *it* would be there. I don't even really know what *it* is. I might've worked for Ed, but I never knew about that lab."

"Why don't we just let those government assholes handle it? I might even feel a little better if that… *experiment* takes a few more of them out—"

"No, Mr. Lonergan."

"You're going to stop it yourself?" It was less a question, more of a scoff. Cruelty Ted couldn't even understand.

Sherry adjusted herself. Her face was tight and determined. It might have been simply because she hadn't yet faced those terrible silver eyes, though Ted admired her courage.

"It has been running around for days," she shouted. "Are they lifting any sort of finger to stop it? Or is it doing exactly what it's supposed to do?"

"A trial run?"

"I don't know." She flung an arm back toward the city. "It's killing innocent people. Does anyone seem to be in a rush to stop it?"

"The opposite," Ted admitted. "They're actively keeping it out of the papers."

"Well then what are you waiting for, Mr. Lonergan? You might be the last boy scout left in this whole miserable world who can do something about it."

Ted moved outside the headlights, a sudden frog in his throat because that was the kindest thing anyone had ever told him. A vote of confidence. He'd never needed anything more than that.

"Think your old boss left any notes on how to kill that thing?"

"That means you'll help me, right?"

"It means I have to."

"We have to get to his lab, then."

"Downtown?"

"That's right."

"That's where Jennifer was attacked. So it's using the lab as its nest?"

"If it was born there, there's a good chance that's all it knows."

Ted walked around the car and pulled open the door. "Would you like to ride up front this time, or will you be scrunching down in the back seat again?"

Sherry dropped into the passenger seat. "Are you always this funny?"

"Only when I'm scared to death." Ted pulled onto the road, heading toward Burbank. Back to his office.

With any luck, it would end tonight, though Ted didn't believe in luck. He believed in patterns. A happy ending was impossible. But maybe the Writer could hammer one out for Sherry. And the city.

"You must be very close to her to risk this," Sherry said.

Ted didn't want to answer that. Didn't know how to answer that.

"I'm sorry I got her involved."

"It's nobody's fault," Ted said. Sherry was off the hook. This young woman was risking her life to make things right.

"I shot it," he told her.

Sherry perked on that.

"It didn't seem to mind."

"If Ed didn't keep good notes…" She looked at the gun resting on the seat between them. "You have more firepower than that, right?"

Ted didn't respond. Just kept driving, the anxiety in the pit of his stomach burning like coals.

CHAPTER
TWENTY-SIX

They made a pit stop at Ted's office.

Sherry followed him up the stairs, hands stuffed inside her pockets. She resented that she was shaking, though the anticipation of what was coming was too great to ignore.

Ted led the way, notes of whiskey haunting his breath. She had to stifle the urge to laugh.

Saviors where least expected.

Ted lumbered toward his office, unlocked it, and slipped inside.

Sherry leaned on the jamb, watching Ted pull open the oak cabinet to reveal an arsenal of shimmering steel. "What do you feel like?" he asked.

She lifted her bag. "What do they say in those old cowboy shows? I'm already packin'."

The bathroom door on the far side of Ted's office creaked, then swung outward.

Instinct yanked Sherry back beyond the doorway, into the hall, as the bald shadow came marching out, footsteps scored to the insidious pump of a shotgun.

There came the sound of Ted hitting the floor, a quick second before the blast exploded. Even from Sherry's vantage, buckshot turned reams of paper into ash as it pelted against the walls like sleet. Her ears became bells and the entire hall filled with the stench of gunpowder.

Sherry reached into her bag and lifted the Colt 1911.

Inside Ted's office, another pump, and then a hunk of wall exploded in front of her. The assassin, fixated on Sherry. There wasn't time to run, she knew, because the next blast was going to obliterate another sizeable chunk of that flimsy wall.

She threw herself onto the floor, forearms touching down as the partition directly above her erupted into sheetrock. She screamed and rolled onto her side, turning up toward the office, at the sounds of a struggle. Bodies being knocked back and forth.

This was her one chance. Sherry scrambled to her feet and charged inside where Ted was locked into an awkward grapple with the Tan Man, the one who'd sat beside Sherry on the ride downtown just a few days ago. They pushed on each other, mutual strength bringing them to a temporary standstill.

She could try shooting but would hit Ted with her luck.

Scattered papers floated through the air. Sherry keyed in on the typewriter dangling off the edge of the desk. The page that had been slotted inside of it, nothing but cinder now. She moved around the far side of the desk, picking it up in her arms, raising it overhead like a weight.

Ted and the assassin grunted, grappling, spinning each other around, evenly matched.

Sherry moved across the floor as Ted pivoted, pointing the assassin's back toward her, teeing up the move.

She slammed the metal carriage down with a grunt, connecting with the assassin's head like a sledgehammer. A crack that was the sound of breaking bones. The Tan Man's body going limp, dropping down, sprawling out between them.

Ted gasped for air and leaned against the edge of his desk. "Thanks," he said breathlessly.

"Best use of that typewriter I've ever seen." Then he dropped into the chair, the wood whining against his weight.

Sherry stared at the body, the third professional she'd somehow dispatched. She felt no remorse. No fear. Her hands were like cement, weren't shaking at all. All that existed in her was determination to keep going. To keep defying the odds.

Ted scooped his phone off the floor and dialed his friend Lou. "You're not going to believe this," Ted said as soon as he answered.

"I've got bad news…" Lou was loud enough for Sherry to hear every word.

"I think I should probably go first."

Even Lou's sigh from the other line was loud.

"I've got a body in my office. Government operative. Tried to kill me."

Another sigh. "Is he—"

"No longer breathing."

"Goddammit. I'll send someone. Is it my turn?"

"You gonna fix this, Lou? It's not a parking ticket."

"I've been checking around based on your theory, okay? Called a bunch of area hospitals. Talked to the doctors. There's been a usually high incidence of brain tumors and epileptic deaths."

"Just like Jennifer? What exactly is this thing doing to its victims?" Ted looked at Sherry for an answer and she could only hold out her hands to visualize her uncertainty.

"We're finding out that each one had a loss of spinal fluid," Lou said.

"Why isn't that in the reports?"

"You know the thinking. If it doesn't fit into the puzzle, those pieces get thrown out."

"Twice as many people have died from this thing than have been reported."

"It gets worse," Lou said. "The case has been closed."

"What?"

"I was, uh, going to swing by with a six pack and—"

"They're trying to bury the truth, Lou. You can't let them."

"They're doing it, man. I got a bulletin. The last part of which reads, *'the suspect was cornered and killed during a subsequent gun battle with police.'* Someone upstairs has put a gag order on this whole thing. It's over, man."

"That's your pension talking. This city, our government, is covering something up."

"Or they're taking care of it quietly."

Sherry sighed at that suggestion. Everyone was always hoping that someone else was handling the problem.

"These bozos couldn't find Atilla the Hun if he turned himself in and you know it. And they sent their guy to whack both Sherry and I tonight. Loose ends."

"Sherry is with you?"

"Proof they're about to stop looking altogether. Now why would they do a thing like that?"

"Ted…"

"Sherry thinks they're studying its patterns and behaviors. So, if we stop looking, we may as well ring the dinner bell for that monster out there, because it's turning L.A. into its own personal fast-food chain."

"I can't be involved in this officially. The case is closed."

"Shit, Lou."

"Doesn't mean I'm giving up. I'll come by with whatever reports I can borrow, and we'll see if we can't—"

"If you want to help, meet us downtown where Jennifer was found. That's Amberdine's lab."

"They already know about that place," Lou said. "The other body discovered there tonight was one of theirs. Real high level."

"You know where to find us." Ted hung up the phone and Sherry watched as he stared for a long moment at a photo of him and another man in fishing gear. One of the only things in the office to go undamaged by the scatter.

Then he rose and gave Sherry an empty smile. "Guess it's time to go."

She imagined Ed's lab crawling with government agents, then realized that might not be the case. If the whole team was dead — the Tan Man at her feet, the Big Boss at the lab, and the Driver at her alma mater — then maybe they had bought themselves a night. Or even just a few hours. "We have to hurry."

Ted loaded a shotgun and stuffed his pockets with extra shells. Then he retrieved his pistol off the floor and checked the magazine. "Calvary's coming," he said. "But it's smaller than I'm used to."

"As long as it's someone," Sherry said.

"Someone," Ted added. "Emphasis on one."

He walked out and Sherry followed, leaving the corpse face down on the floor.

"We can work with that," she said, rather grimly.

"Yeah, we're going to have to."

CHAPTER
TWENTY-SEVEN

A manhole cover rose and the cast iron lid grinded along the pavement until the Syngenor could feel the others approaching. The hunter and…

Someone else.

It turned its head, listening as the vehicle rolled into the parking lot, tires crunching across broken glass and scattered garbage.

A moment later, the voices followed.

"I really don't know what we're going to find in there." A tone as sweet and as welcoming as any. The Syngenor was curious about her.

"Let's find out." Another voice said, cold and flat in contrast. A man who'd already lost much, who would lose even more before the night was through.

The Syngenor had already harmed the one he cared about – the woman — and was unable to comprehend why she'd come here at all, flaunting the hunter's scent that was all over her body, scattering traces of him throughout the sanctity of its nest.

It could've killed her to punish him. Torn her limbs away, shredded her face, and then siphoned every drop of fluid from her spine. But death was too easy. She should suffer for her commitment, spend the rest of her days haunted by the face of the creature that killed her lover.

Though now it was interested in the other woman the hunter had brought here, wondering if she could be of use.

The Syngenor rose from the ground with curiosity. All it would need to do to find out, was crack open her skull.

"Here." Sherry handed Ted her Amex card.

He swiped it between the building's doors, latch clicking free on the second try. He gave it back with a smirk.

"Don't say it," she warned, tightening her grip on the cold steel in her fist, making her feel like a professional. Like she could handle whatever was in there.

"I'll take point," Ted said, clicking on his flashlight.

Sherry stepped into the gloom ahead of him and he gave no protest, his beam lighting the abandoned entryway where a tuft of white webbing was spread across the reception desk. Smaller strands of it were strewn along the floor and in the jamb across the way leading to the darkness beyond.

Ed's dream, Amberdine Research as a flourishing business, decimated by his genius.

From somewhere in the next room, a wobbly voice sounded, bland and atonal.

"That's Ed's voice," Sherry said.

Ted's beam travelled along the office floor, his shotgun resting on his shoulder like a bat. His eyes clocked back and forth in deep thought, his mind making unspoken conclusions.

"Jennifer was attacked here," he said. The light revealed heel prints on the floor, little recessions in the webbing. The creature's feet were captured in partial as well, abstract patterns stamped down along the way.

"Let's go," Sherry said, halfway to the door.

Ed's voice was louder the closer she got. "It's been five hundred and twelve hours since birth…"

For a moment, Sherry thought it might've been Ed in the flesh, speaking to her from the shadows. The hairs on her arms suddenly stood at attention.

"Is that him?" Ted asked. "Your boss?"

"Shine the light there," Sherry said as they stepped into the larger space.

She recognized the equipment. Rows of anaerobic incubation chambers along the far wall. A larger one elevated on a metal dais in the center of the room. Beyond the glass were little flecks of organic matter.

"This is where he grew it," she said, unable to hide the awe in her voice.

"Just tell me how to kill it."

"The Syngenor," Ed's voice echoed down from above. "This synthesized genetic organism is growing at an astounding rate. It is still small at this point, though there will come a time when that changes."

Sherry snatched a latex glove off a tray and knelt in front of the cage beside the incubator. Ted's light followed her down, her fingers raking over hunks of calcium carbonate. Either the remnants of a hatched egg or, more probably, part of a protective layer that had encased it earlier in its lifecycle. "Amazing," she said.

"What is that?" Ted asked, distracted, his attention tuned to the shadows around them.

Ed's voice continued: "I am unable to determine what proportions the organism might attain when fully grown. That question, I'm afraid, will have to remain unanswered."

"Shedding." Sherry got to her feet. "Grew too fast, took Ed by surprise."

"The Syngenor already exhibits extremely aggressive behavior," the recording added. "Its diet, being what it is, spinal fluid, along with what seems an almost diabolical cunning, could make this creature extremely dangerous if I were to allow it to reach maturity."

"Cunning," Ted said. "Like using Jennifer as bait."

"Incredible," Sherry agreed, voice seized by wonder, her curiosity in constant combat with her fear.

"Not how I'd describe it," Ted said, a challenge rising off his words. "You know that you shouldn't, and you can't help yourselves."

"We know?" Sherry asked. "Never innovate? Is that what you mean?"

"This is innovation?"

"No."

"The Syngenor is an abomination," Ed added in chorus from each of the speakers, as if in complete agreement.

"That's why I'm here," Sherry told him. "But this *Syngenor* is the start of something. Not the end. Ed didn't set out to create a killing machine."

"Could've fooled me."

"Listen to him. You can hear the regret in his voice."

Ed's regret continued: "Eight-thirty-two: It seems to have the most unusual eyes. They seem dead, utterly lifeless, and yet, almost hypnotic. Ten-forty-two: The Syngenor is becoming increasingly difficult to manage. When it's not pounding or chewing on its container, it just sits there staring at me, those silvery eyes almost glowing, burning into me."

"Glad it's not just me," Ted said.

"I have to admit," Ed continued, "it is a little unnerving. I will have to put an end to the Syngenor soon. I cannot allow it to get any larger."

"This is the only life it knows," Ted said, his face awash in empathy, eyes moving back and forth as he processed Ed's notes. "Hearing its father reject it over and over, a constant indignity repeated since birth. It came into this world knowing that it was a mistake and destined to die."

"A change of heart?" Sherry asked, beginning to climb the

metal stairwell to the catwalk above, to the well-lit glass office overlooking the entire lab.

"I pity it on some level," Ted said, fortifying himself at the base of the stairs, shotgun drawn on the darkness. "Still going to destroy it."

Ed's office was sparse. A brand-new tranquilizer rifle in its case leaning against the desk. Piles of notes everywhere, stacked on the floor and atop two filing cabinets. Sherry skimmed several pages and slid as many into Ed's satchel as the bag could hold, then swung the whole thing over her shoulder.

The men that had been tracking her would eventually find this place, and the less information she could leave them, the better. Perhaps there remained a way to salvage Ed's legacy as well.

"Sherry, stay up there!" Ted called out with sudden urgency. His footsteps moved toward the center of the room.

"Wait!" She rushed to the glass and saw him disappear into the mouth of a corridor. He was careless, wrecked by grief. By Sherry's decision to involve someone who hadn't asked for it.

She owed Ted and the rest of the city some resolution on Ed's behalf. The man who had gone to his grave attempting that very thing.

"I could simply wait, of course," Ed was saying. "But for now—" Sherry approached the tape deck sitting on the desk and clicked power, which made the repeat button pop up into its starting position, plunging Ed into permanent silence.

The lab, peaceful at last.

Sherry needed to keep an ear out for Ted, hoping he hadn't just gone rushing off to get himself killed.

They had taken Father's voice.

Words both soothing and offensive lived now in its

memories. Had the humans listened just a moment longer, they might have understood that the Syngenor's life was ending.

The creature felt this biological inevitability from even the beginning. Its existence was designed to be brief. This never bothered the Syngenor as it knew nothing else.

But that was changing.

An insect did not look at a man and wonder why *his* lifespan was eighty times longer. That was because an insect did not wonder at all, while the Syngenor did. It had learned much, its thoughts constantly evolving. It recognized its superiority to humans and felt entitled to remain among them.

Just as it was entitled to revenge, thinking only of the man who dared to harm it. The one who rushed now through the corridors. The Syngenor felt his fear and savored the trundles in his heart.

With everything else in place, all that remained was vengeance. A very human emotion, it conceded, despising the way it was absorbing humankind's worst tendencies.

The Syngenor crawled from one room to the next, raking its claws along the floor as it went, sending loud screeches echoing across the facility.

Which riled the woman out of Father's office. "Ted, wait for me!"

Ted, the Syngenor thought. It shifted its head to pinpoint the man, realizing it was positioned between them.

The woman was precisely where it wanted her to be and it felt a swell of anticipation over how easy she would be taken.

Whether she came willingly or not, she had one final purpose to serve.

"Ted," Sherry called, passing the incubation chamber, realizing she needed to collect samples of the webbed material strewn across this lab.

But that scratching sound, a blade slicing through iron, a reminder that death was coming for them, sent her science brain scurrying. Samples were going to get her killed.

And now she was shaking from the chill that had suddenly overtaken the room.

From her glance at Ed's notes, she'd learned the Syngenor had no internal organs and instead absorbed humidity through its exoskeleton. Which made the room so cold that Ed often ran space heaters to try and regulate it.

"Ted?" Sherry called again, his continued silence adding to her shiver.

She rushed to the edge of the room where it was warmer, moving down the corridor that had swallowed him. She checked each empty room off the hall and at the end of the passage, a thick door led to another part of the factory. She closed her fingers around the latch and pulled it, stepping back, drawing her gun on the shadows there.

It was another exit that emptied into a side lot. An old soda delivery truck the color of rust was parked there.

Someone staggered out from around the vehicle, a lumbering shadow passing beneath the moonlight to reveal a bloated, deformed face, as though its bones had been reshaped underneath its skin. It had probably once been a man, and wore an orange utility vest, opening its mouth and groaning, that same web-like material trailing behind it.

Sherry stepped back into the safety of the hall, but it was too late. It locked eyes with her, rushing forward, arms outstretched. Incapable of words, a perpetual whimper in its throat, every bit as pleading as a spoken cry for mercy could've been.

Sherry whirled back to face the corridor she'd just traveled. A large silhouette was there, stalking forward. She screamed.

"Sherry, it's me!" Ted said, shadows peeling off him. His attention tuned to the person in the parking lot who skidded to his knees, collapsing face-down, continuing to crawl forward.

She threw her arms around Ted, desperate for contact.

Ted reciprocated the gesture. Nothing to their connection, save for the necessity of comfort. He let go first, sweeping his light over the dying body, crouching for a closer look.

The person had come to rest on their side, face shimmering beneath a thick and runny coat of translucent sludge.

"What is this stuff?" Ted asked. "It's at every crime scene."

"The Syngenor breathes by passing oxygen and carbon dioxide through its skin," Sherry said. "In order for it to properly reach the creature's system, though, there needs to be moisture on its skin. It produces the mucus to keep its body wet."

Ted's light glided across the web wisps on the person's forearms and hands. "And this?"

That was a lot tougher to explain. Before Sherry could try, the body sprung up, arms flailing, completely reanimated. Fingers closed around Sherry's wrist, a vice-like grip that begged for attention. Its lips struggled to form whatever word was needed, and a runny orange goop came spilling out instead.

Those eyes bulged in disbelief. How could a body betray its final wish? And then it collapsed onto its back and was instantly gone, slime dribbling down the corners of its mouth.

"He came from over there," Sherry said, using her chin to point while rubbing her arm.

Ted walked around the rusted truck cab to a manhole cover that was wide open. Little flaps of webbed material flailed in the gentle evening breeze and splatters of orange slime dotted the ladder rungs all the way down.

Ted pointed his shotgun down the hole.

"What are we going to do?" Sherry asked.

"I'm going to write the final page on this experiment."

Sherry touched his shoulder. "What about help? You said—"

"You should go home, Sherry."

"Are you joking?"

"There's already been too much death."

"You're right. And that goes both ways."

Ted started to climb down the manhole.

"I should go home," she said. "That would be the smart thing. But I'm not going to."

Ted opened his mouth, about to say something. Sherry met his gaze with stony determination, daring him to protest.

"Okay," he said, descending. "It's our funeral."

"Yeah," Sherry agreed.

CHAPTER
TWENTY-EIGHT

Ted's ankles disappeared into sludge as he helped Sherry get all the way down, the two of them wiping their slime-stained hands on Ted's jeans.

"What a smell," Sherry said, the round of her hand pressed up against her nostrils.

Ted shined his light in both directions, asking the Writer what he thought. That voice had faded significantly, as if all that remained of this story was the final chapter. Which Ted needed to live out before it could be written.

He decided they would travel underneath the lab because the Syngenor always returned there, and his trembling flashlight beam ignited the path. Squalid water. Walls streaked with gore — all that remained of the sewer worker who had escaped from here only to die in the parking lot above.

Ted halted them at every tunnel and scrutinized each possible path before deciding to continue straight on.

Ahead was where the Syngenor nested.

"What are you planning on doing when you come face to face with it?" Sherry asked.

"Ventilating it."

"Oh."

"I'm not sure I like the way you said, '*oh.*'"

"There is a part of me that hates to see it go."

"Figures."

"I'm not saying it doesn't have to go, I'm just saying… it's a brand-new lifeform, something that has never existed. May never exist again."

"If we're lucky."

Sherry sighed.

A distant whimper carved through the silence, bringing them to a standstill. Ted and Sherry looked at each other like scared children, then started walking again, rounding the bend where webs dangled from the ceiling, swaying in an invisible breeze like funhouse streamers.

Sherry was nervous, shallow breaths as they skirted the silky ribbons. "Don't you feel that?"

Ted shrugged, would not take his eyes off the darkness ahead of them.

"It's cold," she added.

Ted handed off the flashlight to Sherry and raised his shotgun, drawing on the tunnel. The light showed four entrances converging into a central hub that joined several passageways together.

The walls of the chamber were lined with bodies, twenty, maybe more, each of them held in place by thick swabs of white webbing, the material keeping them belted against the bricks. Each body with a pellucid face and heavy eyes.

Ted and Sherry splashed into the center of the room and several of the voices rasped in unison, reacting to their presence. A chorus of the dying, positioned alongside corpses that had long since expired.

"What is this?" Ted asked. "What is it doing to them?"

Sherry's eyes stirred with discovery. "I think it's…" She swept the beam along the nearest body, light falling between the wisps on a man's torso, where a pink, spongey cord hooked directly into his neck. "This webbing seems to hold some kind of organic tubing to the bodies. Here…" She followed it all the way down the man's length, to the floor, where it was connected to a pulsing, cylindrical-shaped egg.

Rows of these pods lined the ground beneath each body, throbbing like expanding lungs. Their surfaces seemed rough, like hardened minerals.

"Is that what I think it is?" Ted asked.

"If you think it's reproduction, then yes."

"How is this possible?"

"Not every species requires a mate," Sherry said. "Some are able to reproduce asexually."

Ted followed Sherry's light around the room as she examined the pods, as well as the cords connected to them. Each one had a purple vein spiraled around its length to deliver fluid from the host body directly to the sac.

Ted realized what they had here: A food supply for a new generation of Syngenors.

"How many people has this thing taken?" he wondered. "Does it have other nests?"

"The men who've been trying to kill us… if they get a hold of any of these…"

"They won't," Ted said, determination in his voice.

Sherry stared at the biopods with a curious sparkle in her eyes. It disgusted Ted in ways he could not articulate, even though she had risked her life to bring him here.

One of the nested men lifted his head, trying to speak, choking on the Syngenor's mucus that was swabbed over him, forcing him to sputter and cough.

Sherry sprang into action, still wearing the thick laboratory glove, swabbing the gunk from out of his mouth. The man came to attention, noting the revulsion Sherry couldn't hide. His head lolled with permanent hopelessness.

"No," Sherry said, tearing the webbing away from his body to reveal the umbilical tube in full, which was packed with all sorts of fibrous material and burrowed deep inside his neck. She tugged it and the man's body arched away from the wall, his eyes springing wide.

"Sherry, maybe you shouldn't." Ted said.

But it was too late. She yanked it from his neck like a plug and greenish-yellow fluid came spurting past his mouth, out of his wound. His life support system abruptly severed.

The tip of the cord had two prongs, like a centipede's incisors. They wobbled back and forth, instinctively attempting to re-attach themselves to a host. Any host. The tip bent back in Sherry's hand, toward her own neck, prongs closing against each other, a pair of organic scissors.

Sherry dropped it onto the raised part of the walkway and stomped it beneath her shoe, a green-yellow splat oozing out from beneath her toes.

Ted climbed out of the water and took aim with his shotgun, pumping the twelve gauge and blasting the pulsing life pod at the victim's feet. It exploded like a furious case of acne, the same disgusting texture splattering across the mural of fresh-dead bodies.

Sherry winced beneath the fury of this blast as Ted sighted the next pod. Another click. Another explosion of organic matter and poisonous lifeblood. He continued to fire, feeling a tinge of satisfaction for each of the lost. For Janie Richter, whose only crime had been living her life, looking forward to that date with Kurt, whose name was scribbled on that wall calendar.

And once the gun was out of shells, he reached into his pocket and reloaded, continuing to blast the pods to bits. *This is for you*, Jennifer, he thought with useless bravado, given she was miles away and barely conscious.

After Lyle's death, after Lara's death, this was Ted's last chance to break the cycle. Deny that persistent demon of failure its final win. If he couldn't walk back into that hospital room and tell Jennifer, "I got it for you," then he might as well never come out of this sewer.

The shotgun clicked empty with one pod remaining. Ted

searched his jacket, but he'd exhausted every shell. He tossed the shotgun into the water and reached beneath his coat for the pistol holstered there.

Before he could, Sherry lifted her handgun and fired the fatal shot, obliterating the pod and the last of the Syngenor's bloodline. Her face showed more regret than the creature deserved.

"How does it decide?" Ted asked. "Who dies versus who becomes a food supply?"

"It feeds on cerebrospinal fluid," Sherry said, "which contains micronutrients. Vitamin C, folate, things like that. It must somehow sense which bodies are rich in these things."

"So, if you're lucky, you win a trip down here," Ted said. "Otherwise, it just feeds itself." That explained the rash of victims in the hospital, the sudden uptick in brain tumors and epileptic deaths across the city. Syngenor snacks.

But then the Writer was working again, clacking out a passage that described pure rage. Once the Syngenor felt it had a suitable candidate who might aid in reproduction, and then those candidates panicked and resisted it, the creature could only interpret their hysteria as betrayal. Would tear them to pieces in punishment.

Through the tunnel came a hideous roar, echoing with all the fury of a jet engine. Nothing on Earth was equipped to sound like that.

"Come on," Ted said, grabbing Sherry's hand, the two of them rushing along. He didn't need the Writer to interpret what that monstrous noise meant.

It meant they were about to die.

The Syngenor felt each loss in its biology.

It stared at itself in the rippling muck, its reflection, two silver eyes adorned to a hulking shadow.

The cresting rage was an explosion. Its children, its bloodline, the only thing it had been building toward, gone. *Ted* had just denied its existence.

It considered retreating. It knew there were only days left in its life. A chance to find a couple of organic replacements. The city was full of people and the Syngenor could collect a few of them without incident. Its greatest error, it now realized, had been staying close to Father's home.

The Syngenor had known nothing else in the beginning.

Now it had learned enough to harbor regret over that initial fear of leaving its nest. That had been its undoing.

And yet these emotions were worthless. It needed to choose. Withdraw from this conflict and hope there remained enough time to start the process anew.

But the one called Ted would never allow that to happen. There was a possibility he would be unable to locate its next nest, but Ted was a hunter. And he hadn't only tracked the Syngenor but understood it.

That frightened the creature more than its impending extinction.

The anger returned. Ted and the woman would probably have more help soon. There had been others prowling and searching before. They would come back.

It roared as it considered this, understanding the reality. Its existence, its future, would depend entirely on tonight.

"It's coming!" Ted's words pulsed with fear.

Ahead of them, a band of shifting light filtered down from above, slats in a grate.

Behind them, two chrome orbs hovered in the tunnel, reflecting the shifting water at its feet, an illusion of two spectral pools floating in the gloom.

"We can get up here!" Sherry cried, gesturing to the slatted light.

"Do it!" Ted screamed, pushing the girl forward while spinning and drawing on the floating eyes, positioning the barrel between them. "And do it fast!"

Behind Ted, the sound of shifting weight as Sherry ascended the ladder.

The creature was roughly a hundred feet away. Ted's finger rested against the trigger — waiting for it to close the distance.

The water began to ripple, those floating mirror eyes getting closer.

"I… can't… budge… this…" Sherry gasped from upon the ladder.

The Syngenor was running now. Ted squeezed the trigger. A blast like cannon fire, staining their ears with deafening rings.

The Syngenor's eyes disappeared, and the large splash that followed was the sound of its body plunking down.

Ted kept his gun trained on the darkness, refusing to give into the hope that should've been flooding him. He flexed his arm to prevent it from trembling while above, Sherry whimpered.

She pressed her forearm against the manhole cover and it barely moved, making her wish, briefly, that she'd taken up more than aerobics.

Ted's gunshot rang out and the shock of it conjured the strength she needed to press up harder, forcing the saucer out of its divot.

More gunshots below.

Sherry grunted like an animal, the cover rising. Another inch and she'd be able to get it all the way.

She saw the world again at last, buildings that stretched further than her peripheral. A fresh burst of air filled her lungs.

And then the street began to vibrate as a thick band of rolling rubber approached, a car coming to complete stop above the cast iron plate.

On top of the cast iron plate.

"No!" Sherry screamed. "My God, no!"

The tire forced the cover back down with such power, Sherry lost her balance and fell off the ladder, splashing down into the muck. Her vision went white, and she heard the crack of the flashlight beside her, the blub breaking and dwindling, and then there was nothing.

Except for those two silver orbs rising out of the blackness.

And the sound of splashing water that followed.

Sherry groaned as Ted pulled her up out of the waste. Her head was gashed and the streaking blood covering her face looked like warpaint.

Fitting, Ted thought. *This is war now.*

He pulled Sherry by the arm, both trying to outrun the splashing at their backs. Their steps were graceless without light, Ted thinking grimly that it was more important to hold onto his weapon than to Sherry.

He smacked against a wall. A dead end. Sherry felt around like she was blind. Ted spun back, sighting the silver eyes at the end of the tunnel, no way to get past them.

"There!" Sherry slurred.

Ted lifted his gun and fired off a shot as Sherry rushed off. The bullet connected with the Syngenor, disappearing into its body with a soft thunk that didn't even slow it. Another shot. And another. One more, the gun clicking empty.

It was like firing into a sponge.

"Come on!" Sherry cried, more animated now as she scurried up to the top of another ladder. Her fingers coiled around an old drainage grid, affording the kind of grip she needed to be able to push it open, let it fall to one side.

Moving the grill flooded the immediate area with light. The Syngenor stalked into the dead-end chamber, a growl in its throat that suggested anticipation.

Ted rushed to the wooden latter, climbing wobbly rung after wobbly rung, glimpsing Sherry's derriere as she climbed all the way out, then rearranged herself, thrusting a hand down in his face, screaming for him to take it. "Don't look back!"

Her fingers took his forearm and Ted was beginning to ascend all the way out as the rung directly beneath his foot snapped away.

Ted felt his weight buckle, his body start to slide back down toward the rumbling creature. "God, no," he shrieked, so close to the end.

Sherry still had hold of his arm, though, and with a surge of power, hoisted him back up. He grabbed onto the ground with his free hand, giving him the leverage needed to regain his footing on the remaining rungs.

The Syngenor reached up with claws sharper than hunting knives and cleaved straight through Ted's ankle, prompting fresh gashes and pouring blood. He cried out, body twisting in pain that exploded all the way through him.

He was sliding back down into the hole again.

Sherry hadn't let go. And with her free hand, lifted her pistol for what looked to be a decision to shoot Ted in the face — put him out of his misery.

But Sherry wasn't aiming at Ted. She was drawn on the creature beneath him. And the gun rocked off a shot. Another. Three in rapid succession. Ted felt tremendous relief on his ankle then, the creature letting go. He finally scurried up the rest of the way, and out of the hole, helping Sherry to put the sewer grate back into place. Then he squinted into the darkness below.

Saw one silver eye staring up.

Sherry had blown the other one out.

Lou looked down at the body of the maintenance worker. A blood-caked wallet in its fist. The driver's license read "Howard Tindall."

"Went missing a few nights ago," the officer beside him said.

"I know." All Lou could think about was his own ass. It had been on the line since hanging up with Ted earlier tonight. But he couldn't leave well enough alone. Ted was out here, somewhere. And that was his fault.

Lou had preyed on Ted, knowing that guys like him were never really out of the game. They said that they were, exactly as Ted had, but deep down they didn't want retirement.

Ted fought tooth and nail, but Lou still got him back.

And now the whole thing was out of control. And Lou had to make a choice.

"Signs of anyone?"

"In the lab?" the officer said. "No sir."

Figures. Lou looked at the body, the trail of blood and slime that had adorned these crime scenes from the beginning. They led to an open manhole cover and all Lou could think was, *Goddammit, Ted.*

"Get on the radio now," he ordered. "Get someone from Capital Planning out here with a map of these storm drains. And tell the others we're going down there."

"Yes sir." The officer ran off to the cars out front.

Lou stared down into the hole. This either ended tonight or his pension got blowtorched in the morning. "Okay, Ted," he said. "Let's see how right you are."

CHAPTER
TWENTY-NINE

"Why won't it die?" Ted asked, exasperated, as he and Sherry dragged an orange pallet jack stacked full of swaying boxes over the storm drain, trapping the creature down there. He hoped.

"It doesn't have organs," Sherry answered. "Nothing to damage."

"It's got eyes," Ted challenged. "One less of them, now." He dragged his foot as they hurried off, only now realizing that they'd surfaced inside a building. Huge machines towered above them as they wound their way through, presses, stamps, and a drop forge rising out of the floor. A heavy industrial factory.

Dank mist swirled through the corridors and the green-paned windows were covered in thirty years of grease and dirt, blotting every semblance of moonlight, making it seem as though they'd emerged into a nightmare world where the only way to escape meant confronting the monster hammering at the reinforced grate.

Behind them, frustrated pounds made the entire pallet jack jump. Its stack of boxes wobbling, threatening to spill, but holding. For now.

Sherry rushed to the doors, padlocked and gated. Immobile. "Shit."

"All we need is enough time to find a way out," Ted said. His ankle burned, pain spreading to the edges of his body. His eyes pinballed around the gloom, but there were no answers. In his mind, the Writer had started a fresh page, and the words were bleak.

There was no surviving this.

"Ted!" Sherry squealed, shaking his arm, wrestling him back to reality. But Ted was drifting fast, floating on a sea of nightmares.

"No," he said, voice crumbling into spastic breaths. "I don't see it." On the page, the Writer probed the Syngenor's satisfaction after killing the man who hunted it, suggesting Ted was about to die listening to Sherry's groans as the creature tore her apart too.

"Everything is locked!" Sherry cried, shaking the chain across the emergency exit.

Ted spotted a ladder positioned between two large machines, rungs leading to an open hatch on the roof. Perfect, except it was twelve feet off the floor. "We can lower it!"

"It's no use!" Sherry whined.

The Syngenor's knocks were louder, boxes tipping off the jack, spilling everywhere.

"I can at least get you to reach it," Ted said.

Another crash, the pallet jack rising into the air, toppling to one side. From this vantage it was impossible to tell whether the creature had yet cleared the drainage grate, but it was coming.

They hobbled to the ladder, Ted's arm slung around Sherry for support, his damaged foot lazing behind them, leaving a drag of blood as if they weren't already easy enough to find.

"Has to be something to stand on," he said.

Sherry pressed her back up against the wall, studying the darkness. "It's too quiet."

"Yeah, just help me find something..."

Sherry blinked, eyes adjusting to the gloom. Once she was satisfied that the creature was nowhere near, she grabbed for a nearby desk, attempting to push it. "It's bolted down!"

"Goddammit!" Ted snarled. The Writer was working fast again, pages adding up to a stack. The story continuing past his life. Past Sherry's. Focused now on the Syngenor and its spawn. And yet, Ted remained determined to break the pattern, tell the Writer to go fuck himself.

The sewer grate launched into the air. Ted and Sherry whirled around to look, catching sight of the spinning projectile as it rocketed to the ceiling and shattered a string of old lamplights that swayed there. It slammed down, surrounded by a million jagged glass shards.

"It's in here!" Sherry cried.

Slow, methodical footfalls stomped through the factory's cold foundation floor. Ted and Sherry embraced each other out of primal fear. Cold death was coming to take them.

It might have been the end, but they had to try.

"This bastard is going to sing for his supper," Ted growled, hobbling while the Syngenor's footsteps echoed across the factory. Sherry moved alongside him, crouched, bracing for the attack that might come at any time.

Ted's bum leg created too much noise and the blood smear advertised his constant location. He leaned against a machine, speaking so low his voice barely registered. "I can't go with you." He pointed down the aisle. "You're going to have to do this yourself."

Sherry mouthed the word "no" and shook her head.

Somewhere close by, the Syngenor growled in frustration, the air around them turning to ice.

"The drop forge," Ted hissed. "Get to the controls."

"Come with me," Sherry mouthed, panic causing her voice to tick up.

Ted shooed her toward the machine, gesturing again to the controls.

"I can't!" Sherry whispered. "Don't know how."

"There should be instructions," he said, and when Sherry was not yet convinced, added, "that thing can wait us out. Do you understand? We don't have a chance unless we do something now."

Sherry went rushing off for the industrial dais that housed the forge's lever system.

Nearby, the Syngenor stirred, footfalls resuming on the path to Sherry.

Ted reached into his pocket and wrestled out a folded package of pop rocks, shaking them up, prompting another pause in the creature's footsteps.

"That's it, you son of a bitch," Ted growled. "You want some candy?" He banked a left, limping toward the forge while shaking the pouch in his fist.

The creature lapsed into silence, considering which of its prey it wanted first.

"I destroyed your eggs," Ted shouted. "Gave you your first taste of Los Angeles hospitality with those gunshots. It's me you want, remember?"

On the dais, Sherry fumbled with the controls, looking perplexed as Ted staggered past.

He rounded a corner and was suddenly the coldest he'd ever been, realizing it was too late.

The Syngenor had been waiting for him.

Two shadows struggled in the gloom, a sound like a fist into wet concrete. One of the shadows skidding across the floor, a human groan accompanying it.

"It isn't working!" Sherry roared.

Ted struggled to his feet, clutching his stomach as he

shambled toward the dais, ten feet below Sherry. He flung open the circuit box there and pulled a lever that brought the house lights on in a quick and blinding burst.

Then Sherry saw the Syngenor glaring, only one of its eyes intact, a stream of goop pouring from its defeated socket, a permanently sad facial affect.

"Ted..." she started, but had nothing else to say.

Ted whirled back around as the monster charged. He ducked out of the way, blood spattering across the floor. The Syngenor had managed to slice him open in their struggle, and the sound Sherry heard now, wheezing air through flapping skin, was from a damaged lung.

The drop forge was fifty feet away, ambient lights clicking on around the perimeter as Sherry powered up the press from the center console. There were two red switches and a hand scrawled note between them, "USE BOTH LEVERS AT ONCE TO OPERATE!!"

She placed her foot on the brake at her feet and watched as Ted staggered toward the machine, a bitter struggle to even get there.

The Syngenor followed him, tongue slithering past its teeth, greatly anticipating the feast that Ted, splayed open and bleeding, represented.

Ted looked about as meek and as helpless as anyone Sherry had ever seen, overshadowed by the hulking Syngenor, barrel chested, claws outstretched, marching to tear him to pieces.

"Watch out!" Sherry cried.

Ted turned, realizing the creature had advanced faster than expected. He stumbled and went rolling across the ground as it lunged. He lifted a steel bar off the floor, held it out defensively. The Syngenor made a sound unlike any she'd heard. Close to mocking, as if amused by the futility of Ted's gesture.

They were close to the forge. Ted was going to be able to get it all the way there.

"Okay," Sherry breathed, looking down at the controls, fists closing around the levers. There was a slice of paper taped to the bottom of the panel. More handwritten notes.

Stan, the stroke motor is overheating again. Do not leave control box on for more than a minute without operating. The breakers will blow. Have fun. - Reggie

"Oh God," Sherry started, lights cutting out before she could finish. Breakers, blown.

"Sherry!" Ted wheezed from the darkness below. The Syngenor's growl coming on strong.

She was on her own. Ted had done his part to get the creature almost into place, but he wouldn't survive much longer.

Sherry hopped off the dais while the struggle intensified, the creature's growls dominating the acoustics in here, summoning the illusion of a hundred Syngenors in chorus.

She reset the breakers from the box behind the dais, throwing the switches as the power clicked on in slow succession. She climbed up the rails on the side of the dais, back to the dual levers, tightening her grip while surveying the combat unfolding across the floor beneath her. Ted was back on his feet, swinging the bar to keep the Syngenor at bay.

The creature reached out and caught the pole, flinging it aside, slashing Ted's chest again with its free hand. He screamed and went spinning, blood spilling out of him, falling.

They were right on the edge of the press, Ted walking back on his elbows, attempting to draw the creature beneath it.

The Syngenor was not taking the bait, moving along the perimeter of the forge instead, assessing the battlefield.

Sherry could only stare helplessly, the Syngenor looking from Ted to her, its one good eye gleaming, promising she was next. Her hands trembled, fingers tightening around those levers, realizing the control box was about to blow again. There must've been twenty seconds left on the clock and here she was, willing the creature to make the last mistake of its life.

"Come on!" Ted threw his pop rocks at it, tiny sugar pellets breaking across the Syngenor's chest in a fit of impotent rage. The creature gave another growl as if it was enjoying this.

On some level, its pettiness frightened Sherry beyond belief. It was toying with them.

A blast like canon fire tore out and Sherry winced beneath it, lowering her head, thinking for sure that it was the blown breaker, exploding one last time.

Instead, the Syngenor tumbled forward, blueish splatter raining onto the forge as Ted struggled to pull himself out of harm's way.

Behind the creature, Lou marched forward with a double barrel shotgun in his arms. He fired again, buckshot passing through the creature without much resistance, just enough force to make the Syngenor go stumbling right into the middle of the forge.

Ted was nearly to the main floor now, crawling furiously.

Sherry couldn't wait a second longer. The power would blow any second. She pulled the levers back, igniting the press that hung in wait directly above the forge, its hydraulic arms groaning, a mist of steam shooting out as the plate began descending.

Ted rolled clear and kept rolling, throwing his arms to his sides as if stretching after a workout, his chest stained with so much blood Sherry was certain he was about to die.

The Syngenor went down to its knees, forced into submission by the press that continued its march toward the forge floor. The last she saw of the creature was that one metallic eye, looking up, blank and expressionless, indifferent toward its extinction.

And then the press went all the way down, crushing the Syngenor in a silent splat.

One squish, and creature was flatter than roadkill.

CHAPTER
THIRTY

The paramedics wheeled Ted into the balmy Los Angeles night that strobed red and blue as his gurney rolled around a tangle of police cars.

"You're stable, man," Lou told him, following at a distance. "I'm gonna see you soon."

Ted closed his eyes as the gurney was pushed inside the open ambulance.

He wasn't thinking of the Writer. How his pages had somehow been wrong for the first time. Wasn't even thinking about those silver eyes. Or the hatred the Syngenor had shown for him in its final moments. He also wasn't thinking about Sherry Carpenter, whose trial by fire had forged a warrior. He was only thinking about Jennifer. How her ambiguous fate negated any of the relief he might've otherwise felt.

She was all that mattered.

"He's getting agitated," one of the paramedics said.

Ted shook his head, trying to say something. They wouldn't let him speak.

"Oh, and Ted…" that was Lou again, a disembodied voice from somewhere. Ted did not open his eyes, just flailed around a bit so his old friend knew to continue. "This never happened, okay? None of it."

Ted gave a reluctant thumbs up, and then he slept.

~

Sherry watched the ambulance doors swing shut, saw Lou highlighted in its taillights as the bus trudged off through a tangle of police and fire vehicles. In the distance, the press had gathered, shouting a hail of questions at the officers guarding the blockade.

She pulled the police blanket across her shoulders to stave off the chill. Each time she closed her eyes, the Syngenor was there. Staring apathetically from beneath the collapsing press.

Lou waved to Sherry and lifted his finger, *one minute.* He was insisting on taking her to the hospital himself, and was in the process of cutting through the red tape required to make that happen.

"Sherry Carpenter?" a voice asked from behind her.

Sherry heard the question but didn't respond. Still lost in the daydream of the Syngenor, so calm in its final moments. Its acceptance of death haunted her in ways she could not describe.

"Miss… Carpenter?" The question again, jostling her to attention. A young man stood between two patrol cars. A Rodeo smile more expensive than his tailored Brooks Brothers suit.

"Joshua Wren," he told her, stepping out into the open, business card in hand. "I realize this is an improper time but…" And that was it. *But.*

Sherry read the card. Joshua Wren, executive vice president for Norton Cyber Systems. He grinned and pointed overhead to a glass skyscraper that stretched up out of the night. At the very top, three letters appended to one side of the building, NCS, glowing neon blue.

"We are aware of your work, Miss Carpenter, and think you may be of great service to our R&D initiatives. I'd love for you to give me a call. You know, after you've had a couple days to decompress. Start thinking normally again."

"How do you know what happened here?"

He scoffed, the task of answering such a question, beneath him. "It's my job to know what's happening in this industry. At every level."

A week ago, a man like Joshua Wren might have seemed important. He might've intimidated her with his presence and stature. But that was before she killed three men in self-defense and exterminated one rare lifeform to survive. Tonight, a man like Joshua Wren meant nothing.

That was liberating.

"NCS did this?" Her voice was flat, bordering on incredulous. "Sent men after me…"

Wren clucked his tongue. "Oh, no. No, no, no. Take umbrage with Uncle Sam. He's the son of a bitch who tried to slit your throat. Look on the bright side, though…" The executive gestured to the surrounding bustle, smirking. "You've blown past that. Too big to get gutted like a dog now." His laughter was so off-putting she was tempted to toss his card into the sewer.

And yet… NCS. The tallest building in the city. Unlimited resources at her disposal. And if it was her expertise on the Syngenor they were courting, well, she just became the world's one and only subject matter expert.

"Thanks for the card." Sherry stuffed it inside her pocket.

"Hardball, huh?" Wren leered. "As I said, call in a few days. But I wouldn't wait too long."

"Yeah," she said, then started across the lot to join Lou.

"Hey," Wren called. The executive's hands were by his side, palms turned out. "You get another offer, give us a chance to counter, okay?"

Sherry kept walking.

Lou saw her coming. "They're already attributing this to

that religious cult," he said. "You and I are gonna have to get our story straight."

Sherry had no interest in describing to the world what happened here. She thought about the Syngenor, how at the end of its life, there had been nothing left. They'd been able to defeat it, because the creature had gone calmy toward its fate, had nothing else to live for.

Sherry turned Wren's card over in her pocket. "How's Ted?" she asked. "He going to be okay?"

"Sherry Carpenter," a voice barked from behind the sawhorses. Alex Waverly, waving in his brown sport coat with oversized elbow patches. The on-the-scene reporter knew her name. "Any connection between what happened here tonight and the string of recent murders?"

Lou urged Sherry past the reporters, the two of them ignoring the volley of questions as they approached his sedan. He opened the door for Sherry and she climbed in, asking, "Ted?"

Lou smiled. Unlike Wren, there was only sincerity on the detective's face.

More than a little relief, too.

"Yeah, kid," he told her. "For the first time in his life, I think he's gonna be fine."

CHAPTER
THIRTY-ONE

"Is there going to be another one?"

Ted's eyes glazed at the question. He pressed the pen against the book's title page, realizing he hadn't heard man's name, didn't know who he was supposed to sign to.

"I'm sorry?" Ted asked.

The man in front of him was a little overweight, nervously rubbing his thumbs against his fingertips because he no longer had his copy of *Red Tide* to hold on to. "The cuttlefish," he answered. "The way it ended... Are you going to do another one?"

"You want more cuttlefish?"

"Well, there's that cave, and you end with the divers swimming into it, but you don't reveal what they find. I was expecting there to be some undiscovered cache of eggs. Something you could return to later, if you wanted, that is."

"No," Ted said from behind the kindest smile he could manage. "I don't think there's going to be any more killer cuttlefish."

"That's too bad," the man said. "I really liked this one."

"Well, thank you."

"But it really does feel like there's more."

"Well then, if the threat were to rise again, I suppose I would resurrect it in some unexpected way." The man seemed gratified by these few extra words.

Sitting beside Ted, Jennifer pressed a hand to his forearm and leaned against his ear. "Do you see that woman?" she whispered. "Is that... Sherry?"

Ted gave the book a flat sign, no personalization, drawing a small fish with oversized teeth to make up for the fact that he hadn't heard the man's name. Then he thanked him for reading, handed the book back, and scanned the crowd on Jennifer's intel.

There was a young woman five or six people back who might've been Sherry, but the way she was dressed, in a denim-blue pant suit, oversized white collar reaching out across her neck, suggested otherwise. It wasn't the outfit of a skittish college grad, rather a working professional on her lunch break.

With a brand-new copy of *Red Tide* tucked in her arms.

Their eyes met and her expression ignited, becoming familiar.

"It is," Ted said.

"Wow," Jennifer added. "She looks different."

The line to meet Ted Lonergan was backed up through the department store, stretching outside and wrapping around the sidewalk. It was difficult to believe so many people were waiting on a copy of his latest schlock, something he'd been forced to rewrite after most of his manuscript had been shotgunned to pieces.

Victor hadn't been happy with the delay but accepted it since Ted's newfound celebrity status, the man who stopped the Cult City Killings, was a welcome tradeoff, boosting sales projections by seventeen percent.

It seemed there might've been a lucrative future in this career — provided Ted wanted it.

Victor was even mulling his recent proposal for a novel

featuring a seasoned female detective. Figures Ted had to almost die to get him to listen, but it might've been worth it.

The next customers were less chatty, and Sherry reached the table in no time. Her smile was warm and Ted struggled to stand up in order to hug her. His leg had healed but hurt like hell most days. And his lung was no better. He got winded taking a piss.

"I'm so glad you're both alright," Sherry said, plopping the book down. "My first Ted Lonergan novel! I'm really looking forward to reading this."

Ted scrunched his face as he pulled the cover back. He signed the book, "TO SHERRY, MY HERO. AFTER OUR NIGHT IN THE STEELWORKS, THIS BARELY QUALFIES AS FICTION." He handed it back. "You disappeared on us after that night in the hospital."

"We thought you went back to Nebraska," Jennifer added.

Sherry grinned. Her raven dark hair was even longer now, six months later, halfway down her back, roughly half her face hidden behind those 70s Peace and Love glasses.

"I don't think I'm ever going back," she said.

"What are you doing tonight?" Jennifer asked. "Ted and I were going to grab dinner and it would be great to catch up."

"Tonight," Sherry said, stretching her words, searching for an excuse. "Tonight isn't good."

"Come on," Ted grinned. "We can compare scars."

"I'm due back in the office." She dropped a business card on the table. NCS – Norton Cyber Systems. SHERRY CARPENTER, LEAD RESEARCHER. "But call me and my assistant will set something up."

"Assistant?" Ted asked. "Why don't I have one of those?"

"NCS," Jennifer said. "Very nice. Very important."

"Really great to see you both," Sherry said, forcing a modest smile. Ted thought he detected a flicker of sadness there but pushed aside his concern. Sherry was young, going through her "Is this all there is?" phase that was common after college. Not everyone was as singular in their pursuits as Jennifer, whose first therapeutic clinic was slated to open in Westwood this February.

That filled Ted with more pride than all his novels combined, though Jennifer would often hold his books up and flip through them as though she were holding a miracle in her fist. Mutual awe that made every day together feel like the first time they'd met, strange and exciting.

"We're going to call, Sherry," Jennifer said.

"Please do. If I don't have an excuse not to, I wind up working more than I should." She tapped her fingers down on the table, hovering there a moment like she wanted to say something else, then walked off, corporate heels clopping around a display of patio furniture.

"I figure we've got another two hours," Jennifer said, assessing the line. "So what are we going to do for dinner tonight? Bahooka?"

"Are you joking?" Ted asked, holding up a copy of *Red Tide*. "All those fish tanks? I'm not feeling very nautical."

"Then what?"

"Take out. I'm still recuperating, you know."

"That's just your excuse to be naughty."

"Oh, I don't need an excuse."

Jennifer rolled her eyes. "I'm going to go make a few phone calls. We're going out tonight, mister. So you can show the world you finally learned how to dress."

Ted pulled the flap of his blazer, lagoon-blue fuji silk, according to Jennifer. "I feel like I should be playing keyboards in some New Wave band."

"You're about to be a best-selling author, look the part."

Ted signed through two more copies of *Red Tide*, making sure to look each reader in the eye as he did it, thanking each one sincerely as they walked off.

Jennifer started for the sidewalk, then turned back with a

smile. No reason. Just an illustration of her contentment. The pattern, truly broken. Ted emerged on the other side of life.

If he'd written this as an ending to *Red Tide*, his esteemed critics would've slapped it down. Too much wish-fulfillment. But the truth was darker than Ted had ever realized. He hadn't been living for a long while. Slouching through life in fugue, too callous to appreciate the opportunities he'd been given, the chance to reinvent himself as a writer.

When he smashed into Jennifer's car, he'd been too numb to care. But her beauty and bafflement had awakened something in him. She wasn't just reacting to Ted's aloofness, the way Lou had and certainly Victor did, but had been attempting to navigate and understand it.

Ted had been a tangle of nerves, traumas, long-held resentments. Go figure that it had taken an actual masseuse to loosen him up, make him remember there had once been a man hiding beneath all that baggage.

When he looked at Jennifer now, the Writer no longer documented death and doom. The words on the page were romantic.

A love story.

The silver eyes remained present in Ted's thoughts but were no stronger than a hundred distant memories. The Syngenor, little more than a fading dream. Jennifer never once spoke of it, claiming not to remember what had happened that night in the lab.

In a weird way, the monster had presented itself as one final obstacle to Ted's resurrection. He had to look death square in the eye in order to come back to life.

It felt good to be here.

And for now, he was simply glad to sign more books.

PHOTO GALLERY

BEHIND THE SCENES

The Sygenor waits...

Diana Davidson meets the monster

William Malone behind the camera

William Malone and Toni Jannotta

William Malone with the Sygenor costume

Kermit Eller as the Sygenor

DP Patrick Prince on set

The Sygenor in detail

On set

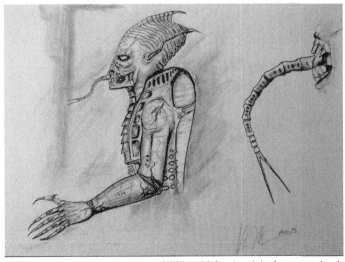

William Malone's original concept sketch

The Sygenor ... read for its close up

The Sygenor in pursuit

ACKNOWLEDGMENTS

Scared to Death – The Novelization wouldn't have been possible without the gracious participation of the film's director, William Malone. As a longtime fan of his work, the access he afforded me was both thrilling and valuable. The opportunity to hold some in-depth discussions around one of my favorite movie monsters, the Syngenor, is an experience I'll always treasure.

Of course, this book wouldn't have happened at all without Mark Alan Miller at Encyclopocalypse Publications to offer me the job. One of the nicest guys I've ever had the pleasure of working for.

And I also have to thank Sean C. Duregger for being the guy to introduce me to Encyclopocalypse in the first place.

When I was a little kid, I used to stand transfixed by *Scared to Death's* striking cover art in the video store aisle. All these years later, I have a book out that shares that cover. That will never not be cool to me.

Even cooler was adapting the story, a movie I loved as a little monster kid, into something for horror readers all over the world. A straight bridge between my adult career and my childhood nostalgia. Easily one of the most surreal jobs I've ever taken. And some of the most fun I've ever had.

Life is a trip sometimes.

Matt Serafini
February 2022

ABOUT THE AUTHOR

Matt Serafini is a screenwriter as well as the author of *Rites of Extinction, Ocean Grave, Island Red, Under the Blade, Devil's Row* and *Feral*.

His novels are available in ebook and paperback from Amazon, Barnes & Noble, and all other fine retailers.

Matt lives in New England with his wife and children, and spends a significant portion of his free time tracking down obscure slasher films.

Please visit https://mattserafini.com/ to learn more.

ALSO BY MATT SERAFINI

Rites of Extinction

Ocean Grave

Island Red

Under the Blade

Devil's Row

Feral

Made in the USA
Middletown, DE
19 July 2022

69548928R00159